The Man from Beyond

Also by Gabriel Brownstein

The Curious Case of
Benjamin Button, Apt. 3 W

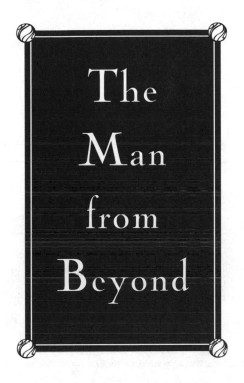

The
Man
from
Beyond

A novel

GABRIEL BROWNSTEIN

W. W. NORTON & COMPANY

NEW YORK   LONDON

For information about permission to reproduce selections
from this book, write to Permissions, W. W. Norton & Company, Inc.,
500 Fifth Avenue, New York, NY 10110

Manufacturing by Quebecor World, Fairfield
Book design by Lovedog Studio
Production manager: Amanda Morrison

Library of Congress Cataloging-in-Publication Data

Brownstein, Gabriel.
The man from beyond : a novel / by Gabriel Brownstein.—1st ed.
p. cm.
ISBN 0-393-05152-8
1. Young women—Fiction. 2. Doyle, Arthur Conan, Sir,
1859–1930—Fiction. 3. Houdini, Harry, 1874–1926—Fiction.
4. Women journalists—Fiction. 5. New York (N.Y.)—Fiction.
6. Spiritualists—Fiction. 7. Spiritualism—Fiction.
8. Magicians—Fiction. I. Title.
PS3602.R75M36 2005
813'.6—dc22
2005011982

W. W. Norton & Company, Inc.
500 Fifth Avenue, New York, N.Y. 10110
www.wwnorton.com

W. W. Norton & Company Ltd.
Castle House, 75/76 Wells Street, London W1T 3QT

1 2 3 4 5 6 7 8 9 0

For my parents

"They say miracles are past, and we have our philosophical persons, to make modern and familiar, things supernatural and causeless. Hence is it that we make trifles of terrors, ensconcing ourselves into seeming knowledge, when we should submit ourselves to an unknown fear."

—Lafew,

in William Shakespeare's *All's Well That Ends Well*

"There is nothing so unnatural as the commonplace."

—Sherlock Holmes,

in Arthur Conan Doyle's "A Case of Identity"

THIS IS A FANTASY. Nothing in it should be taken as fact. Names, places, events, actions, dialogue, headlines, and other details out of history have been distorted here for the purposes of fiction. The real story of Harry Houdini, Arthur Conan Doyle, and the medium Margery is a good one. For a recent account, look to Daniel Stashower's *Teller of Tales: The Life of Arthur Conan Doyle* or Kenneth Silverman's *Houdini!!!* The book that I owe the most to is Houdini's *A Magician Among the Spirits*, without which I would never have imagined this world.

The Man from Beyond

I

SIR ARTHUR CONAN DOYLE sprawls in a beach chair. Under his swimsuit and robe, his chest and belly bulge. White mustaches lift like tusks from his sunburnt face. A man from another continent, another century, a strange creature plopped on the Atlantic City shore, vivid, enormous, and lost, Doyle peers into the surf where the children of his second marriage play with the world's most famous magician. Timothy and Joanna gasp. Houdini pulls pebbles from their ears. He levitates on broken waves. This is his gift to Joanna on her birthday. But hair dye covers only so much. He is no longer the miniature chained Hercules of the old photographs. Houdini's belly sags, his shoulders slope. Scars on his forearms and wrists trace the work of ancient wires, clamps, and handcuffs. Marks from old rough rope run under his armpits and across his chest. Still, his calves and thighs bulge like a wrestler's. He can bend a hotel key between his thumb and finger and, when he needs to, summon creatures from the deep. Now he extends his arms, lowers his face, and as a slow wave approaches, Houdini drinks the ocean. He comes up with his neck tense and wide as a bull's, his wild face a figurehead, mouth roaring. Water explodes from within, lips like a trumpet. A screaming fountain crests in the sky, huge ribbons of it, too much for any man to have swallowed, but when the ribbons land, they are only taffeta. Timothy shouts. Joanna startles. Cries and applause from the shoreline. Smart young men tug their sweethearts. Fathers get down on one knee to point.

"Good show," says Doyle, first to his wife, then to Houdini's.

But he has studied the field deeply, and these little miracles annoy him. What was water—or time, or space—to Houdini? He walked through walls, he escaped bolted chambers. Chained underwater in a coffin of stone, Houdini would not drown. This was transmutation, not legerdemain, and the magician's greatest trick is to appear ordinary. Doyle imagines Houdini at home, the bourgeois demigod for a moment sloughing his corporeal disguise and reaching through an oak table to retrieve a fallen napkin. Of course, he has to deny it. Were Houdini to reveal his true nature, his public would turn insatiable. Doyle cannot blame the charade on cowardice or dishonesty. Houdini is the bravest, most plainspoken man he has ever met, and yet it seems impossible— more than unlikely—that the man fails to understand his magic's underpinnings, its roots in the interconnections between this world and the one beyond.

Doyle's view is obscured by a gathering crowd. He raises himself in his slumped chair. Houdini dangles a hand into the water, then draws up something black and thin. An old fishing line? A strand of seaweed? The magician keeps pulling. Iron finger in the air, he makes a pronouncement, but the words are lost among the surf sounds and gulls' caws, the open space of the beach. An airplane passes, drawing a banner that advertises a new tabloid, the *New York Radio Times*. Timothy, tall and thin, crosses his arms above his chest. Joanna—myopic like her brother, round like her father, short like her mother—giggles. Bess Houdini, Lady Doyle, and Sir Arthur manage uncomfortable smiles. Houdini discovers something large and dripping at the end of his sea line, and he hefts this blob from the shallows. A breaking wave rises to his hips. Now wielding the line so his arm muscles show, Houdini like a cowboy with a lasso twirls the shapeless thing above him and it spreads, an enormous blanket spinning, easy for him to manage now that it's afloat. This sheet rises like a disk, it shines, falls, and swallows Houdini—it lands flat with a slap against the slow seething tide, and the magician is nowhere.

The crowd lurches forward, the view from the beach chairs is obscured. Bess Houdini arranges the skirts of her robe and bathing costume. Lady Doyle, taking the sun through a broad-brimmed hat, says, "The children ought not to spend too long in there. The water is cold, these parts, in August."

"Quite—" Doyle begins, but he is interrupted.

Dead middle between their chairs and the water he appears in a fake beard and carrying a trident, Harry Houdini dressed as the sea god Neptune. Beachgoers whirl. Timothy and Joanna applaud.

"Bravo!" cries Doyle.

Houdini wades back into the water.

Bending casually, he discovers a new toy beneath the waves, a black ball which he rolls from hand to hand. It is made of wood maybe, or rubber, but when he hands it to Timothy the ball gains sixty pounds at least and turns to iron. The boy staggers. Houdini helps him to his feet and as he does so discovers something in Timothy's swim trunks—a pair of handcuffs.

Peals of laughter from the shore. Houdini says something Doyle cannot hear. Smiling Timothy is dumbfounded.

Houdini hands the cuffs to Joanna. Soon the children are locking him up: hands behind his back, the big black ball to his wrists. With a farewell and some comic exaggeration, Houdini tumbles backward into the surf.

Doyle laughs.

A connoisseur of the supernatural, a public proponent of the scientific study of psychical phenomena, Doyle is a predictor if not a prophet of the coming age of religious unification under empirically determined metaphysical principles, the very principles with which Houdini toys. Doyle has come to Atlantic City not only for relaxation but also to investigate a new radio tower which can receive signals from as far away as Pittsburgh. Radio waves—penetrating walls, moving unseen through the ether— mimic the forces tapped by mediums. In the new science of wireless broadcast Doyle sees promising technology for Spiritualism. He has propounded upon the parallel in his Carnegie Hall lectures. New York's Mayor Hylan mocked him, so did Governor Smith. Tabloids spoofed his sermons, and the more serious papers—the *Times*, the *Herald*, the *Sun*, the *World*—belittled him on their front pages. ("It is impossible not to like Sir Arthur," wrote the Pulitzer paper's Dewey Baedeker, "but he resembles nothing so much as a young boy firmly convinced of his own authority and consequently blinded by it.") At the

lectern, Doyle discussed Dr. Dingwall Bird's analyses of ectoplasm, presented the groundbreaking statistical data, weights and
measures and percentages of pressures, the unalterable conclu-
sion that ectoplasm, which moved from gas glow to liquid to gel
to solid around a medium as her trance deepened, manifested in
the material world the presence of etheric forces, and that an
ectoplasmic structure, whether a colloidal figure or a rock-solid
pseudopod (that invisible limb which emerged from between a
medium's legs and so allowed her to lift tables, ring bell boxes,
and toss books and bricks through the air), served as a functional
apparatus through which a medium could allow spirits of the
dead to communicate with the living. The ectoplasmic pseudopod, emerging from the medium's nether parts, captured the
words of the dead as an antenna caught radio broadcasts, and the
medium's body amplified these messages just as through vacuum
tubes the broadcast waves became audible.

It is crazy optimism that allows Doyle to befriend Houdini,
the great debunker of Spiritualists everywhere. Houdini con-
fronts and humiliates Doyle whenever opportunity allows. Just
this morning, the magician spent breakfast attacking Doyle's
beliefs. Pompous, egomaniacal, absurd. "I have, as you know, carried out a number of investigations into the workings of so-called
mediums and miracle-mongers, both here and in Europe."
Houdini over soft-boiled eggs pitched his words as if he were
onstage. "And as yet I have never encountered one who was not
a fraud. But it is important to note that my investigations, as is
proper, have been and will continue to be devoted solely to the
works of professional Spiritualists and never to true believers, or
to noble, well-meaning amateurs such as yourself. You know in

my younger days," Houdini in grave affect, "my wife and I performed as Spiritualists of a sort. We would, as part of a circus
troupe, read the future for crowds. But when I noted the deep
earnestness with which my utterances were received"—that finger in the air—"I felt the game had gone far enough, and I certainly did not relish, then, treading on the sacred feelings of my
admirers. So it is now. And I hope that you do not see me as a
trampler upon your sacred feelings. No. It is precisely because I
respect you that I—who am, in my mind, your partner in explo-
rations of the beyond and never your adversary—hope to steer
you toward truth, particularly in times of weakness or grief when
the ship of your convictions is headed towards the desperate
shoals of deception." And then that little-boy smile, Houdini
charmed by his own speech, and expecting Doyle to be so
equally. Exhausting. But Doyle listens and waits. He is on the
side of truth and expects that soon and naturally enough
Houdini will come over to his side, where lies not only beauty
but the preponderance of evidence.

The ocean is calm. Houdini hasn't come up. And time
stretches, the minutes get weird. Houdini for all they know could
be swimming to Manhattan, but scanning the surf, there is no
sight of him.

"Arthur," says Lady Doyle.

"Mr. Houdini," cries Joanna.

Ten minutes. Fifteen. A child begins bawling. He has performed
stunts a hundred times more dangerous and yet there remains that
worry: the ocean, the bindings, the man there, then gone.

"Get a lifeguard," barks one of the fathers.

But a lifeguard is standing by, uncertain whether to jump into the surf. He doesn't want to bust up the magician's act. Timothy plunges in. Two big bathers follow.

"He's been under," another voice, "how long?"

Doyle knows that all will turn out well, but stands, preferring to play the fool than seem callous. As he rises from his chair, a wind gusts from the ocean. His hat flies off his head. Doyle turns to watch it. The boater glides through the air and sticks—the embarrassment of it—to a beautiful lady's skirt front. She smiles.

"Oh, dear."

Doyle crosses the sand. His wife calls after him, so do his children, but their cries, like the crisis on the shore, dissolve behind him. The woman's face is mesmeric. Doyle needs to get that hat.

"Terribly—" he begins.

"No, Sir Arthur."

Her costume is antique. She carries a parasol, and his round straw hat remains fixed under her waist, right between her legs, its brim beneath her belly.

"Do I?" Doyle stumbles over his sentences. "Have I?"

He notices her companion, his black mustaches.

The woman only smiles. She wears high-heeled lace-up boots on the sand. Are they circus people? The boater hangs on her dress as if her vagina came with a hat rack.

"No." She extends a gloved hand. "We have never had the pleasure, but I suspect you might recognize my name."

"Beg pardon?"

"I do not believe you have made this lady's acquaintance," says the mustaches, anxious-eyed and smiling, unperturbed by the ruckus in the water or the dangling chapeau. "But if you will, I will endeavor to perform introductions at this deliciously serendipitous occasion. Sir Arthur Conan Doyle, allow me to present my wife, known to the world as Margery."

The single name, like Houdini's, is enough. Doyle has seen the articles in *Scientific American*, the photographs of the séances, her hands extended to two editors in the dark, her face clipped out of the photo for discretion's sake, so that a neat blank oval lay between her shoulders. The magazine had offered $5,000 to any medium who could prove genuine otherworldly talent, and Margery had agreed to cooperate with the editors' investigations only if they would set aside questions of money or proof. She was a lady, the magazine explained, but she had talent. Her superluminous pseudopod—invisible in the dark, but lighting the netherworld—extended from her legs in measurable quantities and caught in the ether the voices of spirits long dead. After three sessions, the journal had wanted to award Margery the money, but she had refused. She was a servant of the dead; she was no performer.

"And I, of course, am Dr. Hugo Sabatier," says the mustaches with a flourish of his gloves. "The pleasure, to be sure, is mine."

Doyle dries his hand on the hip of his robe. "Sir Arthur Conan Doyle," he offers.

"Sir Arthur needs no introduction." Sabatier leers amiably, first at the writer, then at the hat.

Doyle knows what holds the thing in place: her pseudopod, that ectoplasmic, etheric arm which emerged from between her legs and at séances wrote messages on slates, threw speaking trumpets across quiet halls, and captured the voices of lost loved ones.

"Odd that we should all be here in Atlantic City," says Sabatier, "and none of us know it."

"Well." Conan Doyle presses down strands of flyaway hair. "I expect—"

"Daddy, Daddy," cries Joanna.

"Father," Timothy calls.

"We ought to meet," says Sabatier, "more formally, I mean. A breakfast, perhaps, tomorrow?"

"Tomorrow," Conan Doyle can only echo him.

His children call.

Margery lifts his hat off her pelvis and offers it with two hands to Conan Doyle.

"I," he says. "Thank you."

"And all this hoo-ha?" asks Sabatier, pointing to the beach.

"Houdini—"

"Drowned, I expect." Grinning from under his mustaches.

"Well—" Conan Doyle begins. But a shout from the shore interrupts him. They turn.

Bent and staggering, Houdini emerges from the breakers twenty yards down the shore. He stands and walks toward the audience, holding aloft his prizes: Lobsters, six of them, claws going crazy.

"Joanna," he calls, "I have caught your birthday supper!"

Cameras flash.

HE WAS gulled by his own imagination, his goodwill made him speak, and in his boldness Doyle never blinked at the newspapers' jeering. He wanted to save the world, thought he was the man to do so. Were you he, you might have made the same mistake. As a young doctor on a whaling ship, Doyle was nicknamed the Great White Diver for his daring. He played cricket so well, competing amateurs mistook him for a pro. A failed eye doctor, he traveled to Germany and there debunked a famous physician's tuberculosis vaccine. Doyle produced on average three books a year. The Sherlock Holmes stories floated England's most popular magazine. His *White Company* rivals Scott for historical romance. A defender of Empire but also of Africans, he spoke and wrote and campaigned against genocide in the Congo. Implored by police departments to investigate, Doyle saved three men wrongly accused of murder. Large-hearted Doyle, though he deplored homosexuality, befriended and championed Oscar Wilde through his trials and imprisonment. Late in life, an overweight famous author, he enlisted in the Boer War and served as a doctor in a tented hospital where typhoid fever struck and hundreds were buried in shallow graves. The old man played football with the troops, well and hard and with two broken ribs.

His humanism led him to renounce Catholicism; he could not believe a Muslim damned by accident of birth. And his scientific bent led him to Spiritualism, but in this he was not alone: Sigmund Freud, William James, and Alfred Russel Wallace all joined the Society for Psychical Research. Doyle alone among them destroyed his reputation in his attempt to spread the light of truth.

II

AFTER SHE GOT THE news, Molly prayed, a thing she always did in secret. Dressed in a nightshirt, glasses off, wavy hair falling, she sat on her college dormitory bed and it came reflexively. She prayed to Jesus. Not apostatically or in revelation or contradiction of her people or her parents, she called the name that to her did not signify the son of God but the absent spirit of comfort. As a child, Molly had believed in angels, and maybe she still did, though she would never admit it. She had heard of them not from her socialist parents or (God forbid) rabbis but in story-books and in songs and on the street at Christmas, had first seen their images hung in shop windows and on evergreens on snowy avenues in December. Nine years old, she had believed in guardian angels and that she might in fact be an angel. Tucked in her bed in the Goodman apartment on Riverside Drive (they had moved uptown to one of those new tall brick apartment towers some years after Molly was born), her brother Carl in the bedroom next door reading Sherlock Holmes or *Ivanhoe* or *The Last of the Mohicans* or maybe *Houdini: Master of Escape*, her father, Abe Goodman, editor of *Progress*, barking and laughing in the dining room full of Marxists and Freudians, lawyers and poets and professors and assorted educated humanist Jews, Molly plumbed the air of her room for singing voices. A secret, invisible arm of her imagination shaped like a butterfly net scooped the space of the clean white plaster-walled room four floors above 89th Street and Riverside Drive. She wanted to catch the humming, chanting spirits of Lenape Indians buried by the railroad tracks near the Hudson, maybe Dutch sea captains or English pirates' wives; she wanted to reach the ancient ghosts of her ancestors Goodman and Thaler, in Vienna or in Berlin. Molly at nine was a dreamy long-haired girl who stared out windows at the river and rain, who clasped her arms around her father's leg and sang.

But sex changed that. Sometime after her twelfth birthday she was wandering the back hall of the apartment, the hall that connected her room and her brother's and the toilet they shared, and she heard a commotion from behind Carl's door. What Molly saw when she pushed it open confused her: two thirteen-year-old boys caught in an embarrassed tableau. On his knees and looking at her was Lyden Silver, the son of her father's best friend, and above him was big dark Carl, who held a rope. Lyden was shirtless, his vest, collar, and undershirt all scattered on Carl's bed, and his pants were off. He wore only undershorts. The rope wrapped around his naked chest twice and it cut lines into his little pectoral muscles and triceps and then went right around his slim waist and thighs, and as Molly's eyes followed the rope trying to figure out what it was doing to Lyden, she felt a tingle.

He had always seemed to her funny-looking, but now she didn't notice Lyden's face, just that skinny white body of taut, bound muscles. He had taken off his clothes to reveal a monster. Lyden and Carl were playing Escape, taking turns. Lyden was flexing his muscles to slack the rope. Before a word came from anyone, Carl leapt across the room. One stride and one big arm swinging, he closed the door, bang, so that Molly's fingers almost got caught, and she had to pull back and blink. But she never forgot that image and sometimes in bed at night she thought not of ghosts or angels but of Lyden Silver's tensed, white, bound body.

Picture Molly at fifteen with her long hair knotted loosely behind her and her round wire glasses on her pretty nose, a glass of wine in her hand. She is laughing. The Silvers are over for dinner, a party as it is so often at the Goodmans'. A nervous journalist from downtown has a dirty collar and stained teeth and a certain romance to his disheveled hair. A bearded guest, recently from Europe, doesn't say much, smokes a pipe, smiles at Molly, and makes her nervous. Abe Goodman is enormous and everywhere, big ramshackle arms and legs like Carl's but with a round gut and a shining bald head. He refills glasses, stalks the room, wine bottle drawn like a six-shooter. He puts that down only to grab a plate of crackers, which he presses at guests violently with two hands. It seems an affectation, as if Abe—the smartest son of Albany haberdashers—is putting on a show of his crudeness, some kind of display of socialist credentials, the way he affects Yiddishisms and the shrugs of downtown distant cousins, but the truth is his manners are better in company than in private. At home with just the wife and kids he will use a finger to spread mayonnaise. Belle, Molly's mother, small and fine-featured, expresses her anxieties differently.

"Sit, sit. Abe, please, that's enough." Which makes Michael and Clarissa Silver laugh. These are the Goodmans' best friends. In summer, the families rent houses together in the leafy Bronx. Michael Silver's red hair has gone prematurely white and his face is shy and round and pink and handsome. Clarissa's maiden name is Lyden, and she looks very much the daughter of a Massachusetts Harvard man that she is: tall with an aristocratic nose and her yellow hair fading. The parents' worst features combine in their son. Lyden has his mother's high forehead and her long Dutch nose, his father's complexion and lips. But there's a power to little red-haired Lyden. Next to big, dark, languorous Carl, he seems quick and compact and ready to explode.

In the living room, with Michael and Clarissa laughing at Abe while Carl slouches in an armchair, big legs sprawling forward, Lyden stands strapped behind his stiff collar and stares straight at Molly. She stops laughing. There is something about his intensity that, even as it attracts, almost frightens her. The two have taken walks together in pastures behind those rented houses in the Bronx. Lyden has never tried to kiss her, but once on the top of a hill he paused, yellow flowers all around and bees buzzing and sweat beading on Molly's brow.

"Do you believe in God?" he asked, out of nowhere. He was standing on a rise and she below him, still hiking with her heavy skirt beating against her legs.

"What's that?" asked Molly, panting a little and moving a hair away from her chin. She had heard the question, but could not believe it.

Lyden's head was set against the clear blue sky, and this hardened the outlines of his face, the high forehead which made it seem at sixteen that he was losing his hair, the long nose, the mouth with its arrogant droop.

"Because I don't," he said, nervous and hesitant. But there was something urgent in his blurting, and she felt that secret monster peeking out from his speech—his desire, his power, all kept on a short, tight leash. "I have been reading," he said, and waved a hand as if to signal there was more. "About the Turks in Armenia. About the Belgians in the Congo. The little, chopped-off hands of children. We live in a horrid age, Molly. You can't, you know," and he stared down at her, "you can't believe in God."

"You're forbidding me?" She laughed.

"I'm just saying. This is the age we live in, Molly." He gestured at the pine trees as though they were his example. "We can't build it on superstition. The only way, the only hope is the brotherhood of man."

"Oh." She could not conceal her disappointment.

Those hands which were now stuffed back in his shy pockets ought to have been after her waist, and that awkward mouth ought to have been kissing her—or at least trying to. Lyden was three years older than she, but now seemed dismally young. While he had been up all night with his histories of atrocities, she had been reading Austen and Brontë, and certain insights into the world were hers. Lyden's talk masked cowardice. The boy was too shy to kiss her.

"I promise," she said dismally. "Never to believe in God." Then she hiked past him toward the hilltop.

But in her dormitory room in Poughkeepsie, she regressed and pleaded. Carl was dead, one of a few hundred in his regiment on a muddy field in Alsace, the green uniform in which he had looked so handsome—it brought out the color in his cheeks, the ferocity of his dark hair—was torn and bloody and his cold body mutilated within. Amateur magician, Carl had pulled scarves from thin air at birthday parties when he was younger, but the crusted red on his chest was no felt rag for him to disappear.

Her mother had pronounced his name like it contained the wonder of great technological advances, "Carl," like "Marconi" or "airplane," as if she were an accidental Edison who had given birth to a great battery of the modern age. And her father pretended not to be interested in his son's successes in love, in school, in tennis, but would ask, when Carl was out of the room, "How many did he score?" Abe assumed his son would take over the publishing business, but Belle's ambitions knew no such limits. A judge? A governor? Senator Goodman? Molly had watched him grow aloof—what others might have called arrogance, the Goodmans saw as princely right.

But something had happened in the last year of prep school to indicate the limits of those rights. Carl had met a girl at a dance and had not been permitted to call on her. Her father would not allow a Jew in his house—made a production about a Jew at a dance—and the frightened girl had told Carl to stay away. Molly had fantasies: Carl would leap the front steps in tennis whites, whack the liveried butler with his racket. Or maybe he would pluck the awful prejudice from behind the girl's ear, the way he did the ace of spades from behind Molly's when she was younger, shuffle it in a deck, and deal out a more harmonious city. There had been fights after he enlisted, chose the army over Yale. For Abe it was treason, his own son tool of the moneyed bosses.

"War to end wars? More like to keep up capitalistic interests.

Why don't you just sign on for the Pinkertons? Go shoot Negroes in Alabama! Safe for democracy! I never dreamed my son would be such a fool."

Carl lit a cigarette and let that hostility linger in the living room, his cool manners in opposition to his father's.

"Abe," said Belle. "You're pushing him."

"I'm not bothered." Carl was an inch taller, and stood erect while Abe slouched; he towered over his father. "It's fine."

"Fine?" said Belle. Her mouth pinched and her eyes squinted. "Sure, it's fine. Go kill yourself. Fine with me. Go. Get shot. Kill German people. They've done terrible things to you, Carl. They're the ones who won't let you see this girl. Yes, I know about the girl, and yes, don't fool yourself, when that cannonball comes rocketing at you and you feel you've got to catch it, your father is right, absolutely, you'll be doing it for Morgans and Rockefellers and Hearst, and believe me, the brother of that Fifth Avenue girl you like, that brother is not going to be standing next to you, there for the next bomb to hit. He's going to be sensibly and comfortably in New Haven, where his father put him, out of harm's way."

"I'm pushing him?" Abe asked.

"Mom. Pop," said Carl. "I'll be fine."

For Molly there seemed to be no choice for Carl but to enlist. She imagined that girl who had refused him—Molly never learned her name—fair-haired and cream-skinned and dressed in an elaborate gown. Rain would beat against the windowpanes of her Fifth Avenue bedroom, and her tears would fall across a page, blurring the words Carl had written from the front. Molly thrilled at the possibilities of heartache.

"He doesn't want to be Jewish," Belle theorized in the living room later when Carl was gone—to take a walk, that's what he'd told everyone, to clear his head. But it was typical, Carl avoiding his family. The new backhanded trick he had learned was how to make himself disappear. "That's what this is about. I'm convinced. Some crazy idea to make himself American. To make himself what his father can't be—"

"You're blaming me?" A glass of wine in one hand, the other raised toward the ceiling. "Was I ever so Jewish? Did I say to him, go, be Jewish? Did I make him even a bar mitzvah? Scientific principles. Read Freud. There is a simple psychological explanation for your son. What he is trying to do is kill me."

When Carl came back from his walk, his parents went quiet. He took off his long gray coat, shook it once in the hall by the elevator, then folded it neatly to be hung in the bathroom. His hair was sleek and wet with rain; he'd gone hatless, no umbrella. Molly had never seen him so beautiful. He was a man and that's what his parents missed. For Molly that explained his enlistment, to be a soldier and not a boy. She was for the romance, the excitement of it.

But sitting on her dormitory bed at Vassar with that telegram in her hand, that romance was a meal that had made her sick.

"Jesus," she moaned.

She begged Him to make it a lie, to bring back the time just twenty minutes before and to make that telegram say something else—some other death, God forbid, any other death, not her brother's. Then, after Jesus, she tried to reach Carl. She concentrated, pulled a trick out of her childhood, stretched her mind across barriers of time and space and life. Her mind like a phantom limb reached hopelessly, stretching eastward over the Atlantic all the way to France and then under the surface of some more metaphorical ocean to the lost Atlantis of the dead. And she felt a spiritual thing, hard and light and warming.

"Oh, Carl." She crumpled the telegram.

Best as she could, Molly composed herself, pinned a black veil under the brim of her hat, and headed home. A locomotive howled as it pulled into the station. Men gripped their hats against the draft. Molly took a seat on the left side of the car, away from the river while the train went south, but she was running against the commuters and because no one sat across the way, her view of the Hudson was clear. Late October and the oaks and maples put on their show. The train passed a marshy patch, a flock of geese rose. The sun set when she was somewhere near the zoo and the Botanical Garden. Streetlights flickered in the trees. The city was a glow that disappeared behind the hills of Inwood, but then it reemerged with its high white finials and bright windows against the blue of evening. Rat-tat-tat, they went above Harlem, tenements and apartment houses, and on the sidewalks below, the Negro city swarmed.

Grand Central, her father waited at the head of the platform. She saw him before he spotted her and Molly could not believe how hunched and ordinary he looked, how old, how frightened, how tired. Abe Goodman was a big man with a powerful head and hands that gripped like vises, but the throng rushed against him and he stood alone in his black raincoat while everyone else was dressed for a clear fall day. He held his hat, showing his baldness. His eyes were wide and tired and the skin sagged from his face and neck. She was a yard away when he recognized her. They hesitated before they embraced, and then all of a sudden were fighting about whether Abe or a redcap would carry her valise.

"You're lugging that yourself?"

"It's nothing." She had packed little more than underwear and a book of poetry.

"Let me." He grabbed.

"Dad."

"Please," he insisted.

She wanted to relent, but before she could hand it over, Abe snatched, wrenched it from her grasp.

"Daddy—Christ! Are you all right?"

"Me?" He looked away, started moving. "Do you want to take a cab or the subway?"

"Dad—"

"Tell me."

"I don't—"

"If you want to take a taxicab we'll take a taxicab, but the subway would be just as easy."

Which was flagrantly perverse.

He bowed his head and charged, bald prow pressing through the rush-hour crowds under the constellations of the painted ceiling, knuckles white with his grip on the handle of her bag. Big shoulders hunched. Commuters startled in his wake. Molly had to hurry to keep up. Her father was more than her frayed personality could stand.

Up the marble stairs Abe charged, onto Vanderbilt Avenue, Molly trailing behind abstractedly and anxious. A newsboy mumbled headlines, an old man had a basket full of puppies. Cabs were circling under the glass awning, and Abe beat a couple dressed in evening wear to a big green one. He stood impatiently by the running board and ordered Molly into the back seat.

"Are you all right?" Molly asked again, after her father gave directions to the driver.

"I'm fine," he said. "You?" When Molly didn't answer—she couldn't—he continued, "I can't say that I'm surprised that he got killed—"

"Jesus—"

"What?"

"It's not a question of—"

"Don't get excited. You're upset, but that's no reason to get—"

"I'm not—"

"Please." He laid his hand on her knee and, to mollify his daughter, told her what a wreck her mother was. "She blames herself, says she should have never let Carl go. Bullshit." He looked away. "I understood this from the start. It's like the time when he was five years old and he liked playing on the railroad tracks—"

"Dad—"

"What?"

"I can't do it this way. Can we? Can we just for a bit?"

"You're upset. I understand. But there's no reason to be so anxious."

Headlights illuminated Abe's face and Molly saw his eyes were wet and rimmed with red. He had not shaved that morning. On his lapel he wore a small ribbon with a cut in it. A trolley passed, the cab moved forward, and as they entered the roadway at the southern end of Central Park, the back seat went dark.

At home there were aunts and uncles, people Molly did not recognize, and of course the Silvers. Clarissa was the first to greet her, shouting, "Belle, Belle, it's Molly!" The apartment smelled of fish and soup and sweets and baking, and Clarissa wore a long black dress and her hair was perched high on her head. She grabbed Molly and swayed and broke out sobbing.

Molly was aware mostly of her father just steps behind her say-ing, "Go, go!" from the foyer. Abe wanted to get into the apart-ment, to lay down her suitcase. He wanted a drink. And the tears that had come to her so easily in her dormitory room at Vassar were nowhere. Molly accepted Clarissa's embrace, rocked in the arms of her beloved neighbor-almost-aunt, but simultaneously felt a distance from her loss, as if it were she who ought to have been consoling Clarissa and not vice versa. How could she even be standing erect?

Her brother had died. She had no business taking trains and taxicabs or hugging Clarissa. She ought to have been lying there on the floor of her dormitory room. Uniformed men ought to have carried her out the door, an ambulance ought to have carted her to her parents' place; she ought to have been crushed. When Molly had unfolded the telegram and seen the greenish paper and its greener ink, the letters of Carl's name had popped off the page through her eyes and smacked the back of her skull. But now, weirdly in possession of her social sensibilities, she felt insufficiently sad.

Michael Silver would be next. She saw him hovering behind Clarissa, little, white-haired, head bent, patiently waiting to kiss her. And she felt Clarissa's bones and thinness. Everyone had gotten old since the summer. And somewhere in the room was her mother. Molly knew she ought to want to see her mother, but really she wanted a bath. She wanted to sit in her bed, to read a newspaper. She wanted to stare out the window as she had as a girl, to see the park and the river and the trains below. Also, she wanted to curl in her mother's lap and sob. It was all too much. Maybe if she could talk to Carl—but before that thought was done she realized there would be no Carl, never again.

Clarissa released Molly, who stumbled and wiped her nose. Michael Silver took her two hands in his.

"I'm so sorry," he said.

Molly tried to talk, but couldn't. Her throat contracted.

Her father took her coat, Clarissa took her hand. The rooms were noisy. Molly was led out of the front hall and into the living room, where in a corner Belle sat in a blue chair, immovable. Either she had not heard Clarissa's cries and did not know Molly was home, or she did not have the energy to respond. Molly walked on shaky legs past the piano, over the green carpet, by the useless mantel with the thick painted canvas above. It was like some big awful dinner party, the worst possible family gathering, and she had to face it without Carl. She needed a joke—that was it—someone who would not take all this quite so seriously.

Two strangers stood close to Belle, one with a plate of cookies, one with a coffee cup, and Belle's hands were in her lap, clenched. She wore a black dress, and her head was uncovered, and there were no pearls, no jewelry around her neck.

"Do you hate me?" she asked without rising when Molly came near.

"It's all right," said the stranger who held the coffee cup. He was tall and clean-shaven, with sad eyes and abundant folds under his chin. On his head he wore a blue yarmulke.

"You know it's my fault," said Belle. "I killed him."

"Sometimes in these cases," said the tall man with the yarmulke, "it is easier to blame oneself than to face the enormity of the loss." His tired, patient eyes peered down at Molly. "My name is Isaac Josephson."

"He's a rabbi," said Belle. "And if he offers another cookie, I'm liable to kill someone. Get that man away from me."

Embarrassed, Rabbi Josephson bent his tragic head.

Behind the chair on which Belle sat was a radiator, and behind the radiator a window. The sky was dark and the lights in the park glowed. No trains stirred below and the traffic on the drive was sparse. A barge moved upriver, a tugboat pushing in its wake. The New Jersey cliffs were invisible, but here and there in the woods above a lighted window glowed.

Molly reached a hand out to her mother, and then Belle grabbed both Molly's arms. Her grip was ferocious, dug like claws into Molly's forearms, and she drew her daughter near. Her head went right into Molly's belly and she let out a cry, wrenching grief, and the room around went temporarily silent. Molly held her mother, not knowing what to do. She glanced backward at the crowd, all of whom stared. She felt like an idiot, thrust onstage, stumbling.

An hour later Lyden arrived. He had taken a train, then a ferry, then a taxicab, a three-legged journey from Princeton. His face had changed since Molly had last seen him, maybe a year and a half before. He wore round tortoiseshell glasses now, and his nose had been broken in a boxing match. He boxed varsity, middleweight, ranked second in the Ivy League. The nose was flatter, no longer aristocratic, and it listed toward the left.

Neither glasses nor nose made Lyden handsome, but both gave his face an inquiring, owlish, ironic look, reminiscent of his father's, and contradictory somehow to both his ferocity and his shyness. He did not take off his coat or his scarf when he came into the Goodmans'. He kissed Belle, he embraced Abe, he answered his mother and father's questions, but he kept his wild-eyed expression until he found Molly. He rushed past the other mourners, nodding at the ones he recognized.

She was in the dining room and hadn't heard of his arrival. She was talking to someone about something—she would never again be sure to whom or about what—when he came through the French doors, long coat flapping. Lyden looked to her like a stranger at first. He reminded her somehow of her brother or some other handsome man. Then she saw the glasses, the broken nose. Whatever canapé had been in her fingers was gone.

He leapt toward her, grabbed her. His coat, tie, and face were cold from the windiness and the outside, but his body warmed her and something in Molly broke. She found not solace in his arms, but recognition. It was as if it had been Lyden she had been looking for in the corners of rooms, Lyden and not her brother. Molly bawled.

Neither said a word. The tears racked her convulsively, and if Lyden had not been there to hold her, she would have fallen.

Why Lyden? Strange that he had been the one she cried to, she thought later that night, so strange also to sleep in her own bedroom. The animals at the foot of the bed shocked her. The books were all aligned and alphabetized, the writing desk looked like a girl's. These were the possessions of someone immensely more optimistic than Molly could imagine she had ever been, and more innocent. In her months away at college Molly was in the business of acquiring sophistication. Lyden Silver, she told herself—how odd, how inappropriate. When he had let her go from that crazy embrace she had nothing to say. And he had been his usual awkward self upon departure, looking down at the ground while their parents exchanged embraces, playing with the buttons of his coat. But when the elevator arrived he had burst out with it.

"Whatever you need, Molly."

And there was another sentence, she was sure, but he did not manage to say it.

"Oh, I'll be all right," she said, and then winced at her lapse in grieving.

But she did feel all right, particularly before and after her cry with Lyden—light-headed, abstracted from her conversations, from everything, but all in all herself, if only lightly tethered to reality, almost as if she had been performing grief when she had sobbed in Lyden's arms, her body doing something at once appropriate and not at all so (hadn't it been her father or mother she ought to have cried with?), her mind floating up near the ceiling. She was not sure she felt it yet, or if she did feel it—the immensity of her loss, how much she had loved her brother—she did not know what it felt like.

The elevator rose in its shaft and she heard the gears clanking. A train passed down by the river and stray dogs barked. The pipes on either side of her bedroom clanked. Toilets flushed, water ran.

Molly was not herself in this bed, which held the strange familiar smells of childhood.

She crept down the narrow hall to Carl's room, where the blinds were drawn and the mirror covered. On his dresser top were his hairbrushes and razors, the metal and polished silver glinting. Streetlights from below kept the room from total darkness. On his desk, she saw the outline of the typewriter and his dictionary. A bottle of ink shone. His high school diploma hung near the books; its glass cover reflected a square of light—a reflection of someone's window across the way. On the dark wooden shelves, the works were kept in an odd semi-chronological order of interest. Molly touched them: the Conan Doyle, Collins, and Scott, the Freud and Marx that lately he had been struggling with. In his closets were tennis rackets and suits and on the top shelves boxes of magic.

She sat on Carl's bed, turned on his reading lamp—something she never would have done while he was living—and looked at the one photograph he kept on his night table, a funny picture of himself and his sister at Coney Island, the summer before last. They were posed in straw hats, a weight lifter on the sand behind them.

Across, on the wall by the door to the room, there was a poster advertising a performance by Houdini, a gift that the Silvers had brought back from England seven years ago and that Abe as an indulgence to his son had had framed. The master of escape was nude, chained, and padlocked, and he faced forward comfortably. Strangely beautiful, he almost resembled Carl—his face was broader and more mature but to Molly's eyes no more confident or powerful or handsome. Molly stared at Houdini, as if she might find comfort there.

Her father had disavowed all personal involvement in sorrow—grief was one of those things like courtesy, like good manners, that Abe Goodman would never claim as his own. And her mother was moaning about how it was her fault—taking this awful wrenching rift in Molly's life and in one crazy, self-pitying swoop claiming all that sadness as her own: "I killed my son"—if grief were a hand of poker, Belle had dealt herself a royal flush. Molly had no language for loss, no experience, and no one to teach her. At school, she admired the tough girls, the ones who smoked and drank, who played with irony and swagger that was useless here. She fell back on Carl's bed, hair all around her, and as she stared at Houdini's face lapsed into sleep.

Sadness and death and exhaustion, how could you joke about that? Those clever Vassar College girls, they would clasp her in irons, wrap her in chains, sack her, box her, and toss her to the bottom of a river. She imagined what it would be like on the way down, soft and pleasurable, like going to sleep, all that cold water seeping in. Molly shut her eyes to feel how the water would flood the box, soak the sack, and give new weight to the chains. It would fill her nostrils and lungs, or, if she were like Houdini, she could slide right out. There would be a choice when the box hit the silt at the bottom of the river. Death or life, the magician could do as he pleased. And at the side of her box, Carl would be knocking.

Molly's breathing deepened. She began to snore. The box side opened and underwater there he was.

"Hello, Mol."

Carl would extend an arm, and she would reach back, right out of her chains.

. . .

SHE WOKE up on his bed feeling close to her brother, and she carried that secret closeness with her to the dining room. All through the coffee and leftover pastries, the three papers that the doorman brought up, she knew Carl was hovering close by. He rode with her to Poughkeepsie. At night he hovered over her dorm-room bed. Silent, illicit, Carl helped her. He found her shoes when she lost them. He came to her aid when she was faced with difficult exam questions. He consoled her when she felt all alone. But this was something that Molly told no one.

In her last year at school, she fell for a girl named Sukey Van Siever, who took Molly on as a pet. Up on the roof of a dormitory past midnight, Sukey taught Molly to smoke. She sang out new poetry. Long, blond, and milk-white, Sukey had a profile like a crescent moon's. She wore her hair short like a boy's, with a stylish flip, and at her urging Molly bobbed her curls. Sukey was rich, led a set of girls whom money allowed to be modern and shocking. They talked of Eliot and petting and jazz, whether or not they liked the poems or kissed many boys—and none of them had been to Harlem. In springtime they rode in a chauffeured car, and Molly sipped whiskey from a flask. Clubby and illegal, the girls laughed on their way to a dance. Molly kissed a boy there, worried he would taste the liquor on her, and a second one, Arnold Greenbaum, at a party the Silvers threw to raise money for deported Reds, but she had never opened her lips to anyone until after graduation, when she went to visit Sukey's Aunt Luna's summerhouse in Newport. The girls walked together on a beach, and alone on a quiet dune after sundown they experimented, touching tongues. It was secret as the cigarettes and funny as the booze, it was safe and fun and they knew that they were shocking. Sukey had kissed other girls, she confessed, but she was madly in love with Molly. The two of them laughed.

August 1922. She was going to work, she was going to be independent. Her father offered Molly a job at *Progress*, but she pushed that aside for lower-paying work at a new tabloid, the *New York Radio Times*, whose slogan went: "Tomorrow's News Today." Molly rented a room in a Greenwich Village walk-up on Gay Street, where the last of the neighborhood Negroes lived. The bathroom was in the hall, and there was a painter, Pignoli, who used the tub to wash his terrier, Goldman. She was bohemian, professional, hard as nails, and even her father's socialism seemed quaint.

Still and all, at night when the streetlights and headlights slung shapes and shadows on her ceiling, Molly lay in her soft single bed and sought out spirits. Nothing she would ever admit to anyone she knew, but she dragged her old butterfly net out of the closet of her imagination and swung it around the room— the folded dressing shade, the photographs pinned to the wall, the books on the shelf (*Ulysses*, first twenty-seven pages cut), the worn armchair, the table with candlesticks, salt and pepper and typewriter and telephone, the gas ring, the coffee percolator, the bottle of bonded whiskey.

Only when she knew she had reached Carl, connected with him, and in this way prayed, could Molly sleep. Then she would get up in the morning to hear the elevated train on Sixth Avenue, the honking horns, and the manic street life of New York—no place out there for a girl who believed in ghosts.

III

T HE HEADLINE READ:

HANDCUFF KING OR KING OF THE SEA?
Magician Harry Houdini here caught frolicking in the
Atlantic City surf with the children of Sherlock Holmes Creator
and Spiritualist True-Believer Sir Arthur Conan Doyle

The *Radio Times* showed it as one of six pictures on its front page, Houdini on a beach in a beard and carrying a trident. His photograph was positioned to the left of Samuel Gompers sweating at a lectern and just below an image of bathing beauty Ellen Murray. Two more photos completed the page: bottom left, the corpse of Brooklyn man Lester Gregarian; and, top corner, Renovated divorcée Maria Vassos Preston, better known to millions as the motion picture vamp Nana Duprés. The front-page photographs went uncredited, but Molly knew who had taken the one of Houdini: Archer Miles, pink-faced Princeton boy out to shoot end-of-summer bathing beauty contests. A dilettante, a ladies' man, a prematurely balding comical cad, Archie had been until this morning the paper's only man in Atlantic City. But Molly had pestered her boss, Frank Farquharson, the paper's editor, into letting her travel all night out to the Jersey shore. She popped out of a phone booth in the lobby of the Ambassador Hotel wearing pants, her cigarette marked with lipstick, and a pair of glasses on her pretty pert nose—her costume enough to baffle the folks from Philadelphia who might never before have seen a nice Jewish socialist-maybe-lesbian from Greenwich Village.

For the first two weeks of her employment at the *Radio Times*, Farquharson had stuck her on cosmetology. It was a kind of science, he said, he needed women readers, and a woman writer had special insights into the field. From the first, Molly had wanted out of it. Makeup and fashion were not what she wanted to write—too superficial, too girlish—and then, when the paper's arts writer had taken ill, she had volunteered to cover Doyle's lectures at Carnegie Hall. Farquharson gave the okay: Molly was a Vassar girl, and he thought she might get the literary angle. But the truth was she had not gone in for Sherlock Holmes stories as a kid or for any of Doyle's adventure romances; that had been her brother's stuff. She only knew what everyone else knew: hansom cabs, London fog, and Elementary, my dear Watson. Still, off she went to see Doyle after his ship docked, half ready to mock him, and out of thirty-odd reporters was the only woman present. She had imagined a loopy, eccentric Englishman, effeminate and thin, wearing maybe a cape and leaning on a gold-handled cane, so she was surprised when she saw him: huge, reasonable, and frank, a healthy, middle-aged elephant ready to talk about anything, baseball, Jack Dempsey, Germany, or ghosts.

He said he was looking forward to seeing the American version of cricket. As a sometime boxer and former military man, he wasn't surprised by the champion's behavior: Doyle found it commonplace that courage in the ring should be conjoined with cowardice when it came to the battlefield. He had visited Germany, and he spoke with feeling. The suffering he had seen in Berlin was wickedness, no way to treat a fallen enemy. Good sportsmanship demanded that one offer a hand up. When the reporters teased him about his religion—"Are there cigars in the afterlife?" "Prohibition in the world beyond?"—Doyle gave as good as he got. He explained that Spiritualism offered a more manly and scientific set of beliefs than any he had encountered elsewhere. Where other religions demanded acceptance on faith, he explained, Spiritualism offered concrete proof of its tenets. And there was nothing cultish about it, he argued, no sense of us versus them, no chosen people or heathens condemned to eternal purgatory. Doyle wanted to disabuse the press of the notion that he had come to his beliefs only after the death of his son Kingsley, who had been killed in the fields of France. Nevertheless, he admitted, he had received no small measure of comfort when a medium had helped him contact his dear lost child, and the hope to spread that comfort was among the motivations for present task.

"Hume, Gibbon, Tom Paine, and a line of writers who culminated in the Huxleys and Ingersolls of the Victorian era," he said, "cleaned the whole universe of psychic power and left it a mere clockwork mechanical wonder swinging in a vast vacuo, with no sign of intelligence outside our own pygmy brains."

A big bull of a man, so bright, so sure of himself, so heart-breakingly misguided—it was embarrassing, but who could fail to be impressed? By the time Molly saw him take the podium at Carnegie Hall, this aristoctratic behemoth showing off doctored photographs and proclaiming them revealed truth, she had given up her plans of making fun of him. Doyle held forth solemnly and pedantically. He showed off his photographs, double exposures which he claimed showed war dead swarming over grieving London crowds. He described the Bird Protocols, systematic procedures through which the Columbia University chemist Dingwall Bird proposed that a medium's power could be authenticated, and he showed pictures of mediums blowing into glass tubes, hovering books before their faces. It stabbed at Molly—his physical largeness, his intellectual desperation, his refusal to acknowlege the reality of death. She was a good reporter, accurate, sympathetic, and with a gift for a quick, sharp phrase, but as soon as she had filed her story she was sent back to women's work. It frustrated her. So when Molly heard about Doyle and Houdini in Atlantic City, she went knocking on her editor's door.

"It's nothing I believe in, but . . ."

She had once taken a course on comparative religion and knew a little something about Spiritualism. Speaking quickly and without his responding, Molly explained to Farquharson how it might fit into his paper. The celebrity angle would sell, she said, and the Spiritualists were scientists of sorts, Christian Scientists in reverse—they found holiness through technological means, photographs and scientific studies. Of course, she insisted, the very idea of talking ghosts was ridiculous, still . ...

Farquharson was a long-boned, white-bearded, ugly man, a shouter, a bully, and a bigot, but he was no more frightening in his tirades than Abe Goodman could be. He had no patience for mysticism or vogue words like "technological," but unflappable Molly stood in the door to his dim office, pitching her story away. In his green eyeshade he studied his desk—clippings and paste and scissors and ink. Molly smiled at the top of his head, at his big bony shoulders with their too-tight suspenders. Farquharson sent a long finger into his ear, fishing for a stray bit of wax. He reached across the desk for a letter opener.

"You're not going to turn my paper into some kind of ladies' preaching pulpit?"

"God, no. I said, didn't I? I don't for a minute think—" And she laughed nervously, uncharacteristically. "You don't think—"

"Well," he said, "get on it."

And that was that.

The paper's temporary offices were housed in an old die-cutting plant by the East River, and from the pressroom one could see the docks where the dump trucks tipped their loads into garbage scows by the bridge. In the first-floor lobby—where just before dawn you could feel the presses rumble—there was a model of the proposed Herald Square Radio Times Building, complete with broadcast tower, motion picture theater, and a long roof garden that could serve as a zeppelin landing dock. The paper had invested in the latest telephotography equipment—pictures could be transmitted to home base from far away—and headlines were broadcast from a huge antenna on the roof at noon and midnight. The pressroom had sleek, modern telephones on every desk. The back pages carried a mass of scientific advertisement: Eveready batteries, for example, "The Air Is Full of Things You Shouldn't Miss." The rest of the press told you what happened yesterday, the *Radio Times* covered the future: a page devoted to business and another to science ("the new student of radio is sometimes puzzled by the word 'impendence'"), a daily list of new inventions (an automatic shoe-shine machine, an electrically driven pitting saw for cling peaches, a trouble-shovel easily carried in an automobile), and occasional articles with a sociological slant ("The Advantages of Being a Chinaman," by Han Cho Lee). Above the elevator bank was the motto: TOMORROW'S NEWS TODAY. Molly called Sukey Van Siever to cancel their evening plans, left the building, took a taxicab to her Gay Street apartment, and packed a bag for the trip to New Jersey. She rode a ferry and a train all night, sleeplessly. Now, in the lobby of the hotel, she stubbed out her cigarette in a bucket of sand and crossed the lobby toward a corner with six wing-backed chairs.

She found an empty one less comfortable than it looked, puffy and pillowed but angled so that her back would not fit. The lobby clock edged from a quarter after twelve toward twelve-thirty. She had slipped the bellboy her own dollar, and two more to the maître d'. For three bucks, she learned the Doyles had a reservation for lunch with the Houdinis, but she distrusted her informants. What if the family had changed its plans, gone fishing or rented a boat? The elevator doors opened, two children trotted out, Molly hoped they were Doyle's, but they were followed by other parents: a short man in a homburg and his too-tall wife. The voice of doubt spoke up in her head, and as usual, it took on her father's rhythms: Nothing important could possibly happen here in the Ambassador Hotel, two old farts talking about ghosts. By pushing her editor and running out here, she had potentially strung her own noose. If she came home empty-handed, it would be nobody's fault but her own, and soon enough she would be writing more articles about lipstick, or worse, she would get fired and have to go begging for work from her dad.

Molly imagined Abe haranguing her: What was she doing out here with these seaside mishegass when William Z. Foster, an American labor hero, rotted in a midwestern jail? She dropped the *Radio Times* on a table and picked up a copy of yesterday evening's *Graphic*. Bernarr Macfadden's brand-new brainchild, the tabloid aimed low—murders, bobbed-hair bandits, horses at the track—but it was her competition and like the *Radio Times* cast its faith in technology. The *Graphic*'s trademark was the composite photo, pictographs cobbling together bedrooms and lovers and smoking guns. For the Atlantic City story—covered on its Entertainments page—a startled Conan Doyle was superimposed near a big-breasted girl and Houdini triumphant in the surf. Molly read a column inch of the paper's "All-Seeing Eye":

How the great Magi has grown portly and slow! But don't take this reporter's word for it, sneak a peek at his latest picture show—if you dare! *The Man from* Where?!? Still, what a show he puts on for the kiddies! Is this what's next for Houdini? Entertaining tots at the seashore? No, the handcuff king should hang it up. Cufflink king might be more his speed—*largo!*

Hovering between the prose and the pictograph was a block-print illustration, a mystic-looking eyeball afloat on black ink, but Molly knew the column's source was more prosaic than that: Alton Grimm, whom she expected to see here, lurking among the potted palms and plush carpets of the lobby, in town for the beauty pageants, but leaning in on her story. Tall and ghoulish, with diseased teeth and fingernails, if there was any gallantry about Alton Grimm it came from his honest pleasure in sticking his nose in other people's business. He had a leering, awful grin, gums riding so high that his face resembled a skull. The thought of this man's competition fired her rage. Molly turned from his column and flipped through the *Graphic* idly. She was reading an article titled "Why Jews Excel at Basketball," a picture of Nate Holman with a ball, when a cry from the desk clerk interrupted her.

"Sir Arthur!" the clerk called. "Mr. Conan Doyle?"

Molly looked up to see him there with his wife and kids, moving from the elevators to the restaurant. Doyle paused by the front desk, grandfatherly and distracted, sorting through his mail. He might have been a successful brewer or a retired prizefighter, here for a weekend by the surf. No one would have guessed a literary man, much less a religious crusader. His clothes were good but quiet. His bulk and energy made his wife and children seem small. The adolescents, hopping around him, looked younger than they actually were. Lady Doyle stood at a distance. She had been, so Molly had read, a great beauty when he had first met her, a talented horse rider. She had nursed Doyle's first wife through her final illness, but there was nothing about her now to suggest tenderness or vivacity. Her face was thin behind tiny reflecting glasses, her dress long and gray and stiff. She clasped her hands tensely in front of her. Her upper lip twitched. Lady Doyle boasted mediumistic powers, so Molly had learned when working her way through the *Radio Times'* library of old clippings, and had raised her children to believe that life was transient and death far more comfortable.

Points and nudges, from around the room people noticed the famous man. Doyle opened an envelope and unfolded a page. His wife came close, whispering. Doyle set his papers down, stuffed one page into his jacket pocket, said something to the clerk, and then with a wave of both arms herded his children toward the dining room. The family vanished. Molly frowned. Again her father's voice came to her. There was no clear story here, nothing to follow from day to day. "Genial Fellow Harbors Peculiar Religious Convictions," what kind of headline was that? Smarter for her to hop back on the train, rush back to the city, and write about the latest in rouge. There were new books on child-rearing on her desk at work. Molly bit her thumb. But maybe the family angle could work. If she spent a day with them by the hotel pool, maybe they would agree to talk, to discuss the benefits and complexities of bringing up children the Spiritualist way. Were there difficulties at school? Were the children, so comfortable with death, any more confident in life?

Her head throbbed from lack of sleep, the bumpy night on the train. Molly arranged the leg of her pants, suddenly self-conscious about her clothing. What would Sukey Van Siever say about that: Molly at poolside asking child-rearing advice from a zealot? For Sukey, all Molly's professional ambitions were dull. That Molly wanted to work, to support herself, to be independent, it smacked to her of asexual earnestness, as if pretty little Molly secretly wanted to be a kind of suffragette or temperance campaigner. The room on Gay Street was all right, thought Sukey, something romantic about that. Even the typewriter could be forgiven, if only Molly were a poet and not a newspaperwoman. And Sir Arthur Conan Doyle—the dullness of it was tragic. Of course we all have immortal souls, said Sukey, but where was the fun in fussing about it? Molly picked her head up, saw the elevator doors open, and blinked. There was Harry Houdini.

The space of the big lobby collapsed. One of the smaller men in the room, he possessed the place entirely. Houdini's face, perhaps because it was so familiar, loomed larger than everyone else's, hair black, skin pale, and eyes—even far away—demonic. He was polite. He signed an autograph for a child. He was graceful and yet in his neat motions, even in his smile, lurked some mad, violent energy. He lifted a finger in the air, he laughed. His simplest gesture contained possibility. At any moment, he might levitate, vanish, or fly. And when Houdini was out of view, Molly could not even remember his wife's face. The glare of the magician's fame had turned that woman invisible.

She shot up from her chair, went to the restaurant doorway, and peeked. The maître d' approached. Molly shook her head, eyes on Houdini. At the Doyles' table, he bowed, black hair shining. Everyone watched him, the diners struggling not to stare.

A quarter for the busboy, and Molly scribbled down their lunch orders—*HH: Chicken/ CD: Roast Beef*. A dollar more to the maître d' and he took her card to them, Molly Goodman, the *Radio Times*, apologizing for the interruption and wondering if the gentlemen might spare a minute for scientific discussion when the families were done with their meal. Then, not waiting for a reply—she did not want to give them the chance to refuse her—Molly dashed back to her uncomfortable chair, heart beating madly.

She picked up a copy of the *World*, but could not focus on its front-page articles about trade and tariffs. What the hell am I doing here? she thought. Magic tricks, mediums, chasing old men who chase ghosts? But if she could get an interview with Houdini or Doyle. Oh dear, thought Molly. Here she was staking out celebrities, competing with Alton Grimm, the parasyphilitic gossip columnist, and hoping beyond hope for a fight between friends. A public spat between Houdini and Doyle would make great copy. The possibility of success made success look cheap.

Archer Miles, the photographer from her paper, strolled through the lobby, hat in one hand and a pretty girl in the other. Molly thought to wave, but decided he would not see her. Archie's eyes were fixed entirely on his girl—she was blond with a sweet complexion. Her head wobbled as she talked, conversation that to look at Miles's pink comprehensive face was delightful, amusing, and true.

He swung his legs leisurely. His forehead shone in the lights. The girl made mincing steps. She was just the kind Molly would expect to see with Archie Miles, a swimsuit-competition blonde. She knew she ought to call out, to get him to snap a few pictures to go with whatever article she was writing, but she didn't want anything to do with him. Molly made justifications: that there really was, at this point, no story; that Archie's presence—and his camera's—might fudge her chances at an interview. But the truth was she didn't like him. He was too confident in his charms, too sure he charmed everyone. What would Archie think, she wondered, if he learned that she hated him? He might even be hurt. And Molly didn't want to hurt Archie, so at the last minute she called his name. But too late. He had already left the lobby.

"He hasn't fucked her," said Alton Grimm, the All-Seeing Eye, who had appeared as if out of nowhere to sit next to her.

"Excuse me?"

"If he had fucked her, he wouldn't be listening to her with that chipper little smile."

Jets of smoke came from his nostrils. Skin flaked in blisters off his brow. Grimm offered Molly a cigarette, and though she accepted, she was careful not to touch his flaking fingernails.

AT FIFTEEN MINUTES past one o'clock, the Doyles left the restaurant, first the children, then Lady Doyle, and last Sir Arthur. Molly appeared before him at the bottom of the lobby steps.

"Good afternoon." Bright as a bunny. "You got my card?"

"I beg your pardon?"

"The *Radio Times*? I sent a note?"

"Of course," said Doyle, "Miss Greenstein."

Lady Doyle glared.

"Goodman," said Molly.

He nodded. "Terribly." His wife put a hand on each child and steered them down the three short steps and away from the reporter. Sir Arthur tried to follow.

"I'll be a minute, really," said Molly.

Doyle sighed. "But this afternoon, unfortunately." He looked at his wife, who waited close by. "We are otherwise—we find our time quite—"

"I went and saw that radio tower. The one you mentioned in your interview with the *Herald*. The one with the enormous capacity—"

"Ah?"

"I was interested from a scientific angle. I work for the scientific paper, you know. *The Radio Times*, Tomorrow's News Today. We're eager to explore the Spiritualist view."

"Indeed." Doyle glanced from Molly to his wife. "I have a press agent, you know." He fumbled through his pockets and found a card. "There. In New York. Mr. Samuel Waxman. The name, the mailing address, and telephone number are all there for you. And if your paper should like to arrange an interview, please address your inquiries to Mr. Waxman, a very competent gentleman, may I say—"

"I understand you're here with Houdini." Molly would not let him get past her. She had not traveled all the way from the city for his press agent's card.

"Yes." Doyle nodded. "Well, we must be—"

"I'd love to interview—" Molly began.

"Ah." He looked down at her. "But Houdini's his own man, you know. I don't dare speak for Houdini. And I must—"

"So are there any new developments?"

"My dear—"

"Nothing planned for this evening? The *Radio Times* is willing to devote considerable attention to this story and—"

"Young lady." Lady Doyle stepped forward. "I find this highly irregular, to accost a gentleman on holiday with his family and—"

"Apologies." Molly hated her, this dried-out Victorian in her many-buttoned dress, wet blue eyes furious behind her spectacles. "Apologies," Molly said again. "I was just wondering if there were any developments in—" But before she could get out another word, she was interrupted.

Lady Doyle gazed up to the entrance to the restaurant, and Molly's eyes followed. There at the landing was Harry Houdini. He had been watching, he had heard every word.

"Tonight," he announced, raising that finger, "there will indeed be developments, a séance. With the Conan Doyles and also with"—he paused, extending his hand to present himself— "Houdini."

"My wife," Conan Doyle whispered, the huge man taking Molly by the arm. "My wife will—privately and not for publication—offer Houdini a demonstration of spirit writing. Tonight. Not for publication, mind you." He shot a glance at Houdini. "And I tell you this only because I have been forced to do so, and if you should honor my confidence, I am certain—"

"And I will be honored," said Houdini, advancing and bowing left and right, "to spend the evening with my good friend Sir Arthur Conan Doyle and with his lovely and noble wife, my Lady Doyle. There is no need to hide this from the newspapers, Sir Arthur. I understand your gentlemanly discretion, but it is not the American style. No. I state it freely: How I yearn to witness Lady Doyle's talents and to experience firsthand their effects."

"It's this evening, then?" asked Molly, scribbling notes.

Houdini gripped her elbow and drew her from Doyle's grasp.

"I have," he began, "as I am sure you know, carried out a number of investigations into the workings of many so-called mediums and miracle-mongers, both here and in Europe." He spoke the same words as he had the other day to Conan Doyle, Houdini all the while watching Molly's pencil move across her page. "But it is important to note that my investigations, as is proper, have been and will continue to be devoted solely to the works of professional Spiritualists." Doyle looked on, discomfited and awestruck, but Houdini continued undeterred. "We would, as part of a traveling circus troupe, read the future for crowds." Molly pulled at the string at the end of her pencil, freeing up a nub of fresh lead. "I most certainly did not relish, then, treading on the sacred feelings of my admirers." He slowed his speech, making sure she got every word, and Molly kept scribbling until he was done. "The same is true now of the sacred feelings of my friends, and I will witness Lady Doyle's performance tonight in the spirit of friendship and not investigation."

He nodded, signaling the interview was done.

Molly turned toward Bess Houdini, a small woman in green, with large eyes set wide in a delicate face. "And will you be attending the séance tonight?" she asked.

But Sir Arthur answered for her. "We would of course be happy, more than happy, to have Mrs. Houdini at our table, and perhaps sometime soon we will, but it is important, when crossing over into the world beyond and entering the domain of purely psychical forces, to maintain a balance of belief and doubt, and, you know, two doubters might tip the balance such that our little table might prove less than congenial to any sojourners from the beyond."

"I suppose that means I would not be—"

"Certainly not," said Lady Doyle to Molly.

And they were gone.

She got herself a table at the restaurant, and with the last of her cash ordered coffee and drank it with a plate of wet scrambled eggs. Molly was not three bites in when Alton Grimm pulled up a chair and dropped his stained straw hat near the creamer. Sparse eyebrows climbed his scaly forehead. He had seen her with the Doyles and Houdinis.

"Oh, yeah." Molly gave only the vaguest information. "They're gathering in the Doyles' rooms tonight." Between bites and swallows. "Some kind of Spiritualist problem. I don't know."

Grimm frowned. Probably, even if she had been more generous and specific, he would not have shared his news with her: that this morning in the Embassy Hotel, just one block down the boardwalk, he had seen Doyle breakfasting with the famous medium Margery.

THE SUN SETS. The clouds go from white to orange to gray. On the Heinz pier, a hundred bulbs light the number 57. In the Doyles' rooms, curtains are drawn, lights out, and the three sitters hold hands in the darkness. Doyle signals, and they release each other. With a trembling match, he lights his candle. The flame's reflection doubles in his wife's glasses. She shuts her eyes, runs her fingers over the pen and paper that are arranged in front of her. Houdini bows his head, and Doyle watches, trying to gauge his friend's seriousness, his willingness to muzzle attack-dog doubts.

"I shall rest my pen," says Lady Doyle, "and there will follow a period of quiet. Then you will ask your questions. If we are all firm in our hopes and if we are fortunate, the spirit hand shall travel the distance between the two worlds and move my own hand. But for this to happen, we must all three rely absolutely on one another's concentration and good fellowship. The responsibility"—and she gave Houdini a meaningful glance—"is divided equally amongst us."

"I will do my honest level best." Houdini looks up at her. "Everything honest friendship requires. Lady Doyle," he adds, "you cannot know what it would mean to me if I were to speak to my mother."

She closes her eyes.

Against the room's quiet they hear the distant surf sounds, the breakers, the laughter of strollers on the boardwalk, the push-carts' creaking wheels, and far away, squawking car horns and motors. Doyle's eyes move from his wife to Houdini, whose body at rest is kinetic. The magician watches Lady Doyle, his attentiveness exaggerated as if for a crowd. Lady Doyle's eyes flutter. Houdini looks toward Conan Doyle, who nods.

"Can you read my mind?"

Her pen begins a slow, ink-spitting orbit that resolves itself into smaller circles and finally letters and words:

I always read your mind, my darling.

Sir Arthur leans forward. Another shape is forming under Lady Doyle's pen, this one on the top right-hand corner of the page.

"Was your mother religious?" whispers Doyle.

Houdini nods. Lady Doyle has drawn a cross.

"Have you any news for me?" asks Houdini.

The pen scratches, skids, then gains momentum. The first O and H are clumsy, but the work accelerates and soon letters are running one into the next.

Oh my darling son thank GOD I am through—I have tried of
so often now I am happy Why of course—I want to talk to my
beloved boy my beloved friends—thank you with all my heart
for you have answered the cry of my heartgod bless

Her pen hops and slides like a one-legged dancer. Conan Doyle
bends toward candle. The yellow flame colors his skin.

Never had a mother such a son tellhim not to grieve   soon
he'll get the evidence he needs tell him I want him to write in
his own home on his own to me I shall come to him in his own
home and it will be so much better he is so dear to me and I am
preparing him a sweet home here for him in God's good time he
shall join me—

When the page is filled Doyle snatches it off the stack gingerly as
if it were a cake on a grill. His wife's pen lands on the paper
beneath and does not pause in its scribbling.

I am so happy in this life so large and so free and so joyous and
oh my sorrow is that my beloved boy has not known how often
I have been with him all the while here anyway from my hearts
darling it is so different here so lovely so lofty and all sweetness
around one nothing that hurts and we see our beloved ones on
earth and know they will all see us soon that is such joy such
courage—oh tell him I love him more than ever and that there
are no years there is no distance and his goodness fills my soul
with gladness and thankfulness oh just—it is me it is me let him

*know it is me—I have bridged the gap at last the gulf oh thank
you for now I shall at long last be at peace*

Her pen slips. It spins across the table. Houdini remains
rigidly attentive, while his hand, its own creature, snatches the
thing midflight. Lady Doyle slumps, puts a hand to her jaw, and
moves it right and left, as if she has been punched there. Her
husband fixes her a glass of water. Then, while she drinks, Doyle
gathers the pages, orders them, and hands them to Houdini. The
magician pulls out glasses from his jacket's breast pocket.
Leaning toward Doyle, he points to letters and words, and nods
seriously as his friend interprets. Lady Doyle sips her drink.

"Well?" asks Doyle, when Houdini has put the pages down.

"Thank you," says Houdini.

"But—"

"Thank you."

"Are you saying that you remain unconvinced?"

"No such thing."

"Bravo!" cries Conan Doyle.

But, "I am convinced," says the magician, "convinced as ever
of your goodwill, of your wife's goodwill, and of her integrity. I
have never for a moment needed convincing of any of this. As to
the existence of spirits," he continues, "of my mother's spirit—
well, you may know that I feel my mother's spirit with me every
day, watching me, my mother's loving soul—"

Doyle slaps the table. "Just as the writing has it! There you
are: your mother's voice. And as you say, my dear Houdini, there
can be no doubt of the source, my wife is no trickster—"

"Sir Arthur—"

"What you have witnessed"—Doyle will not be interrupted—
"is the power of plain, honest trust, nothing supersophisticated,
nothing could be more logical. We have come together and
given ourselves over to the spirit world, and the spirit of your
good mother has responded. There we have it. So, as you are an
honest fellow, you'll admit to an honest day's work: Shall we cor-
ral that reporting woman we saw this afternoon, that Miss
Goodman of the *Telegram Times*, and have headlines in the
morning to the effect of 'Houdini Sees the Light'? You see, my
good man, it is simply a matter of faith—"

"It is a matter of faith," says Houdini.

"Are you suggesting—"

Still in his chair, leaning back slightly, Houdini stacks the
sheets of spirit writing and aligns the paper's edges. He folds the
sheets neatly. He is about to put them in his jacket pocket when
he stops.

"Believe me," he says, "I accepted your invitation here
tonight with some hesitation. I do not, in any way, want to take
advantage of your trust, your faith, or your hospitality."

"But, tell me, do you persist in your doubts?"

"Perhaps," says Houdini, "perhaps it is too large a fact to swallow whole. Perhaps it takes time to digest these things." He gestures with the papers. "You see, Lady Doyle, Sir Arthur, I admire
both of you so. People of substance, of genuine character. I
admire your sincerity, gentility, dignity. And this is of course all I
had wanted for years." He takes the paper in both hands, fum-
bling uncharacteristically. "To speak with my beloved mother—
Sir Arthur, I know you feel something of this in the loss of your
son, as if a central part of one's soul has departed, a missing piece

of one's very own life. My mother." He cannot speak. The pit beneath the candle flame overflows with wax. "It is not a fact one can take in all at once."

"You seem," says Lady Doyle, "genuinely moved."

"I am," Houdini tells her. "Perhaps I can take these pages, bring them back to my hotel room, examine them—"

"Of course," says Sir Arthur.

"Be assured," Lady Doyle chimes in, "none of the words on those pages are mine."

"I see," says Houdini, and now everyone in the room is standing.

"It is not difficult," Lady Doyle insists, her natural reserve counterbalanced by an urge to help. "It is not difficult, and—I rarely if ever disagree with husband, but here I must—it is not simply a matter of faith. It is a matter of spirit, I tell you. I know that I speak for Sir Arthur when I tell you that what you have in your hand is evidence."

"Evidence," her husband echoes.

"One can," she insists, "I am not entirely certain of it, but I suspect that one can be almost entirely without faith—almost entirely—and still have some success in this writing. Sir Arthur claims that I have a gift for it, that the spirits find my hand congenial to the task"—her upper lip makes its slight hop—"but I tell you, I insist, it is not a matter of talent. I do not fight against them, that is all. And it is only struggle against them, only active doubt that chases the hand away. If one is willing to withhold doubt and one is ready and does not protest in any way consciously or unconsciously, why, then the spirits come. All that is required is that blessed blankness and serenity."

"I see," says Houdini.

"Perhaps," Conan Doyle suggests, "in order to make the conversion complete, Houdini ought to take a turn at spirit writing. No—I am in earnest. We all read what the spirit said: Your mother asked that you make the attempt at writing, at home, she said, but you might as well start here, among friends—she acknowledged us as friends who mean you good entirely. Now, then, you cannot argue with that; one ought to obey one's mother. Follow my wife's lead. Take up the pen and paper. Remember her advice and see what comes of it: Passivity above all, relaxation of the instinct to doubt. Nothing could be simpler. If nothing comes of it, we try again; if success, well, then—success!" With a chuckle. "So be a good lad and have a seat. Listen to your mother. Try your hand. There is nothing to fear, unless one fears the love of the spirits beyond."

The candle burns low. The curtains billow. Soon all three are sitting.

"One strives," Lady Doyle gives instruction, "to sever the link between mind and hand. You must let a greater intelligence drive you."

"How does one know," Houdini wonders, "that there is a greater intelligence?"

"One knows." Her smile is surprisingly pretty. "One must know."

So he takes her pen, which he could have swallowed or multiplied or made disappear, and he lets it scratch the paper.

"Let your mind go blank," says Lady Doyle. "Absolutely blank. When the mind is blank, the spirits work."

Houdini obediently shuts his eyes. He exhales and the three sit quietly. The pen wavers but produces nothing. Wax collects on the tabletop. Doyle fingers his mustache while Houdini's head rocks above his powerful shoulders. The pen inches one way and another, tracing a groove.

"Blank," whispers Lady Doyle.

And as she says the word the candle snuffs. In darkness and quiet, they hear the pen scratching. Doyle's eyes adjust to the half-light. Houdini barely moves. He might be half asleep, but for his pen, which wavers oddly, then falls from his hand. Doyle stands, finds a light switch.

In the center of the page, in a childish, angular hand, is a single word: *Margery*.

"Ha!" cries Doyle.

"What do you mean?" asks Houdini.

"There's your evidence. Will you call yourself a fraud?"

"I have no idea what you are implying," Houdini protests. "We were just discussing her, over lunch, in connection with this very—"

"No. I shall count this, Houdini, as your first and happiest defeat."

"But we spoke of her this afternoon, and clearly my mind, distracted, fell back to our earlier conversation—and under the circumstances of the evening the association is not at all surprising—"

"No words crossed your mind?" asks Lady Doyle.

"Not one."

"Not one!" Sir Arthur booms.

"Surely there can be explanations other than spirits. We are not aware of everything that—"

"No," says Conan Doyle, "most of us are in deep ignorance of the spirit world which you, my dear friend, are experiencing right here, right now, in the most immediate and personal sensations, and yet, even though the strongest possible evidence lies before you, evidence produced by your own hand, you continue to doubt." He smiles. "Fascinating, is it not? The thing to study, the true fascination, is not the existence of another plane of being, which, if one pauses to think, exists as surely as does one's own right hand, but the complex justifications, caveats, and ratiocinations, the work that we do to deny the existence of that world. She was here tonight, Houdini."

"Who?"

Doyle points to the page.

"Margery?" It is too much.

"She was here, governing your hand."

"You wrote her name," says Lady Doyle.

"I think she is challenging you, Houdini. I think she is daring you to attend her séance, Thursday next in Pleasant Valley, where she and Dr. Sabatier live. And when you come"—he points at Houdini—"you shall arrive as a believer. No tricks, no tomfoolery. No tests. Just come, be receptive, and we shall see."

"Margery?" Houdini looks away. "Challenging me? Governing my hand? Well. I accept. Of course. Whatever, wherever her challenge, let her name her terms—I accept."

V

THE DOWNTOWN PRESSES ROLLED. Evening papers got folded and bundled and lobbed into the backs of trucks, then hawked at street corners and kiosks all over town. By the time Houdini had made it to the Doyles' hotel suite, subway trash cans were crammed with copies of the "All-Seeing Eye":

> Spirit voices say somewhere in Surf City Sir Arthur Conan Doyle will introduce everyone's favorite unbeliever to medium-of-the-moment Margery. Mrs. Houdini won't be allowed in the door—and that rustle you hear, folks, is the sound of ghostly tongues wagging.

The *Graphic* found itself in Molly's hands just after she filed her story, and as she scanned Alton Grimm's prose, her stomach turned.

Farquharson called to bring her home. Flat, uncompromising, long-distance from New York, he didn't make threats or use obscenities, just reminded Molly that she had been scooped not only by a gossip columnist but by the camera jockey from her own paper. Archer Miles had come up with another photo from her beat, and it would run on page one: Arthur Conan Doyle in a rolling chair, smiling as he took a ride down the boardwalk. Only one of the sentences she had phoned in would run, somewhere on page six, lost amid a clutter of curiosity pieces, appended to a wire service version of the story Grimm had broken.

"Goodman," her editor had said, "I'm not paying you to sunbathe or model swimsuits."

Molly protested, argued that Grimm had it wrong: Margery was not at the séance in the Doyles' room last night. As she spoke she felt her temper rise.

"Say what you want," said Farquharson. "See me in my office when you get back."

The line went dead, and Molly got to work, canvassing the garage and the maids and the kitchen, anywhere she might get information. She was nearly out of cash, had spent almost a week's salary on tickets, lodging, food, and bribes, and it wasn't at all clear that Farquharson would reimburse her. Still, she got what she needed: The Doyles and Houdinis were set to check out the next morning and as far as she could gather they would be traveling in separate limousines to Manhattan. Molly got out a map and tried to anticipate their route, then moved between the garage and the lobby that morning, smoking cigarettes.

Somehow, she missed them, lost sight of a driver for fifteen minutes, and then within the half hour both parties were gone. Undaunted, but nearly panicked, Molly bought a train ticket home, hoping beyond hope that she would catch at least one of them at the Hoboken Ferry—if not there, then at their hotel rooms in town. She would find out what had happened at the spirit demonstration that Lady Doyle had performed. Whether Farquharson would run the story or not, she would prove to him that she and not Alton Grimm had it right: Margery had not met Houdini. And just before noon, as she stood by the ferry docks wearing a broad-brimmed hat and carrying binoculars, Molly contemplated her disaster. She had badgered her boss and made promises and spent money. Coming home empty-handed, she would be fired.

Seagulls climbed against the wind. Gallant men ran errands across the trolley tracks between the train and ferry depots, in front of the half-abandoned stables. Scattered vacationers showed no sense of holiday. The weekend was over. Impatient feet kicked stones. Nervous glances shot at the pier, the boats, the river, and the big white buildings of Manhattan. The glare of noon reflected off Molly's glasses. She took off her hat and walked toward some high ground, where she could see the cars as they pulled in. Her hair, brownish under the awnings of the train station, glowed golden in the sun. She had skipped breakfast, so bought some roast corn at a stand, but what she got from the salt and butter was the smell of humiliation. The end of the week would find her asking her father for a job.

She checked her watch. Five minutes before the next ferry would depart. The cars had boarded. Molly knew she should jump on, give up, go home. A second bite of the salted blandness and she had to fight nausea. She imagined what Sukey would say, or at least Sukey's blithe face, how little it would interest her if Molly got fired. And her father would be all smiles and consolation and quick to offer work at *Progress*. Her mother, Molly figured, might be more circumspect. If Molly had not come home with a story (so Belle's reasoning), she must not have wanted one; she was capable enough, so her failure had to signal ambivalence. Did she want to work for that paper—did she want to be a reporter at all? The thought of her mother's psychological syllogisms nagged at her. She didn't understand her own story, what a story was, or even how to chase one.

What was she doing here for instance, on the ferry dock? She could spend hours watching cars, trains, boats, and people move in and out and back and forth, but she was kidding herself if she thought she was doing anything but stalling. Did she still believe in magic, that by wishing for it, news would come to her? And if Conan Doyle appeared, what would she ask him, and what answer could he give her that would justify her time? She was a coward, so Molly told herself, she was standing here at the docks because she was frightened of what might happen when she went back to the city. The thought of her own cowardice only made her angrier. Molly scanned the lines for tickets. She looked for limousines approaching. A man in sunglasses turned toward her and smiled. She did not recognize him until he tipped his cap and showed his baldness to the sun.

"Goodman!" It was Archer Miles, trotting toward her in summer whites. "What are you doing standing there? Waiting for some butter-and-egg man of yours?"

"Waiting for the ferry," she said with a shrug.

"Why not take this one?"

"Waiting for a friend." She affected casualness.

"Applesauce," he said. "Ain't I a friend?"

She avoided the question, looking around to see if the hotel blonde was nearby. "I thought you were staying in Atlantic City."

"Workaday Johnny," Miles told her. "I head in and out, back and forth."

Workaday Johnny, Molly thought contemptuously—his father's shipping lines, his penthouse hotel address. She said nothing, but her face must have betrayed her.

"You're not sore at me?"

"Sore?"

An awkward silence passed, both knowing that their paper had for the last two days carried pictures he had taken of people she ought to have been covering, and meanwhile had run no stories of hers. Miles was right, they should have been friends. They were the college kids on the paper's staff. But there it was, Molly didn't like him.

Their silence was punctured gracelessly by the ferry's horn.

"Guess I got to run." He paused, wiping his own chin. "Little bit of butter, right there, left side."

The ferry hooted once more. Molly did what she could with her napkin.

"Hey, I know what I'll do." Miles was backing away, waving his sunglasses. "I'll tell old Farquharson you tipped me off to it. I'll tell the old man I would never have gotten the pictures unless you told me where to go."

"Right," said Molly. "Triple my humiliation."

But he didn't hear, cupped a hand to signal as much, then tripped away for the boat. As he ran, the tail of his jacket rose, and Molly watched, idly considering the shape of his behind.

The ferry horn sounded one last time. The lines were drawn in, the engines groaned, the reeking Hudson, greenish brown with sewage and waste, churned as propellers roared. Molly looked up at the rail where passengers had gathered to watch the departing shore, and there saw a big gray-haired father smiling with his girl—Sir Arthur Conan Doyle and his daughter Joanna, watching the docks recede. His glasses went white; light off the water reflecting against the lenses, and then maybe he was look-ing in Molly's direction, but it couldn't matter now. She cursed. She found a bench and lit a cigarette. Pigeons fought over a dis-carded half roll. Molly had a vision of the ferry ride: Archer Miles, scurrying between some ex-debutante soon-to-be-fiancée in Manhattan and some farmer's-daughter bathing suit model on the Jersey shore, was sure to bump into Doyle mid-Hudson, while the writer was deep in conference with some great ghost, maybe Abraham Lincoln come back for casual chitchat. Cheerful Miles would oblige the pair, pull out his Kodak, and snap a few shots, afterward conducting interviews and acting as amanuensis to the assassinated president. After docking, Archie would taxi off to the *Radio Times* to type up his news: *"Honest Abe Calls Prohibition a Bust—Urges New Yorkers to Vote Democrat."* Soon, very soon, she would be reviewing Yiddish theater for *Progress*. Or maybe she would never return to New York. She saw the docks across the river, the massive Nabisco factory, the red brick buildings, the white towers. Seen from this distance Manhattan appeared less a human habitation than an enormous machine, consuming and disgorging boats and trains, billowing smoke, gleaming stone. Molly tossed her cigarette and ground it under the toe of her pump. This story, this trip to New Jersey, it was all a wild, stupid attempt to escape her life, and it had failed.

Oh, Carl, she thought, God help me. Tears were forming in the corners of her eyes. She fought them back. They were pathetic, self-indulgent. Help me, Carl, help me get ahold of myself.

She bit her lip to stop her praying, stood up on the bench, one last survey of the incoming cars, and—yes, that was it, that big black Packard over there. She did not need to check the license plate against her notes, she had already memorized the number. She hopped back down on her bench, hoping she had not made a spectacle of herself. The question now was how to approach. Help, Carl, help. She would feel like a lunatic running across the lot of parked cars to rap on his window, and yet there was no guarantee he would leave his car in the short ride across the river, and she could lose him easily at the docks on 23rd Street.

She pulled out her notes to review them. A short, dark-haired man hovered nearby on the periphery of her vision. She kept her eyes away from him. Her bob, her lipstick, her cigarette, these thrilled the out-of-town guys, who thought she was the thing they had been promised by the modern age: the pretty college girl who wanted it. They asked for a cigarette or the time, and then next came an offer, a soda pop or something stronger. This one seemed stiff, almost nervous. Molly was still sitting but about to stand, heading for Houdini's car, hoping to blow past her sudden suitor.

But he blocked her way.

"Excuse me," he said, and his voice was half familiar. "You are Miss Goodman."

"Do I?"

He was standing between her and the sun. He tipped his hat, and the loss of its shade only made it harder to make out his features. She put a hand to her forehead and squinted.

"You are the reporter I spoke with yesterday." A wave of his powerful hand. "You recognize me."

"Why—"

"Come." Houdini beckoned.

Molly stood.

And she followed as if in a trance across the baking asphalt. He opened the back door and invited her into his limousine. The back of his car was dark and curtained, even more capacious than it looked from outside. Two cushioned benches faced each other. One was empty, the other held Houdini's wife. Molly slid into the open banquette and the magician followed her.

"I congratulate you on your pursuit of me," the magician said. "Take out your pencil and pad."

In the darkness of the car, Molly rummaged through her clutch. There was a small notebook, a short, discontinuous novel about life at Princeton, a pack of cigarettes, lipstick, her glasses case, tissues. *Pencil.* Molly prayed for one. *Pencil.* Then Houdini's hand materialized in the darkness holding a beautiful pen. It had been a mistake, he announced, for him to avoid her in the lobby of the hotel this morning. (He said this simply; Houdini could appear to her or not as he saw fit.) But he had read his mail and the newspapers as he had traveled from Atlantic City to this ferry port and he was incensed by the innuendo he had found there.

"It is not easy," said Houdini, "to be in my position."

And he leaned forward, his right hand just above the paper on which Molly was ready to write. He glared at her, waiting. So she wrote, *It is not easy to be in my position.* Satisfied, Houdini continued.

"There are some questions," he said, "which may arise before the public. I have been considering how best to address these. I am determined, without delay, to resolve uncertainties. So it is that I have brought you here. I have not the time to speak with newspaper reporters all over the city, and I will allow for no ambiguities to be reported regarding the séance given to me last night by the Lady Doyle in the presence of her husband, Sir Arthur." And he offered the date, time, and place of the spirit writing, as if he were giving a deposition in court. "For it was I who sat at the table, I and not, as it has been reported in yours and other newspapers, the so-called medium Margery."

Molly did as he expected. She wrote down every word.

"After more than thirty years' experience in the realm of mystery," he said, watching her pen as he spoke, "I have never seen a mystery, and I have never visited a séance, which I could not fully explain. I have had a note from Sir Arthur Conan Doyle this morning which intimates that I, Houdini, was awed and perplexed by the events of the evening in question. Sir Arthur goes further. He states unequivocally that in the course of the séance, I, Harry Houdini, was in the presence of my dear mother's spirit—that Lady Doyle's writing summoned the spirit of my dear, beloved mother—and it is my obligation, because of the dangers faced by investigators of psychic phenomena, and because of the reputation I have earned, to quash these misconceptions thoroughly and before they can be misconstrued by a wider audience."

The ferry's horn blew. The driver, seated behind a partition and with his back to Molly, slipped the car in gear and edged it toward the boat. Molly wrote as fast as she could, flipped one page, and began the next.

"Lady Doyle told me that she was automatically writing a letter which was guided by the spirit of my beloved, sainted mother. Every boy who has ever had a worshiping mother and has lost earthly touch knows the feeling which will come over anyone at the thought of sensing the presence of his mother." Houdini paused, allowing Molly to catch up. "I must tell you that there was not the slightest idea of my having felt my mother's presence. Not once. And the letter that followed, in Lady Doyle's hand, I cannot possibly accept as having been written or inspired by the soul or spirit of my sweet mother." Houdini proceeded to offer proof: that the cross on the paper could not have been put there by the spirit of his mother. "My mother was religious, yes, but a rabbi's wife, a believing Jew." And furthermore, it had seemed impossible to him that his mother would comprehend the language in which the letter was written. "Although she had lived in America for almost fifty years, she could not read, speak, or write English, and the Spiritualists claim that when you are possessed by a spirit who does not speak your language, you automatically write, speak, or sing in the language of the deceased." The car edged onto the ferry. Houdini became excited. "Yesterday was the anniversary of my mother's birth, her birthday, you know, and I cannot imagine that she would fail to make any mention of this. I understand that this alone signifies little, but combined with the other proofs—it is indisputable. My beloved, departed mother, may she rest in peace, had no part in the letter written by Lady Doyle.

"And as to that other claim of Doyle's," he started all over again, "that I was overtaken by supernatural forces because of my having written the word *Margery* on a piece of paper"—and here his pointing finger became a fist—"I must emphatically state that this was not, as the Conan Doyles would have it, an instance of spirit writing, of my body being overtaken, spiritually, by the etheric arm of the miracle-monger of Pleasant Valley no! I must emphatically state that this writing was an act of my own volition. I had the name in my mind and there was not the slightest chance of it having been more than a deliberate mystification on my part, or let us say a kindlier word regarding my thought, a. . . ." He paused, voice dropping to a lower register. "A coincidence. They believed otherwise and perhaps my unwillingness to offend them had something to do with their confusion, but the hand that wrote that word and the mind behind that hand belonged to Houdini and to Houdini alone."

Molly scribbled away, hoping to capture the scrambled logic of his sentences. Was Houdini claiming that he had deliberately misled the Doyles? Was he telling her what he would not tell them? She had no time to ask. The magician continued.

"I have the highest esteem for both Sir Arthur and his wife," he said, "but I am setting this down, letting you know the truth, so that no false claims regarding these events are made without such claims facing immediate, published contradiction. It must be understood that the spirit of Sir Arthur Conan Doyle's friend Margery never once guided the hand of Houdini." And quick as light that famous hand vanished. "That is all," he said.

The car hauled itself over the bumps of the dock and into the ferry. It parked among a set of black, blue, and green automobiles, all their engines cooling, Fords and Chevrolets and REO Speedwagons packed in so close none could maneuver, a space that smelled like a stable.

"But why," Molly began, and then turned her sentences around. "If you think any deceit was practiced, what do you imagine the Conan Doyles' motives might have been? Are you suggesting that Sir Arthur and Lady Doyle—"

"The Doyles' motives are beyond reproach," said Houdini. "Set that down: that their motives are beyond reproach. And I, Houdini, whatever the world may think, am no mind reader. I am, as you know, a scientific practitioner of illusion—the only honest one in existence today. You believe in science, my dear, don't you?" And Molly nodded. "Then you know that I cannot tell you their thoughts. But set this down, too: The hand of Margery never demonstrated any power, at any time, over the hand of Houdini."

"Are you calling Lady Doyle a fraud?"

"Young lady!" said Bess Houdini.

"And are you saying—" Molly was not going to be told what to write; she was going to press him. "Are you saying that you wrote the name Margery deliberately, in order to somehow fool the Conan Doyles?"

"You seem to be suggesting that either I, Houdini, or the Conan Doyles, noble people whose motives I again say are beyond reproach, were practicing some kind of scheme," said Houdini. "I find that suggestion offensive. I am not interested in schemes. I am interested in truth. And the truth is that my mother was not present and that Margery had no influence on my hand." He leaned across her lap to open the door of the automobile. "You may depart now."

"But," said Molly, "I had another question regarding—"

"If you have not purchased a ticket, my man will purchase one for you."

She opened her mouth.

"I tell you, Miss Goodman, that is all."

Molly smiled and surrendered.

The air was close and smelled of seawater, gasoline, and horse piss. She threaded her way between cars and trucks. A straw hat peeked out of a driver's-side window. A stranger called out something lewd. Molly found a spiral stairway, its banister corroded by long exposure to salt air. Gulls were cawing above, shadows against the blue sky. She held her purse tightly. Farquharson could not fire a girl coming home with this.

And she began to plan: what hotels she would have to call to find Conan Doyle, what questions she would have to ask him. The ferry's ride across the water was easy and slow, and she saw the spires of office towers through the hole at the top of the stairs, the Woolworth Tower, intricate Gothic high points, and then, as she got closer toward the opening, more of its sheer modern face. She climbed out onto the green wood planks of the passenger deck, crowded with benches and the cries of families, and saw the whole expanse of Manhattan coming close.

Molly hit the shore like an invading army.

VI

A S A SOPHOMORE AT Princeton, Lyden Silver was
the second-ranked middleweight boxer in the Ivy League.
He was short but quick, and punched with a savageness unexpected in such a quiet boy. He would have been ranked first if
not for what had happened to him on the day his father traveled
up to Cambridge to see Lyden fight. Michael Silver was a prominent lawyer, would become almost famous after the war for
defending suspected Communists in the time of the Palmer raids,
but was then known in the Boston area mainly for having married the Cambridge beauty Clarissa Lyden, and in New York for
being a cousin of the gangster Leopold "Goldy" Silverstein.
Those who disliked Lyden called his pugilism Semitic, sneaky,
and relentless, and though as an adolescent he had trained at the
uptown Harmonie Club, it was as though his fighting rose up,
like his father, from the Lower East Side. Even as an undergraduate, Lyden was not glib, not given to smiles. His shyness was

partly an attempt to compensate for the inner fury that he expressed so vividly in the boxing ring, but shyness was also of a piece with his decency, a natural social deference—something he had been born with, like his orange hair or pale eyes. But his shyness never won him many friends.

That day when his father traveled up to Cambridge to see him fight, Lyden faced Thomas French, the popular champion, a good-looking Harvard senior undefeated that year, who promised privately before the match to knock the Jewish kid all the way back to Europe. French came out swinging, underestimated his opponent, threw a left cross at Lyden's head, and missed badly. He was off balance when Lyden counterpunched, a right to the belly that took the air out of Harvard. French doubled over, and this shocked even Lyden, who popped the champ on his head so he fell. The crowd began to boo, and it wasn't until after the fight that Lyden understood why. The blow to the belly was ruled below the belt. That seemed the only explanation for French's crumpling. But Lyden knew where his fist had hit. He stood in the ring, nineteen years old, sweaty and bruised and being jeered unfairly by a hundred men in a gym. From the Crimson side came hisses and grumbling, but the traveling Princeton boosters were worse. Articles after the fight called his father a Red, his uncle a murderer, and there was a move to have Lyden expelled; he'd disgraced the school. Lyden could not enlist on account of color blindness, and so the only manly thing, he thought, was to stick it out. He quit boxing. His best friend died at war. He was snubbed everywhere he went, even—perhaps especially—by the Jews at Princeton who argued that (a) Lyden was not a Jew, he was the child of a gentile mother; and (b) that he had disgraced

Jews all over the country. Lyden devoted himself to his studies and to solitary physical exercise. After college, he went to law school, and then to work for his father. In the courtroom he found an outlet for his fury that suited him almost as well as had the boxing ring. While her undergraduate years had brought Molly apart from her parents, his time at Princeton had drawn Lyden closer to his. He still lived with them in his old room on the sixth floor just two stories above the Goodmans.

On the subway uptown, he read the *Radio Times*, only one article in it. Houdini made arguments which Doyle refuted. The cross on the paper was not a sectarian symbol but a holy one, placed on the page by Lady Doyle to ward off low influences. The language of the writing did not signify. Language was for the living; the communication of the dead could fill any idiom as water any vase. As to birthdays, what could be more meaningless from the perspective of eternity? Lyden wore a beard, sign of his radicalism, and his Welsh Margotson collar was beaten down by the heat and the working day. Early September, his parents were just back from the Bronx, but he had been holding down the office all alone. The train was crowded with warehousemen, dockworkers, stockbrokers, and it was murder, windows open to the grit of the tunnel, commuters packed tightly, and everyone trying to read his own paper and not get too intimate with his neighbor's sweat. Lyden looked over the eight hundred words twice. He had read Sherlock Holmes as a boy and had idolized Houdini, but the way they talked now—he didn't understand it. Lyden was sure that this was his fault; if Molly was interested, it must have been compelling. He was hopelessly romantically inexperienced. She was beyond him; Lyden understood that. He was to see her tonight, and was ready to be humiliated by his stammer, by his stupid shyness and bottled passion. The train pulled into 79th Street at six-thirty, so he got out to stroll the last blocks, checking the time as he went. The anniversary of Carl's birthday—the fact would go unmentioned but underlie the dinner—and it was supposed to be like old times, the Goodmans and the Silvers, except that Carl was dead and he and Molly were no longer children. Flowers were sold in bins on the corner of 83rd Street. Lyden paused. It was too much to bring them, but he didn't want to come empty-handed. There was a bouquet of blooms whose name he could not remember, long-stemmed with bunches of small blue blossoms. He bought them and then felt self-conscious, carrying them like a lover up Broadway and then westward to his parents' apartment building where he had grown up and where he still lived, carrying them speechlessly toward the Goodmans' door.

Behind which there was chaos, Abe Goodman in his underwear. He had taken off the jacket, vest, and pants he wore to *Progress*, but had not yet dressed for dinner. "A challie?" he called. Sabbath bread sat in the center of the table, gleaming where light from the electric chandelier played off its rounds, with a silver candlestick on either side and the blue china marshaled all around.

"Get dressed!" Belle screamed from the kitchen, where she was with the new girl, supervising.

"For Michael Silver we get a challie?"

If Belle heard, she pretended not to, and gave directions for the boiling of dumplings and the slicing of fruit.

"I don't understand." Abe stood alone in the French doors between the living and dining rooms, surveying the table with its stacks of soup bowls and first- and second-course plates, its rows of forks and spoons. "A production for the Silvers?"

"Abe," Belle shouted. "Will you please? They'll be coming."

"Shabbas." Bouncing the word like it was a rubber ball, his accent all affectation, Abe lifted the bread from its board and held it up for inspection. That was how Belle found him, Abe and the loaf like Hamlet and a skull.

"She doesn't know how to do strudel." Belle wore pearls and pearl earrings and a frilled apron over her dress.

"She'll learn." Abe put the bread down and picked up a whole tomato from the sideboard. This he munched as if it were an apple.

"She'll never learn."

"Who's the seventh?" A seed fell on his undershirt.

"Molly's bringing a friend."

"A friend? And so the challah—"

"A girl. Some Vassar friend of—"

"For Lyden, then?" Abe looked cunning. "What, some kind of special—Do you still expect Molly to take an interest in Lyden?"

"If you don't get dressed," Belle sighed, "they'll take an interest in your briefs." A clatter of dishes in the kitchen. "Your sweet Polish rose has once again ruined dinner. Three times this week," she added. "A disaster."

The girl in question was bright and pretty and right off the boat and had been hired only six days ago. She was good at cleaning, quick and furious, and had all the wrong experiences, a tough life forty miles from Gdansk, where her grandmother had a bakery. She chopped apples thickly and, sure she would please the Goodmans, rolled a dough made of oil, flour, and egg; she flapped the stuffing into loaves with lumps of fruit protruding. She worked quickly to impress, tried always to keep a few steps ahead, and Belle had to correct everything. So she took the extra time to show her the pan and how to make the sweeter German dough with lumps of brown sugar and handfuls of nuts. To Raizel, it was all dazzling. She was a pretty, plump girl, with just the rudiments of English, intimidated by the Goodmans' wealth, but more than willing to show her usefulness and aspirations to American life. Every morning she bought the *Daily News*, and worked out the phrases that corresponded with the photographs. Abe lectured her over his coffee, practicing his impossible Yiddish—really a mishmash of the German and Hebrew he had studied in school—and explaining incomprehensibly the complex combination of heroism and corruption of Al Smith, the differences between communism, socialism, and American progressivism, and the ways in which the stock market acted as a tool to extract blood from the American worker. All lost on Raizel.

"She's a lovely girl," said Belle, "beautiful. But our kitchen is not the right place—"

"She's very intelligent."

"Please." Belle shrugged. "Just get dressed. They'll be here."

In the kitchen, the soup steamed and the girl was hacking the roast. She chopped and sweated as if she were in competition to show how many slices she could make an hour. For Belle, the cutting was the most important part, the meat had to be sliced thinly and against the grain so that it peeled off in nearly translucent strips, the knife's metal visible behind the brown diamonds of flesh.

"Here, here, let me show."

The girl moved away, only to stare with distrust at the skimpy portions that the lady of the house found so elegant. Belle laid down the knife and washed her hands in the tap.

"Just as thinly as you can, then put it back with the onions and tomatoes. We'll serve it on the blue platter. Parsley all around."

She wiped her hands on a checked towel, glanced over her shoulder as she left the kitchen, only to see the girl again in combat with the meat, rendering slabs with bulges and thin spots and dangling tangles of fat. This idea of fresh-off-the-boat, train-it-yourself immigrant help was Abe's craziness. Everything for him had to be social uplift. She untied her apron, hung it in a closet on a peg. From the living room, she heard grunting, her husband rearranging furniture.

"Please?"

It was five minutes to seven, the guests about due. He was still in his undershorts and sleeveless white shirt. Sweat beaded from the end of his nose. Bulges and bends showed in the rug. The marble-topped coffee table stood a yard from the sofa and one blue armchair floated in the center of the room.

"Abe?"

"The corner looked cramped." He wiped his hands. "When did Molly say she would be here? Is she really bringing that friend?"

"Abe. Get dressed. Don't be nervous. She just doesn't want to work for your newspaper, okay? Your daughter loves you."

"Dressed. Don't worry." He waved a dismissing hand. "I just have to." And he hefted the blue chair off the rug.

"I'll leave you to your hernia."

At ten after seven, the doorbell rang. Lyden was the first to arrive. He felt an unwanted suitor at the Goodmans' door, wooing with his damp shirt and too many flowers.

But to Belle, he did not appear as anything but Lyden, whom she had known since he was a baby: a good friend's son, almost a nephew, and since the death of Carl wrapped in passionate, bittersweet affection. She was not used to seeing him in his city clothes, and today he was surprisingly handsome. Still short, but wide-shouldered, and maybe it was the glasses but he seemed to have matured into his face. His fine suit and good shoes were kept up carelessly. His gallant, shy manner hid his natural athleticism. Belle cried out over the flowers and gave him a kiss. Lyden laughed, a little embarrassed, and then apologized.

"No, no. Everyone else is even later!" She had her apron in her left hand, bad business in the kitchen. In the foyer, they could smell the smoke. "I just—you'll have to excuse me. I'll give these to the girl. She's new—she's just. Molly will be delighted."

"They're not for Molly," said Lyden, too quickly.

"No?" Belle smiled. "For me? Why, thank you, Mr. Silver." And Lyden blushed.

Abe was in his bedroom, the door ajar. The steam-borne smell of his shaving soap wafted into the foyer along with the carbon from the kitchen. Lyden, hat in hand, took one look down the narrow hall to what had once been Carl's room, where as a child he had played. Back there lay Molly's little bed, her toy animals, the pink spread—or had they redecorated, he reminded himself, made Molly's room into Belle's study, the old bed still there for occasional guests, while Carl's room remained mostly untouched and unused, some kind of dark museum? He stepped into the living room, thinking of childhood birthday parties and balloons, teenage surreptitious whiskey, and, of course, sitting shiva for Carl. Lyden was studying a painting above the mantel—thick gobs of oil paint indicating the iron scaffold of a building, hellish reds for sunset beyond, and the black silhouette of a worker, arms extended either in triumph or despair—when Abe entered in dishabille.

"Lyden!" he shouted, surprised and genial. Pants on, shirt unbuttoned, he was working a link in a cuff. "I didn't hear the bell." Shaving foam sprouted from behind an ear. "Do you need a drink? Is the girl getting you a drink? Where's Belle? Can I take your hat?"

"It's nice to see you." Lyden pivoted neatly as a dancer.

"Red or white? I get it from a Frenchman in the East Thirties, can't do better."

"I'll get it. I know where you keep it. You should—"

Abe raised his hands. "I'm the host."

"That's you." Lyden smiled. "But don't you want to . . ." With a gesture he tried to indicate Abe's shirtsleeves.

When the doorbell rang again, Abe was still in the living room fussing over Lyden.

"Mr. Goodman," cried Belle, coming out of the kitchen once again and removing for the third time her apron. "Get dressed, will you, please?" And then, lowering her voice, "We should be like normal people. We should have a regular in the kitchen, a Negro, someone who knows their business. This crazy girl—"

"She's fine, will you?" Abe jerked his arm away. "We're having a conversation."

"You're not dressed."

"He cares?" Abe pointed at Lyden, who could only blush.

"To the bedroom, Abe," said Belle, "and come back wearing shoes."

He shrugged, and his long feet in black socks made their way through the foyer, behind his door, which this time he shut. Belle went to the door holding her apron, and hoping it was Molly or the Silvers and not, please God, Molly's fancy friend. She could converse ably with Fifth Avenue money, but only if her husband was decently clothed and the smoke gone from her kitchen. Lyden, anxious in the living room, relaxed when he heard the sound of his mother's voice. He checked his watch again: Molly, twenty minutes late and counting.

ACROSS TOWN, she was clock-watching, too.

"Darling," said Sukey, when she caught Molly at it, "they don't have pretty girls to parties because we're prompt."

"Course," said Molly, and she tried her best to smile.

She was not herself. She had made a mistake, inviting Sukey to dinner. Her friend would only make her parents anxious, and Sukey would find the Goodmans appalling. When she had made the invitation, Molly had come up with justifications: that Sukey's presence would protect her, provide a buffer against her parents' raving, but by now she had reversed that logic. Sukey was going to see where she had come from, her birth in anxious comedy, her father the raging radical with his ghetto affectations, her mother's awful ambitions toward respectability. She was going to see it all.

"I'm thrilled." Sukey sat at her dressing table surrounded by jewelry, cosmetics, brushes, and combs. "I'm sure I'll love your family. My fear, of course, is that they will despise me." And she darted a desperate look behind her. "You don't think they will?"

"I don't think you have to—"

"Oh, it's true," said Sukey. "You're ashamed. Just as I thought. Well, well." She had a scarf in each hand and couldn't choose between them. "How do you like me?" The green flattered the green of her eyes, the pink the pink of her skin.

"Hmm." Molly tried to get the tone right. "You'll be beautiful in both."

"Shameless flirt."

The vaulted rooms of the Van Siever mansion, the gaudy gilded moldings, the cool solarium with its bubbling pool, the enormous dining room table—all this had become in Molly's eyes if not normal at least instructive. As she watched Sukey primp, she thought: This is how it's done. Molly was perched on a lion's-foot ottoman, her face half reflected in the bottom corner of Sukey's grand mirror. She leaned forward to see herself better, and to watch Sukey's application of lipstick, envying the freedom that came with money, wildness that smacked of security, and her reflection looked wan next to her spangled friend's. Molly went uncharacteristically quiet.

She had spent the morning running sheets of paper into the roller of her typewriter, planting a few letters on each page, then ripping the pages out again, as if her job were to crumple them into balls. She complained to telephone operators, and demanded that copy boys run to the library for files for her, she ate a tuna fish sandwich for lunch and upset her stomach further with too much coffee, then stood in a hotel lobby for hours waiting for Rudolph Valentino, and met only his manager, who told the groaning pack of reporters that the Sheikh was indisposed. Behind her in the lobby, Dewey Baedeker of the *World* joined Alton Grimm of the *Graphic* in indecent speculation. Molly's success on the Doyle-Houdini story had bumped her up from the women's interest section, and now she was covering personalities. She did her best with what the manager gave her, phoned in a story that was more or less pointless and would anyway be ruined by rewrite, then rushed uptown via an orange taxicab she could not afford, hoping she would not worry her mother by arriving late, and hoping she would not make Sukey late, either.

Sukey had complained to Molly earlier in the day, calling her at her desk at the *Radio Times* and declaring that she could not possibly arrive alone at the Goodmans'. She had just come home from a session of rigorous psychoanalysis, she needed support, the company of the woman who loved her. So at six-thirty with the sun sinking and the city still hot, Molly had dashed up the steps of the Van Siever mansion, feeling ridiculous as she handed her cloche hat to the footman. A maid had led Molly from the front hall through the tinkling solarium, up a side stairway behind a door to Sukey's chambers, through the boudoir to the bath, where Sukey lay under a sheaf of bubbles, drinking gin, smoking a cigarette, and flipping through the *Saturday Evening Post.*

"Christ, we're going to be late."

"How can you speak to me that way, darling? I'm on the absolute verge of a breakdown."

And now Molly checked her watch. Twenty past seven. In ten minutes more, her mother would be beset with images of her corpse; Belle had been like that even before Carl's death, perched on the edge of disaster. Sukey set down her lipstick and stood from her dressing table.

"Courage before going?"

"What the hell," Molly said.

The drink was Sukey's third or fourth (depending on how one did the counting) of the afternoon, and Molly's first at the end of an exhausting day. Light-headed afterward, they traipsed down the stairs arm in arm. The footman ran into the street with a whistle, and when the cab pulled up and he opened the front door, Molly felt her head tingle with Fifth Avenue romance.

Through woolly Central Park and in the back seat of the cab, Sukey chattered on about Negroes. Dr. Capoulosse kept African and Asiatic talismans and totems in his waiting room and office and today—"I always shock him with my personal remarks!"—Sukey had asked the psychiatrist about these, and then she and Dr. Capoulosse had had the most absolutely frank and exciting discussion of primitivism. By the doctor's reckoning, the Negro senses of spirit and sex were twinned—Capoulosse pointed to the shouting songs and wild dancing common in their churches—a remarkable combining of superego and id, he said, the higher and the lower impulses, impossible in the more intellectually developed races, yet instructive and key to the mental health and vibrance of the coloreds. Sukey thought her salvation lay in jazz.

"Balls," said Molly.

"That's what I love about you, darling, your mouth!" And she dove across the seat to kiss it, just once, before flying back in howling laughter to her own corner, hands hiding her lips, while Molly rearranged her glasses and cap.

The cab slowed as it rounded the corner onto 89th Street. An unfamiliar doorman stood guard in braid and epaulets. When she came uptown from her rooms on Gay Street, Molly was usually struck by the high ceilings of her parents' building, the wealth and solidity of Riverside Drive, but from Sukey's it all felt cheap and machine-made, and Sukey in the lobby mirror looked like a creature of rare plumage. Her own clothes seemed dowdy and professional; she was one of the drab pigeons of the city. Molly checked her mouth. Had the lipstick smudged? The elevator came, the engine clanked, the pulleys rose, Molly checked the old porter's watch; it was a quarter past eight. When she was a child and unashamed of her sense of spirits, Molly had claimed she could feel what she called "worry waves" emanating from Apartment 4A. With her nurse in the park, if Carl got into mischief and they were half an hour late returning, little Molly thought she could sense it, the anxious energy throbbing from her mother's brain—the children late, the children lost—and she felt it now, those uneasy waves, as if the martini at Sukey's had numbed her to them, but with proximity the vibrating intimations had finally broken through. Beneath her tough shell, she was still a dutiful girl and vulnerable to them.

"Thank God you're alive," said Belle when she opened the door. "I telephoned your aunt," she said to Sukey, by way of greeting.

"Christ, Mother," said Molly, in lieu of hello.

"Relax, relax," said her father. "Come in. Abe Goodman." He extended a hand to Sukey. "My God, you're dressed for a night of dancing."

"Will there be dancing?" Sukey asked with a laugh.

"You telephoned her aunt?"

"Why do you care who I telephone?"

Molly made a face.

"Fret not," said Belle. "She was lovely, had no idea who I was or what I was talking about. But Molly"—she grew confidential—"I need your help."

Standing by the small hall separating foyer from kitchen, Molly caught the smell of carbon and smoke. Meanwhile, from the living room, the Silvers rose to greet her. Michael stretched out his arms, Clarissa beamed, and Lyden followed sheepishly. He looked up, she caught his eye, and Molly thought his familiar face so handsome—but then she was caught up in Michael's arms, and bussing Clarissa, and Lyden stood back and smoked. There was no servant there to take hats, wraps, or pocketbooks, and Abe snatched at everything. He grabbed her little bag from Sukey. She laughed.

"Everyone into the living room," Abe shouted, while Clarissa held Sukey's one hand in her two.

But Belle tugged Molly desperately by the arm. "I need you." And then, lowering her voice to a whisper, "The girl has ruined everything. It's a disaster, I tell you, nothing to eat."

Anxious Molly watched Sukey ignore Lyden, and wondered how long her friend could mistake her father for a clown. In the kitchen, they toured the wreckage of dinner: roast cold and slaughtered, strudels topped in carbon, black potatoes stacked in the sink. Raizel, the pretty girl in the maid's uniform, had already been fired, and sat with her head on the kitchen counter, sobbing.

"I can't believe you telephoned," Molly began when they were alone.

"Enough," Belle interrupted. "Do you see this disaster? I telephoned, yes. I'm a terrible person. Okay, get used to it. It's time you accepted the fact that your mother is a social liability. But please, can I have your attention for a moment? There is a catastrophe at hand. Look, will you just, at the strudels."

Molly pulled a cigarette case from the handbag she had kept from her father.

"You're smoking?"

She ignored her mother, lit up, and poked a fork in the pastries. She draped her gray jacket over a kitchen chair and rolled up her sleeves.

"Here's what you do," said Molly. "Get a bottle of white wine. Pour yourself a glass, pour one for me, and another for this poor girl here. Then sit back and let me take care of things."

The potatoes were charred but still firm, the roast badly sliced but tasty. Molly pressed a few dollars into the girl's hands, directed her to a nearby bakery. "She can't," cried Belle, "she barely speaks English!" But Molly drew a map on the back of a brown paper bag, making sure nothing would get lost in translation. Then, with her mother still insisting it wasn't possible for the girl to go to the bakery, that it was far too late at night (besides, was it right to give her cash?), Molly faced the meat. She arranged its awful slices at a slant, snipping off lumps, and resetting the cooked tomatoes and slices of onions, laying it all down comfortably in the red-brown sauce and assuring her mother that cold meat was perfectly right for a warm September dinner. Belle rubbed her hands and made baleful predictions. Molly worked the potatoes. The skins were ruined but the meat salvageable. She was a slob in day-to-day life, but faced with a specific task Molly could execute it neatly. She cut off the damaged parts, sliced the rest into a bowl with green onions and parsley, then doused them with oil, salt, and vinegar so the white cubes shone.

"You don't have a lemon?" she asked her mother, who looked on with astonishment.

"Where did you learn this?"

"Pass me the pepper mill, Ma."

Then, without removing her apron, she peeked into the living room, where Sukey was still ignoring Lyden and shocking the middle-aged men.

"My psychoanalyst," she was saying, "considers it onanistic—"

"You're seeing a psychoanalyst?"

"Isn't everyone?"

"Whatever for?"

"Why, Mr. Silver, for my sexual problems, of course."

Clarissa laughed. Michael looked aghast. Finally, dinner.

"Will you look at that?" crowed Michael Silver as Molly brought in the bowl of potatoes. "A great journalist, a modern woman, and still she handles the kitchen. Is that salad French?"

"She came into my kitchen," said Belle, "and she took it over."

"Like she will someday my paper. No, I'm serious. No, let me." Abe was out of his chair, grabbing the bowl from her hands. "Where's Raizel? Belle, what did you do with Raizel? No, please. Let me. Relax."

"It looks beautiful," said Lyden, with a cough.

Sukey nudged Molly under the table, recognizing a lover when she saw one.

And whatever control Molly had wielded over the meat and potatoes was surrendered completely to the crowd. Belle and Michael disapproved of Sukey—her gems, her hair, her laughter, her naked legs. As soon as she sat down, Molly knew it. Abe leered at the pretty girl. Clarissa wanted to befriend her. And Sukey found everyone amusing, so said her little taps under the table, her meaningful glances, and her raised brows. Five minutes into the meal, Molly resented everyone. Clarissa Silver tried too hard, smiled at Molly's friend, but flailed for conversation. Her father pawed the roast. Lyden gritted his teeth. The Goodmans' dining room was wide, with a generous high ceiling. Two windows had views of the river and the palisades, another faced downtown, trees and rooftops, buildings, train tracks, the gray Hudson leading toward docks and the harbor. Most of the furniture had been bought before the war when Molly was nine and the family had moved into the apartment, but the best pieces— like the sideboard and the chandelier—had come from Belle's parents and the carpet was authentic Turkish and beautifully made. Still, in contrast to the marble rooms of the Van Siever mansion, her parents' place felt cozy and stodgy and hopelessly bourgeois. At her parents' every slip in diction or manners (a mix of affectation, failure, and familiarity), Sukey darted a smile Molly's way, and Molly remembered Capoulosse's discourse on Negroes and wondered what the doctor might have thought of the mental health of the Gilded Ghetto Jews.

"We sent the girl for dessert," Molly's mother apologized, "but I think she ran away with the money."

"I certainly would." Sukey giggled. "Were I her."

"I'll bet," said Belle.

Molly choked. Sukey laughed. Clarissa patted her on the shoulder. Lyden stared at Molly, and as he stared Molly's anger turned on him. What had she ever seen in him? Why was he always so goddamn serious? Under the lights his hair gleamed like belly lox. She hated Jews, she hated gentiles, also lesbians, also heterosexuals. She wanted to go home.

Abe opened a third bottle of wine. He had drunk most of the second and much of the first. And when the plates were empty and everyone was awkwardly wishing the girl would return with dessert, he slapped the table so the wine glasses jumped.

"It's horseshit!"

"What?"

"The hokum. Your boyfriend." He pointed the bread knife at Molly.

"Who?"

"You know. That man you write about."

"Houdini," Belle whispered sweetly.

But Abe shrugged off his wife's mocking tone. "No. Not Mr. Weiss. You know his real name was Weiss? A rabbi's son. A genuine Jewish-American hero. From Wisconsin! But I'm not talking about him. My son admired Houdini"—facing Sukey now—"and I always encouraged the admiration. We had a poster of him in Carl's room, you know. Didn't—who gave it to him?"

"We did," said Michael Silver. "Got it in England."

"I'm not talking about that." Abe waved a hand. "The other guy. Sir Englishman. It's tough to lose a son at war, I should know, but don't go crazy. What's his name? The soldier, the knight, the guy who used to write mysteries, your boyfriend—"

"Sir Arthur Conan Doyle?" asked Molly.

"Exactly." Abe slapped the table again. Without getting up from his chair, he reached an enormous arm to the sideboard and grabbed a pear. He bit off the top and spat out the stem. "What a schmuck. Those lectures at Carnegie Hall. What interests me is that this is such an upper-class phenomenon." He gestured with the dripping fruit. "It has to do if you ask me with the breakdown of widespread faith in Christianity and organized religion and an attempt in the age of science and industry to keep the working-man bamboozled—and Molly, if you wrote for my paper, if I allowed anyone at my paper to write about this shit, and of course, darling, I would allow you, I would encourage you, that's a promise, and not because you're my daughter but because you have the genuine gift, the gift for the story. Read what she writes. Of course she doesn't believe in that crap—"

"Of course not," said Belle.

"But you have a reporter like this girl on staff, you maybe give a little direction, but cultivate for God's sake her interests—are you listening to me? I'm not just saying because she's my daughter. But as I was saying, it's the same old anti-materialist message, just delivered in a new envelope they hope will look a little more modern: Don't look at this world, look at the next. That's science? Bullshit! And you know of course why they want the working man to look at the next world, it's because in this world they are schtupping him up the—"

"Abe!" Belle cried.

He gestured with his knife.

"Schtupping?" asked Sukey.

Belle gave the table a significant look. Then she said, "It has nothing to do with the working man, Abe. I have read Molly's articles carefully, and I think they are wonderful. And of course she doesn't believe, she's too smart for that. But I don't think, Abe, that she needs another point of view, Abe, especially not one about the proletariat. Her point of view is just fine. But if you look at these two gentlemen, what you will see, I believe, are men in different stages of morbid continuation of the Oedipal struggle. With Conan Doyle, his son was killed at war—off to war to fight for the good of the Empire his father loved. Of course, it drove him crazy. Guilt, sadness. It's different, Abe, yes—no, let me talk here—Abe, it's not the same as with you. The two are unrelated. Let me finish. And with Mr. Houdini, clearly, it's all about his mother. Read the article. All he does is talk about his mother. He's fixated. Please, help yourself to more potatoes, Lyden. And what's more, look at these séances. Invariably, it's old men tying up young women in the dark—"

"Absolutely!" Sukey burst in. "And look at Houdini, a man who likes to be tied up naked!"

"Forgive me," said Clarissa Silver, "but this is a subject that, whether or not we take it seriously, and I do believe Molly takes it seriously, has been given deep consideration by some of the great minds of our time. Why, Dr. Freud himself is, as we sit here and speak, a member of the Society for Psychical Research, publishing, as a matter of fact, in their journals. So we cannot dismiss this all as some form of sexual perversion—"

Great protests around the table. No one was dismissing Molly's work. Everyone claimed the highest esteem for and greatest pride in Molly, and meanwhile Molly turned over a piece of meat with her fork. She looked at Lyden and found again that he was staring. Clarissa Silver went on about Dr.

Freud, and then she spoke of her father, and then about mystics she had known. Clarissa pressed forward with her stories, trying to hold together the party through sheer force of personal anecdote. And Michael Silver smiled at his wife dotingly, and Sukey turned shocking or cute, and Lyden had the nerve to just stare at Molly, nervously, sympathetically, and decently as—Molly's mind strained for simile—a potato.

"And the most astonishing thing," said Clarissa, "that she told me was about a certain medium—you've written about her, haven't you Molly? She goes by the name Margery, but she is actually the daughter of a former acquaintance of mine, the eminent Cambridge psychiatrist, Dr. Humboldt Twist. Extraordinary coincidence, her real name is Mary Twist—"

"Mary Twist!" Sukey fairly shouted. "Why, Molly, do you remember Mary Twist? Oh, it must be the same. Why, this is incredible! She was the absolute scandal of Poughkeepsie!"

"My Lord, you know her?"

Molly could not believe they were speaking on the same subject. Also she could not remember the girl. "Mary Twist?"

"Humboldt, of course," said Clarissa, "was the only child of Dr. Omicron Twist, who made quite a name for himself regarding diseases of the blood, and was the most popular lecturer at Harvard Medical School—and his mother was Virginia Humboldt Twist, a sad, sad tale. A woman prone to terrible nervous ailments. Tragic, really." Margery's mother—Molly felt she should be getting out her pencil, taking notes, but Clarissa went on, "Some say she fell into the Charles, some say she was pushed. At any rate, dear Humboldt as a young man had the most magnificent white-blond hair and was adored by all the young women of Cambridge. A charming young man, and of course quite brilliant. If his father had not sent him abroad for his studies, who knows what might have happened? As it was, he married an Italian woman. The daughter of a count, I believe—"

"You'll have to tell me this slowly," said Molly, and her voice felt not her own.

But Sukey was off: "Mary Twist, you know, she had the most scandalous, the most absolutely! And so beautiful, it was shocking, really. We all were in love with her, weren't we, Molly? She had a veritable harem of freshman girls, I tell you. But there was that attempt on her life—"

Belle gasped, turned Victorian. "Is this what you do at Vassar?"

"Oh, dear!" Clarissa laughed.

"Well, here's Molly's next story," said Michael Silver.

"What do you mean?" asked Molly. "I can't. This is just rumor. You *both* knew her?" And it *was* a story. Though she felt herself pulled into it, Molly resisted.

"Sure. You could write the story of this mystic, this Margery." But Michael was nervous, conscious of stepping on toes. "The dinner party can serve as your sources. Maybe."

There was a long pause at the table, friendly stares, everyone waiting for Molly to speak.

"I mean, it's not a story." Molly became hesitant, looking first at her father and then at a picture of Carl that hung on the wall. "But it's amazing. Mary Twist. You mean you both knew her?" And she remembered Houdini inviting her into his car. She had an eerie, tingling feeling, her chair rising off the floor.

"What do you mean, it's no story?" Belle protested. Years at the margins of the newspaper business gave her expertise.

"Everything they have been saying, the true identity of Margery. That Margery is really Mary Twist—you went to school with her. Clarissa knows her parents. And this history of psychological troubles in her family, wouldn't it be of interest?"

"You could write it for *Progress*," Abe said.

Molly bit her lip. She wasn't sure she remembered Mary Twist, but maybe—tall, beautiful, dark hair, pink skin, thin and tragic—was she imagining? Molly had read the articles, of course, declamations about her power in *Scientific American* magazine. But she was not going to let her mother tell her what to do, no more than she would write for her father. She looked away from the table back at the picture of Carl. Above the sideboard, her parents had hung the framed photograph. Where once there had been a small dark painting in the Dutch style of a man pushing a wheelbarrow up a hill, there was now a portrait taken on his sixteenth birthday. The luminous face split Molly in two, because it showed at once the arrogant handsome boy she now recognized, and also little-girl Molly's ideal of adult romance. Carl's was her father's face, but so much more handsome. Molly looked at the picture, then back at the table.

"This is just gossip," she said.

"Yes." Lyden burst out. "You expect Molly to write about that?" A vein in his neck throbbed. "No. She's in the right, don't you see? To publish this woman's sex scandals, her mother's illness, her grandmother's death—to ruin this girl's life, and why? Because you people know a little tattle? Molly works for a tabloid, but that's—well, it's respectable, at least, and there's no reason to imagine she would traffic in this kind of. . . ." He let his voice trail off. Even his parents were staring. "Sorry," he said.

There was silence at the table. Molly looked at Sukey, who opened her eyes wide for effect. She looked at Lyden, who glanced down at his plate, conscious that he had gone too far, shown everyone that he cared too much. Molly felt a sudden strange hovering, apart from it all. Margery was Mary Twist, whose family Clarissa Silver had known in Boston, whom she herself had known at school. The story was revealing itself, as if written before she got to it.

Her father said, "Of course, Lyden, no one is suggesting that she stoop to that kind of gossip, but there is no doubt that this knowledge could inform her work."

Both Lyden and he were now looking at Molly, but at that moment she could not talk. Her eyes rose up to the picture of Carl, her heart made a flip.

"Excuse me," Molly said, and she dashed off to the bathroom.

The doorbell rang. Raizel returned with an enormous cheesecake she had found at an unheard-of Italian bakery half a mile away. Molly snatched her bag from the kitchen, almost hid in her old bedroom, now converted to her mother's study and hung with a family portrait circa 1909. She stumbled past the closet, the bookshelves with her father's Judaica, and toward Carl's bedroom door. She put her hand on the knob shaped like an octagonal glass jewel. "Oh, buddy," Molly said. Then she ducked into the bathroom, pulled a lighter and cigarette from her bag, and stepped inevitably into the tub, more from habit than fear of being caught.

It was a trick she had learned from Carl when they were kids; she remembered catching him smoking in there when he was dressed for a dance, his polished shoes against the porcelain basin, Carl squatting in his best dark suit. Molly crouched as he had, blew smoke through a crack at the bottom of the window, and watched the drip from the tap, and the bathtub's copper stain. Her heels clanked against the basin. Mary Twist and Margery, Sukey and Clarissa.

"Oh, Carl," she prayed involuntarily.

ON THE roof garden of the Park Hotel, Doyle feels as he did on the beach: as though he is naked and she a figure in a dream. Her long gloves, veil, that dress from another era—a dress his mother might have worn had she been taller, thinner, more elegant and beautiful. Tears well in Doyle's eyes; it's her prettiness, her youth. Her skirt billows and she seems to have no legs under it. She floats above the carpet, levitating, and her frozen smile seems separate from her face. Eyes lurk behind the veil, and Doyle knows she knows him. He expects the table to rise when she sits, imagines the extension of that ectoplasmic pseudopod. Last night he reread Dingwall Bird's work on pseudopods, how the pseudopod was invisible in the light, yet how sunlight could be congenial to its power, how the pseudopod was built on the substance of dream and yet was powerful as any lever. He has met many mediums, but never one with such palpable gifts.

Margery illuminates the rooftop as the sun does the Hudson, the row houses, docks and factories, the spires of churches and the towers downtown. Sabatier sits beside her and lays his hand on his wife's arm, just where the glove meets the elbow. He sets her arm on the tabletop as if setting the arm of a phonograph on a spinning disk, and she speaks.

"We do not want to convince the world. We would rather provide a haven for those who already are convinced. I am not here for the education of doubters, but for the hopes and beliefs of those who understand and honor my gifts. No honor is due me—none at all. I understand myself as an instrument to be played by the dead, and to play for those who honestly seek enlightenment and contact with their lost beloveds. I am to be used sparingly, and only by the honorable. You, for instance, Sir Arthur, and men of like minds."

Her husband watches her as she speaks, keeping time with the nodding of his head. The waiter moves around the table, refilling glasses with ice and water. Margery does not pause when he comes her way. Her smile is unbending. Nirvana lies over his left shoulder, a cloud above Brooklyn.

"What I really imagine," Dr. Sabatier cuts in, "when I go off into my dreams and fantasies, I think that my wife's future lies not in proselytizing or proof, but in retreat. If we could create a place, and I do not imagine it would cost a tremendous amount of money, a few sympathetic friends could help us and then it would be built, if we could create such a place, almost a resort in the country, where seekers could come and practice safely— mediums and believers alike, honest Spiritualists, seeking comfort in contact with the beyond, and not for ugly things like proof. I believe. You believe. We do not need proof. Proof is in the resting of the eyes on my dear wife. And frankly, I do not want any doubters—like your friend Houdini—I do not relish the thought of them near her. Why, it is like inviting to the ballet some Philistine who expects the dancers to score points, or somehow to offer incontrovertible proof of their beauty. This is art, not science. These doubters, these Philistines, they are as useful to me as are false mediums. If I had my dream, I would set up shop, so to speak, away from the doubters and the frauds that plague us, a few acres in the woods, a library, modest residences. Believers could come for a weekend, a year, a lifetime of study and reflection." He laughs, then sighs. "But it's only a dream, Sir Arthur. We live in a humble cottage. I have retired from my position at the college. We are supported only by generous gifts from friends, gifts for which we never ask." Again, nervous laughter. "Why, otherwise they would not be gifts. I fear we never shall have the resources to construct my fantasy."

Doyle crosses his arms. He feels beneath the fabric of the jacket the wallet that sits in his breast pocket, comfortably stuffed with cash, rising and falling with the beat of his heart.

VII

HOUDINI LIES SUBMERGED in his big bathtub. Police handcuffs clasp his wrists, bolted irons hold his ankles. Chains communicate between the two restraints, the chains padlocked twice to a steel belt at his middle.

At seven years old, he could hang upside down and pick up sewing needles with his eyelids. As a young magician, he apprenticed to a locksmith, learned the trick of every file, bolt, and tumbler, and could pick anything that came into the shop. In his twenties, Houdini encountered a Chinese magician and then practiced until he learned the man's best trick; using raw potatoes strung with wire, he worked until he could swallow and regurgitate a billiard ball. He could swell his wrists and shrink them, thread a needle with his toes. The muscles at the center of his hand were developed so he could palm a quarter without a finger's moving. He had trained his anal sphincter to carry a tool kit encased in wax, producible within seconds. The calluses on his feet were thick enough to hide small rods of steel.

Now he pulls those feet to his hands, chains dragging against the tub's specially designed basin. He finds a lockpick in the left heel, inserts it not into the keyhole of the right handcuff but into its lock, the gap where serrated tongue meets open mouth. Here, opposite the hinge, lies the manacle's weak spot. With quick, practiced jerks, Houdini beats the cuff against the steel around his middle, levering open the bracelet. Water splashes across the bathroom floor. The clock on the sink keeps ticking. A second lockpick rests in his gut; Houdini forces this to his tongue. With his teeth he skins the wax from the tool. Blood rises in the water. Pick into padlock, easy as turning a doorknob, he tricks the thing open, then collects the metal—locks, chains, and irons—on his belly, Houdini supine underwater, sending bubbles out his nose.

Here he stays, willing endurance. He shuts his eyes and imagines the second hand running, the clock's ticks. Thoughts fly to his latest motion picture, to his wife downstairs. His lungs burn. His throat muscles twitch. Lights flash on the back of his eyelids. He drives himself close as possible to dying, then bursts into the air.

Houdini smiles at the mirror. His penis wags in its gray pubic nest, middle-aged gut bouncing.

"THESE PICTURES are not occult," said Arthur Conan Doyle from the lectern. "But they are psychic, because everything that emanates from the brain is psychic. They are not supernatural. Nothing is. They are preternatural in the sense that they are not known to our ordinary senses."

Below him sat the convened Society of American Magicians. Houdini had invited Doyle in part as an apology for having attacked him in the press, and there was much surprise when Doyle accepted the invitation. At the *Radio Times* they wondered, would he strike back at Houdini? Would Houdini again humiliate his friend? In the balcony, Molly worried for Doyle. He seemed lost and vague, and she could not stand to see him present again those silly pictures of dead queens and great presidents standing before attentive Spiritualists.

"What's emanating from his brain?" asked Archie Miles, who had been assigned as her photographer.

"Zip it," said Molly.

Onstage, Doyle continued. "It is the effect," he said, "of the joining on the one hand of the imagination, and on the other hand some power of materialization. The imagination, I may say, comes from me—the materialization, from elsewhere. There would be great danger if the original were shown instead of the counterfeit, but what you will see is a living presentiment. Now if the house lights will be dimmed and the film projector operated." Doyle shuffled his papers and stepped back from the podium. "We shall see."

And he found his way slowly to a seat beside Houdini. Behind the celebrities were seated tycoons: Adolf Ochs, Bernard Gimbel, and E. F. Albee. The auditorium went black. The assembled journalists, magicians, and guests rearranged themselves. The blank screen showed all white, then numbers, darkness punctuated by scratches and hairs, slithering abstract snakes in the shadow play, before the image established itself: a forest, something moving within.

Molly had only seen still spirit photography, never before a movie. She wondered what would happen here, in this jungle. A head emerged from the foliage, a reptile, its horned nose gesturing. Its face poked out with two more horns on its forehead. Something exotic, something South American, but it looked like a dinosaur; a bone shield like a mane ringed its forehead. The creature coiled, then bounded like a cat, its movements perfect and lifelike, the triceratops' skips and jumps as smooth as a Keystone Kop tumbling into a barrel.

"Jesus shit," said Molly.

Archie Miles chuckled, and she hated his bald-headed silhouette.

Scraps of dust, then. Small hairs flickered. Residue on the lens projected on-screen. The next moving image was a valley, a white sun low in the sky, enormous mountains that climbed to stony peaks. The silhouette of a bird, then a flock of birds, then, as the camera eased down from its aerial height—how did they get so high?—a vulture sprang from a ledge. Or was it a bat? It had wide wings with claws emerging at their second fold, an enormous head with a curved crown and a needle-nosed beak. Beside it, the trees looked tiny. A woman screamed and her screams were contagious, the audience gasping. Molly wished she could get a look at the face of Houdini or of Mr. Ochs. Surely the *Times* would know how to react to this; it seemed to her miraculous.

The pterodactyl dived, its talons whipped across the bough of a tree. There was no struggle, just a jerk of the monster's head and the ape in its claws went limp. Laboriously now, it flew upward to its rocky perch, encumbered by the weight of the corpse. The young dinosaurs, mewling soundlessly, pecked at the fur and flesh. It was disgusting. It was superreal. The screen went blank, to the shuffling and shouts of the crowd.

Miles said, "The Spiritualists are going to make a killing in pictures," and all around her confused magicians clamored. No one there had seen anything like this before. Molly could not understand it.

A brontosaurus emerged from its swamp, heavy bellied, stump-legged, and enormous. Smaller creatures trotted by its side. The big dinosaur swayed its rubber neck, and then the whole film went red. A volcano erupted, a forest burned. On-screen, lava flowed, rocks hurtled, and everywhere monsters drowned. Molly, over-come, shrieked and grabbed Archie Miles by the arm.

Afterward, Doyle was triumphant. And though by now the reporters understood the stunt, that he had showed the conven-tioneers some clips from the upcoming movie version of his book *The Lost World*, Doyle would not let on—he was still busy pulling their general leg, hinting that it was spirit work, knowing half the audience had thought it real. "Photographic representations of the imagined world, surely," he said, "but the world is always being imagined." And then, in answer to a shouted question from Molly, "But my dear Miss Goodman, what will appear in your paper tomorrow, if not your imaginings?" The magicians were irritated, all claimed not to have been fooled, but their shouts while the film was playing and their irritation afterward scored points for Conan Doyle. He had had them for a moment mystified and afraid. Archie Miles flashed his camera, and so did a dozen others, and Sir Arthur smiled. His illusion—if not the trick of the movie, then the act as a befuddled stooge—had fooled the illusionists.

Reporters called in to their papers. Molly huddled in a corner with Miles. She tried to get all the details straight. Archie knew something about film, and explained what he could about motion picture camera work, and a little bit about animation.

"Okay, kid," he said out front of the theater. "This is what I know: The book is called *The Lost World,* and the hero is named Professor Challenger, and Wallace Beery is going to play him in the picture show. Obviously, the science of this movie is incredible. You saw what they did, and the way they do it is with clay and rubber creatures, hanging them on wires, adjusting their bodies, and shooting the thing frame by frame. It's not like a bunch of stills. You have a clicker attached to the camera, and it controls the flow of the shooting. So between the camera and the models, if you know how to use them, you can make a bird fly slow or fast. See? They did it beautifully. And didn't you love those segments with the tinted film? The lava scene, when the whole movie turned red? I can't wait to see the whole thing— God, I loved those books when I was a kid. And you weren't alone, kid; you saw the way that sorcerer's convention acted? A bunch of four-flushers, if you ask me. Served them right. But this is what the *Radio Times* should be writing about, not the Spiritualism, but the science of entertainment. That's the future, if you ask me."

"Wait, wait," said Molly, "go back and tell me again how they made the creatures move."

A janitor swept up programs and cigarette butts. The members of the magicians' society were off to a reception to which journalists were not invited. Archie sent his work back to the office via a boy in a taxicab, then stayed while Molly in a phone booth got the whole story straight: When the movie was coming out, how the movie was made, whether this was a planned part of the film's publicity, how Doyle had pulled one over on the magicians by pretending it was spirit photography. She knew copy might cut out half of the details, but she liked for her own satisfaction to get them straight. Miles was smiling when she was done.

"Christ," Molly said, "I hope you're right about all you told me."

"Course I'm right."

"Then I'm in your debt."

"You want to repay me?" And he asked if he could buy her dinner.

Maybe, Molly thought, she hadn't given Archer Miles his due.

The lights of the avenue were ringed in mist, the headlights of automobiles glowing cones. She caught the scent of Archie's cologne and shaving lotion as it mingled with the mist. Good clothes, and his hat concealed his baldness. He was a big man but carried himself as if it were a joke: the clothes, the baldness, his soft good looks, that they were walking so close to one another. He said something that made Molly laugh and the rain started up again and she hid under his umbrella. The place he picked was off Sixth Avenue, a town house converted into apartments. Rain pooled in the seams of the granite sidewalk, made islands and archipelagos out of the cobbles in the street. He led her away from the stoop, down through the gate three steps to the garden floor. Deeper puddles there, and he helped her around them, and again, without knowing why, Molly laughed.

She could hear the violin within and smell the garlic cooking. The door was opened by an old woman with a floral apron and a smile. Archie introduced her, and from the look in the old woman's eye, Molly knew she wasn't the first girl he had taken here. A few steps down past a hat rack, a coat rack, and an umbrella stand, around the newel post of the stairway that led upward to the residential floors, and Molly's eyes adjusted to the low long room, checkerboard tablecloths, candles in wine bottles, and happy men twirling spaghetti on forks. She took off her wrap; Archie handed it to the proprietress. He ordered a bottle of wine that would have cost her half a week's salary. In the bathroom, Molly dropped her glasses in her purse.

Generous plates of pasta came out from the steaming kitchen, and Archie gave names to everything exotic, even the green vegetable fried in oil. He fanned a few more bills after dinner for a bubbly summer wine, which they drank while spooning tiramisu, and Archie told her what that name meant in Italian. Molly was stupidly drunk well past midnight, when an accordion band took over from the violinist. The tables were pushed against the wall. Everyone got up and danced. And though Molly was not a practiced dancer, Archie led her easily. They were laughing as they left up the stairs and onto deserted 26th Street, wet and clean with rain. Archie wore her cap and she his fedora. He invited her up to his place, but Molly declined.

"You're a good girl, ain't you?" he said.

"Good enough."

He rode her home in a taxi and kissed her as the streets flew by, all of it a joke, all of it perfectly natural. Archie was gallant, paid for the cab, and led her to the door of her building on Gay Street, where he wished her goodnight with a hilarious bow. And when she stood in the foyer with its once-red carpet, its table with a vase of dried flowers and an overlarge Bakelite ashtray, Molly felt light-headed and happy and an absolute fraud. It wasn't her, dancing in a slummy speakeasy with a handsome man—it wasn't her, but it was pleasant.

She climbed the stairs to the third floor, drunk but too tired to sleep. She wanted to take a bath, but Pignoli the painter had left dog hairs in the tub again, washing that awful pooch, Goldman. Past three A.M. Molly kicked his door hard enough to wake him, and the little terrier began to howl. Home at last, she sat on the edge of the bed and tossed her shoes across the floor. It was pleasant, dancing like that, but it did not feel real. Sukey said it: that Molly was too serious, too driven by work, never out to have fun. Archie had said it, that she was a good girl. What was it that had made her despise him for so long, why had he made her so uncomfortable when they first met? Molly decided that she hadn't liked him because he was attractive, that she was afraid of sex, afraid of men—that's why she was playing around with a woman. She groaned.

There was the bottle of whiskey on the top shelf of her cabinet, but Molly was already drunk. It was late and tomorrow she had to work.

Oh, God, she remembered, she was meeting her father for breakfast.

But she liked Archie Miles. Archie was smart. What had he said about Spiritualists, that their reasoning was off? He had done it very elegantly, driven the knife of argument into their illogical hearts. "Scientists should stay out of that business," he said. "Don't empiricism nix the feelings of faith?" And in retrospect she wondered if he was doing this so casually, but nonetheless to impress her, as if he had known that talking smart might relax her. Empiricism, some word. Tautological, that was another. Then he said he had just the right adjective to describe the color of her eyes. She closed those eyes, slipped out of her dress, left it in a puddle on the floor. He was playing with her, Molly knew it. He knew that she needed to think he was smart in order for her to forgive herself for dancing.

Sukey would have loved Archie, she thought, and he would probably love Sukey, too. Molly sighed. Why hadn't she gone to his room with him? And would he invite her again?

WHEN HE gets to his suite, Doyle tiptoes through the dark rooms, peeking in on his wife and children. He hangs up his coat. Fired up by his triumph, he is unable to rest. Doyle fixes himself a drink. Fidgeting around the room, he picks up a copy of *Time* magazine, reads an article about long-distance cinema, still pictures being transmitted from Washington to Philadelphia, motion pictures beamed from one room to the next, light reflected then chopped into bits by a radio eye, then mailed off into the ether, from which it can be recomposed. Astounding stuff, he's not sure he understands it all.

Doyle stands. He looks out the window. Lights in the Argus-eyed buildings, the sound of revelry downstairs, a phonograph, "Whatever Became of Hinky Dinky Parlay Vous?" Down the avenue bulbs flick on and off in sequence on a movie theater's marquee, lights running in a circle. That and the article in the magazine make Doyle think of a film he has recently seen, one that attempted to explain Einsteinian thought: Squiggling lines underwater were revealed to be straight when seen from the air, a rocket that shot up vertically flew at an arc when contemplated in relation to the earth's rotation and curve, and then time itself— But this is where the mathematician lost Doyle, Einstein playing with physics like a conjurer with a coin. But if those thoughts qualified as science, why not his research?

He loosens his tie. He leans farther out the window, lets the misty rain settle on his cheeks and chin. Fords race the avenue. What the world needs, he decides, is an Einstein of mortality. Near this city of the future, in this country of the present— Sabatier is right, there must be a place to which mediums and Spiritualists can retreat, a place from which spiritual light could spread, light emanating like radio waves, like electricity, to be transmitted to the country and the world.

VIII

THE NEXT MORNING TIMOTHY Conan Doyle
sinks. The boy brings his wrists to his ankles, pretending
he is chained. His blond hair rises as his body drops. The tiles at
the base of the pool come close. Rolling, Timothy sees lights play
on the surface, and in the distance of the shallow end his sister's
legs. Is that his sister? At its edges, the white world resolves into
obscurity. A diver breaks the surface toward the middle of the
pool. This is what it's like, thinks Timothy. As the material is to
the spiritual, so the underwater to the world above. The surface
is the sky, the limit of our view, and we are all down below,
believing that we must hold our breaths, that there is no more to
the universe beyond than the surface's fractured glow. To break
through one need only defy the rules. If he would breathe right
now, he might emerge not into poolside tiles and the mixed
smell of chlorine and mildew, but to something livelier and love-
lier, emerge not by swimming but through transmutation. Maybe

that's Houdini's trick, just defy the rules, relax, breathe. Allow oneself to drown, to fade in and out of the higher world. At the bottom of the pool, he lies on his side. The diver races toward him. If he were to breath in, thinks Timothy, his father would appreciate the bravery, but on the other hand he doesn't want to upset his mother. And so, before the lifeguard reaches him, he loses his imaginary cuffs and chains and swims upward. The life-guard arches like a dolphin, and the two break the surface one after the other.

"Kid, don't scare me like that, hey?"

A HEAVY KNOT of men at the door of Kortchmar's, the steam and garlic and onions and frying fat. Hairy-knuckled hands and men barking, fat ties flapping on fatter bellies, laugh-ter and argument, the cash register ringing, dirty plates into sinks, toasted bagels, eggs on a long, greased griddle with pota-toes and onions. Molly edged her way through the Yiddish-English crowd at the door, not another woman in the place. Before she got to the counter with its displays of chubs and her-ring, tubs of cream cheese and pickled onions and sturgeons split and smoked, she was recognized. "Hey, hey!" said a fat man in an apron. But he got slapped by his partner, who brandished an enormous fish-slicing knife. "She's mine you're talking about, my darling—look at her!" Molly blew kisses, killing the countermen, and moved into the long dining room with its ceiling fans and Formica tabletops.

Abe Goodman ruled the big round table in the back, and he was up from his chair with big arms spread wide, expostulating.

Michael Silver, also standing, waved two limp hands at Abe, miming rejection, wincing and looking away. Their breakfast companions were finishing coffee, slipping on jackets, yelling about checks. Some shirked and tried to pay less, some waved five-dollar bills, but even the ones who wanted to pay exactly what they owed came in for abuse.

Michael Silver, turning in disgust from Abe, was the first to spot her. "Mol!" He planted a wet kiss on her. "Now you've come, now, when I have to go down to Henry Street!"

"What is it?"

"Nothing. Settlement houses, women's clubs, everybody wants a piece of me."

"Look," Abe thundered. "You wouldn't get to talk to her even if you didn't have to run." He reached a big arm through the crowd, gripping Molly. "She's all mine, Mike. I'm not going to let any of you near her."

"Ah, she's beautiful." Michael Silver's hand was on her shoulder, luxuriating. "Isn't she beautiful?"

"Gorgeous," chimed in a man whose name she could not place. His eyes were heavy-lidded, his nose protruded—these gatherings of her father's always felt like bar mitzvahs or marriages, a dozen men indistinguishable from her father's cousins.

"This is news, big shot?" Abe was jolly in his contempt. "That my daughter is beautiful?"

"Ah, but gorgeous," said Michael Silver, and he moved his hands, showing her off.

Molly nudged him. "You're pretty good-looking yourself."

"I am taking her away from you." Abe grabbed his jacket and coffee cup, whose contents sloshed over an empty cup of juice.

"Maishe, I'm picking up and going to another table. Maishe! My daughter!"

But the dairy's proprietor had already noticed, and wiping his hands on his stained apron came over to visit. "I never see this girl anymore, such a beautiful girl. Like a shiksa, Abe—"

"We're moving!"

Maishe laughed. "I've been reading you," he told Molly, while Abe impatiently stood by and jiggled a chair. "And I got a question. This Conan Doyle, he's a smart man, no? These detective stories, he couldn't be such a dummy. So what's he doing with these pictures? This—I don't know how to say. And you, you're writing about it like it's—"

"You don't think she believes in that shit?" shouted Abe, voice carrying above the noisy room.

"I think she is doing great," said Maishe.

"Thank you," said Molly.

"But like your father said—"

"Did I say she wasn't doing good?" Nearly apoplectic. "All I said is I wanted to have breakfast with my daughter. Over there, maybe. When she's done taking questions from you fine gentlemen."

Maishe shrugged and kissed Molly. Michael Silver wished her goodbye for the seventh time. Molly followed her father to a table by the window, saying, "Excuse me," to the old man who cleared plates.

"Mike's a pain in the ass, but his wife is dying, so go easy on him. Also he'd like you to marry his son."

"What—who—" Molly had not yet taken off her cap. "Did you say—"

"Before I forget, he gave me a letter for you. From Lyden, he was here, he didn't want to hand it over, but I made him—I said, Look, she'll be here, I'll give it to her, for what do you need the post office?"

"Pop!" She grabbed his hand but not the envelope. "Did you say that Clarissa is—"

"Heart palpitations." Abe scooped sugar into his coffee. "Mike said she had some last night. Maybe it's nothing. I think it's nothing. But you know Mike, he worries. Asshole. So you're still really working that crap, I see. Pictures of dead people or not-actually-dead people, or what is it now, dinosaurs?"

"Pop, just tell me about Clarissa. And why do you have a letter from Lyden, anyway?"

"He wanted to put it in the mailbox—"

"So put it in the mailbox, tell me about Clarissa, and for God's sake lay off about my work."

"I didn't bring it up." Hands in the air, Abe surrendered. "You were talking to Maishe about the article and I just had a thought. Anyway." He reached out to grab a waiter by the pants leg. "She wants a bagel, whitefish, no, sturgeon for my daughter, a cup of coffee, let her put in the milk and sugar, she's independent that way, grapefruit juice is good, and you have maybe fruit cup?" His Yiddish affectations grew stronger below Fourteenth Street. "Did I order right?"

"Pop!" She tried to fix her eyes on him, but his kept darting away. "What is the story with Clarissa Silver?"

"You should write the Silvers a note."

"What is this with her heart palpitations?"

"Heart palpitations," echoed Abe with a shrug.

"Pop, you told me she was—"

"Who said anything about dying?" His hand reached across the table. "You get so upset. Why are you getting so upset? What did I say to upset you? Heart palpitations, big deal. You shouldn't get so excited. No." Opening his blue eyes wide, Abe about to discuss something delicate. "Your mother is concerned—"

"About Clarissa?"

"Fuck Clarissa." A dismissive wave. "Heart palpitations. Everyone has heart palpitations. I have heart palpitations." He downed his coffee. "Healthy as a horse." And he laid Lyden's note unconsciously by his plate. "No. You know how your mother gets." And Abe did a little pantomime puppet show, dangling his fingers over his napkin. "Nyeh, nyeh, nyeh, nyeh."

"I have no idea what you're talking about."

"The truth is—I think—now don't get upset. I didn't say anything yet. At least until I tell the story, relax." The old black waiter passed and again Abe grabbed him. "I'm going to need another bagel. Salt. Heavy on the butter." The old man's eyes blurred. "He heard me, right?"

"I'm not upset. I'm just confused now. Please tell me—"

"Clarissa is a little sick. That's the truth, she has a little trouble—"

"She looks terrific." Molly tucked her hair behind her ears.

"She does look terrific." He relaxed back into his chair. "And I'm sure she'll be fine, but Silver, he gets ideas, he gets worries. Write him a note, will you?"

"A get-well note?"

"No, no, no. About her heart you did not hear that from me.

But the thing I'm trying to discuss with you is your mother—you promise you won't get upset?"

"If it's not a get-well note, what kind of note are you suggesting I write? And do I drop it in the mail, or do you want to deliver it by hand, like Lyden's note? Are you in competition with the postmaster general?"

"You'll take the letter?"

"Put it in the mail and I'll get it."

"I don't understand. But you promise, right? You promise you won't get upset." If it was a question, Abe didn't wait for the answer. "We were all happy to see you. We were. But the feeling that your mother had—she just. . . . She thought you ignored the Silvers, that they might have been hurt, insulted, and also, you'll forgive me for mentioning it, but she wasn't so crazy about your choice of friend."

Molly glowered.

"You promised you wouldn't get angry."

"Pop," she said, her voice flat as her pale gray eyes. "I don't give a crap what you think about my friends."

"She was dressed like a streetwalker."

"I'm leaving." Molly stood.

"Don't." He reached across the table, grabbed her wrist. "Forgive me, okay? Please forgive me. I know. I was wrong. Whatever I said. I'm sorry. It's the way I am, I can't help it. Look, I'm your father. Forgive me, hey? Oh, Molly—what comes out of my mouth? Half the time, even I don't know. Your mother gets upset and it's difficult for everyone. Just relax, okay? Accept my apology."

Molly shrugged. "I'll stick around. I need more coffee. I need some food." Her stomach was settling, earlier bicarbonate of soda taking effect against her late night out and her drinking. "But don't get nasty about my friends."

They sat in silence, spreading cream cheese, cutting tomatoes, sipping coffee, munching fish. The crowd thinned, empty tables appeared. Abe's eyebrows beetled and spread, his jaw working a thick piece of bread. Molly took her sturgeon lightly and drank coffee as if it were medicine.

"Anyway," Abe said while chewing, "you don't want to work with your father, that's it?"

"Pop—"

"I'm just asking, that's all. No harm in asking. But are you happy, that's what I want to know."

"I'm happy, Pop."

"I don't believe it."

"It's a job, Pop. I understand you don't approve of the stories I cover, but I'm on the front page. And I made that story mine— Doyle, Houdini—no one gave it to me, I fought for that."

"Will you?" He put down his cutlery. "You're going to lecture me on what's a story? You're going to tell me what's page one? Okay, you say you want independence, but then you tell me you have to fight to get a story there. You want independence? I can give you independence—"

Molly laughed.

"I'm being serious here. A lot of people would listen to Abe Goodman, a lot of people starting out in the newspaper business would be interested in his advice. And I'll tell you, it is possible for a reporter to move from the kind of paper you're working on and the kinds of stories you're writing to things that are more substantial, more gratifying, more serious. But I tell you, people get marked. People confuse the reporter with the story he writes. You could spend your whole life working on cheese, on filler, on crap. Which would be a shame. Listen, I admire your brains, Molly, really. Every one of those assholes"—he gestured at the empty round table—"thinks you're beautiful, a real doll, but believe me, maybe one or two recognize your intelligence, let alone your talent. They love you. A sweet face—they think they know you. No idea you're as tough as the goddamn pavement. They never pay attention to your brains. Believe me. Genuinely, even though I'm your father, I admire. Not just because I'm your father, I think you could make a hell of an editor. You could take over *Progress* one day—"

"Pop, for now—"

"Will you? I'm making an offer no one in town is going to make. Nobody is going to talk to a fucking schoolgirl about being an editor. You're not going to get a better job, and I'm not doing it out of charity. I'm putting my heart on the table here."

Molly couldn't swallow.

"Look, the newspaper business is going to shit. The Hearsts, the Knights, they're buying up papers all over the country. And good papers fall apart every year. I'm getting old—"

"Pop—"

"Look, it's not only Clarissa Silver you should worry about—"

"What do you mean?"

"Nothing critical, but I'm not going to be around forever. I made a paper. That's something. I'm proud of that. But I'm also proud of my daughter. Other fathers, they would look at a girl like you and say, What's the matter? Twenty-two, beautiful, how come she hasn't got a husband? I won't say your mother is ashamed, but we both wonder: Why can't Molly live in our house? Is there something wrong with our apartment? Is it not big enough?"

Molly lit a cigarette.

"You're smoking now?"

"I'm smoking." A trick she had maybe unconsciously learned from Carl, something to occupy her hands and mouth, a way to maintain poise in the face of Abe's onslaught. The hunching of his shoulders, the rocking of his head, his fists pressing on the table, all the motions echoed in her skull, in her hangover, as if his sentences were beating not just on her headache but on her psyche. "Maybe you should give this line a rest. Maybe you should go back to the note I should write to the Silvers."

But he ignored her, was watching the smoke rise from her burnt match. "Right. Of course you're smoking. Why shouldn't a woman smoke? Get modern, this is what I tell your mother. I say, Our Molly is a modern girl. This is not to be ashamed of, this is to be proud." Their coffee got refilled. Abe continued: "So to my modern girl I say, do I want somebody else, anybody else at my paper? Of course not. I am blessed—this is what I tell every-one—I am blessed with a modern daughter. What's the matter with Molly, why isn't she married, why does she work so hard, a beautiful girl, a nice girl like that living in Greenwich Village? I could give them a fistful of newspaper clippings, but what would they see? This Weiss business—Houdini, Shmoudini, his name is Weiss—this tomorrow's news today. What the hell is that? Thank you very much, but I want today's paper. It's killing me, really it is." He shook his big head, his pale face pink with busted capillaries. Blood and feeling ran close to the top. "Spirits. Spooks. Magicians. What do you need this—"

"We've been through this, Pop." She didn't want to make a scene. She retreated far into herself, staring at him with unforgiving, unwavering gray eyes.

"I'm not saying it's a bad job. It's a fine job for some palooka just in from Des Moines, but for you? With your college education—for my daughter, the future editor—"

"Pop." And she laid down her words carefully against his sloppy aggression, conscious of his vulnerability, and desperate to preserve his dignity as well as her own. "Let's talk about something else."

"I could give you your own column. Whatever you want to write." His guileless eyes came to a rest. "I'm the easiest man to work for. Do you ever even think of it? I mean, seriously? Is it an option with you?"

"We could talk about the theater. Mayor Hylan. Babe Ruth—"

"I don't understand. Is it me? Is it personal? I mean, you could take a job somewhere else. As a matter of fact, I was just talking to Lapides, Irv Lapides—don't look at me like that, you just talked to him, Molly, two minutes ago. Lapides at the *Post*— you're never going to get anywhere if you don't keep track of people. Anyway, he's a creep but no idiot and he says he can get you on staff. An evening paper, Molly, and a respectable one— evening paper means not so many late nights—"

She grabbed his pointing hand.

"Dad," she said, still holding his wrist in her fingers. "I'm not going to work for you."

"Not this year? Or not ever? Am I that horrible?"

"Oh, Pop. You're wonderful." She let go. "But you're impossible. Tell me about that letter from Lyden—"

"Oh, Lyden, what a schmuck. He dropped the letter, and you know what your Freudian mother would say: That couldn't be an accident. He dropped the letter and I saw it addressed to you, I grabbed it. He tried to take it away, the schmuck, but I told him I was going to see you—Will you take it, Molly? Because I promised I'd give it to you, and if you don't get it, well, then he'll think I pocketed it or something like that."

She took the letter, imagining Lyden Silver humiliated, enraged, and wanting to break Abe Goodman's jaw. "You shouldn't stick your fingers in other people's business," she said.

"That's news," said Abe, and he sighed, his large shoulders falling. "Do you remember," he asked, "when I took you to see Houdini when you were kids? It was a terrible mistake. Carl, of course, Carl loved it, but you were three years old and it scared the pants off you."

"We went to a theater?"

"No, no, he was doing one of those crazy promotions. He had a show going, and you know how he used to do it. A public stunt in a public place. Herald Square, I think. They hung him, I can't remember, was it from a crane or a building? Carl and Lyden jumping up and down to see. They put him in a straitjacket and hung him, like from chains. People were pointing and gasping, and my little girl started to cry. Oy, she started bawling. I thought it was perfect for you. Such an idiot, I thought you would enjoy. But what did I know? Like usual, nothing. Houdini struggles, he kicks off the jacket—I'm a newspaperman, I'm supposed to be

watching careful, but instead I'm on my knees on Broadway, saying to my little girl, It's okay, it's okay. The man is going to be
okay. He does this for a living. God knows what I said. I was such
an idiot to take you there. Your mother told me not to take you.
Anyway, the magician gets free, the crowd applauds, but not my
Molly. She is crying for the rest of the afternoon. All you did was
cry. Clinging to your daddy. In those days, I used to be able to do
something for you. I could put you on my knee. For weeks you
had nightmares. And I used to sit by you, thinking what an asshole I had been."

IX

THAT SEPTEMBER, THE HUMAN FLY fell thirty
stories to his death while trying to climb a skyscraper in
Chicago. Houdini released a new movie, *The Man from Beyond*,
which, like his other films, flopped. Its hero was a century-old
man found trapped in ice who, defrosted and resuscitated, proved
as adept at escape as had the noble princes or romantic thieves
that Houdini had played in earlier adventures. Handcuffs, strait-
jackets, nothing could hold him, but on film this shocked no
one. In movies anyone could be magic. Mabel Normand tied to a
railroad track slipped free as the engine closed in, Fatty Arbuckle
danced like a pretty girl, and Buster Keaton exited Wild West
saloon doors to enter the busy heart of Los Angeles. Houdini's
stage magnetism vanished on film. Those hypnotic eyes looked
anxious. He cast himself always as the romantic lead, but insisted
when playing love scenes that his wife be on the set, and he
glanced offscreen each time the Man from Beyond kissed his

lady. As he had when he was younger, Houdini showed off his naked body. He could not shake his tendency to strip. But middle-aged, he was old and pasty and his chest had tits.

THE REVIEWS in the papers tell the story: *The Man from Beyond* is panned wherever it is mentioned. Doyle tucks them into his briefcase, then jolts forward as his driver brakes. He draws the curtain to see 114th Street lined with pretty brownstones. In the rising sun, signposts and hydrants cast long shadows. A boy rides a bicycle westward. Doyle turns to watch the knickered kid pass, and when he glances back there's Houdini, who glides down his stoop, moving like a dancing master and smiling like a maître d'. Tipping his cap, stepping into Doyle's car, heading off on a tour Doyle had planned, Houdini plays the host.

"You have seen the papers this morning."

"Hmm?" says Conan Doyle, surprised that Houdini would mention the attacks on his movie. "You mean that terrible accident in Chicago?"

"Full of it. Free publicity. This river jump will do the trick."

"Oh, yes. The river jump. I read something—I had meant to speak with you—are you quite certain this is absolutely necessary?"

"Necessary?" The wheels begin to roll. "Well, if you mean by 'necessary' the sort of thing any actor or film company manager is required to do in the ordinary business of releasing a motion picture, no. Not 'necessary.' But," Houdini continues, "is it among the most brilliant strokes of promotional genius to be seen this year? Of course, I am not the man to boast and say so, but hear me out, Sir Arthur, in America I have incalculable experience in this realm, and with the new motion picture of your work arriving so soon in theaters, *The Forgotten World*—"

"*The Lost World.*"

"Yes. Those magnificent dinosaurs. A brilliant idea, and not so different from the notion that animates my picture. See, he is a man from a lost world—but preserved! Astonishingly! I suppose that is the difference between your picture and my own. That I, the hero, am a relic from another age, and not the villains, you know. The villains are real people, not dinosaurs. It is a crucial difference. Have you seen the picture?"

"Not yet, but I have read the notices—"

"Notices are unimportant. Particularly in the motion picture business, and you must hear me out, Sir Arthur. What is important is to speak directly to the audience. Hence: the river jump!"

"Isn't that a bit dangerous?" asks Doyle. "And haven't they seen it before, your jumping into a river? I cannot see how it would induce anyone to see a picture show about—"

Houdini pats Doyle's knee. "This is precisely what my money men have been telling me. But it is foolishness, as I will explain. You see, what is necessary here is a keen understanding of the public mind. Now, I ask you, in the public mind, what figure is more admired, more esteemed, in the public mind, than Houdini? As you ponder the question, quickly, you will realize that there is no one else in whose case the public mind is so forced to struggle. You see, where I once was the Handcuff King I am now seen in a different light. The public comes to me with questions of a philosophical and spiritual nature. So I must remind them why they loved me first, and for such a task there is nothing like a genuine dazzlement of the sort that no other per-

former in the world is capable. Only one"—he raised his finger—
"Houdini!"

The driver heads east to avoid Broadway traffic. Houdini's
neighborhood fades into Harlem, tire shops next to churches
next to barbers, goods for sale on the avenues, men in green and
burgundy suits, shouts and laughter. A fruit cart, the broad-
brimmed hats. A street preacher waves a Bible. But past Mount
Morris Park everyone turns blond, the signs Finnish, the clothing plainer. The bearded shouter on a corner is a Red, his book
some kind of manifesto. The city is full of cities, and as Doyle
watches it pass he thinks it instructive from a Spiritualist view,
these manifestations of material lives with their imperfect repeti-
tions and transnational echos.

"You know," Houdini continues, "in the river scene, when I,
as the Man from Beyond, swim the mouth of Niagara, audiences
will not believe what they are seeing—will not believe it, and
not in the sense that they will be dazzled and confused as by your
dinosaurs. They will not wonder if what they see is real or not.
No, they will be so shocked by the power of the event that they
will assume they are witnessing cinematic trickery. But no—there
is no trickery. It is I. The power and development of Houdini
struggling against nature's most terrifying force. The real made
mystifying, not the mystification made to seem real. We developed our own methods for capturing the action. They will never
believe that what they are witnessing is life!"

"I fail to understand." Doyle shifts in the back seat. "If they
won't believe it, why make it part of the show? After all, isn't
that the point—to make them believe?"

"But this is precisely my argument, precisely!" He claps his hands. "That Houdini is the only honest, the only scientific practitioner of astonishments both on stage and on film—and this is precisely why the name Houdini is recognized and admired in all corners of the globe. Yes. No mechanical wonders and cinematic mystifications. Honesty. Integrity. And it is the river jump, a feat of daring, one no other performer would attempt, at least not under the same scientific conditions of scrutiny—the river jump will remind audiences around the world of the power of Houdini."

Bumps in the road as the car makes its way over trolley tracks, and Doyle glimpses an El train lumbering toward the Bronx. Past High Bridge Park and its reservoir, the Packard's shining hood climbs uphill into the sunshine. Houses thin, traffic stalls, they approach the Broadway drawbridge. Stupid to invite Houdini, thinks Doyle, to drag Margery and Sabatier into this business of proving themselves, when after all in her sublime confidence Margery has nothing to prove. Combat with Houdini, he thinks, is no place for a lady, and there is little chance Houdini will recognize her gifts; and yet the chance tempts him—if only he can convince the man! Earlier this morning on the way uptown, Doyle had imagined discussing his ideas about relativity with Houdini, explaining his developing theory about perspective and belief, but of course it was impossible to have a reasoned discourse with the man. Still it had to be explained somehow: that the existence of spirits depended on a willingness to perceive them, and this was not as his enemies would have it, J. M. Barrie pixie-dust and Tinkerbell, if-you-believe-in-fairies-clap-your-hands, but a psychical question with metaphysical implications. The world existed only insofar as one was able to perceive it, if only in the sense that

Bishop Berkeley had propounded, and in that sense Doyle's position on the relativity of souls was not Einsteinian but commonplace. He never argued that belief constructed anything, no castles in the sky, only that belief was the opening of an internal eye, as necessary for apprehending Spiritual phenomena as the opening of the physical eye was for apprehending light. As an eye doctor, he had operated on cataracts, treated glaucoma, washed and sutured eyeballs, but always his patients had wanted to see. Strange how in the case of spiritual vision men wished for blindness, became overcautious, frighteningly so. Fooled once by a charlatan, they would never see a doctor, suffering from that awful fallacy that if one was a fake, all were. This morning, Doyle had considered the hypothetical rocket ship in the film about Einstein, the shifting vision of time. The doubter stood earthbound, perceived the planet's curve as a flat line to the horizon, when faith was the aircraft that allowed one to comprehend not only the true shape of the globe, but also one's own misapprehension. Here was Doyle the aviator, motor running, asking Houdini to hop aboard his airplane, and there stood Houdini, arms crossed, eyes shut, petulant and earthbound, claiming that he didn't need a flying machine to tell the difference between round and flat.

Slowly they cross the old steel bridge into the Bronx. Beneath them the churning waters of Spuyten Duyvil, to the right the old Croton Aqueduct, to their left the palisades. A tug shoves a barge upriver, whitecaps in the late summer breeze. The slow road, built for horse carts, winds through the shady towns of Westchester County, main streets of commuter towns near fields and farms, hints of autumn in the maples and elms. Early September, apples ripen in the orchards. As the ride continues

north, Houdini's agitation resolves itself, first into a set of pronouncements on the happiness of a drive in the country, then
into a kind of nervous performance of relaxation, and then, in
the flickering light of the back of the car, his face sags impassively, his hands lie limp in his lap. Doyle checks his watch. In
some twenty minutes they will be arriving at Margery's. The car
lurches onto an bumpy road, and Houdini touches his lips. A
minute later Doyle breaks the silence.

"Now," he says, "my dear Houdini, I have particularly high
hopes in this woman."

"Indeed. I am aware."

"And so the afternoon calls for some delicacy."

"Delicacy?" Houdini jerks to life. "Who is more delicate than
I? No, I understand completely. I am enormously obliged to you,
Sir Arthur, and I put myself entirely in your hands."

"Yes, of course. But the point is, and I don't know how many
times I have put this to you, but we are their guests, the guests of
the Sabatiers, and we must at the very least be good guests. They
are treating us to a séance, you know, and let us think of it as if
they were treating us to a piano recital, or a bit of fine food,
nothing one would dare—"

"I am eager to see what they've cooked up."

"This is precisely—this is—look here, Houdini, were they laying out breakfast, I very much doubt you would attack the
poached egg as a detective would a murder case—"

"Ah, but you are the writer of detective stories. And I if they
told me the egg was a goose's when I knew it was a chicken's,
honesty would compel me to point out the lie. It is not polite to
allow one's friends to be deceived."

"Indeed. However, the point I am making, the point is—I understand that you have your doubts, but—how to put it—"

"I come with an open mind."

"I am afraid that's what you said about my wife's spirit writing, and the next day I opened the newspapers—"

"Sir Arthur, this is unfair. This is distinctly unfair. You have my word that I spoke to that reporter only in a spirit of consideration—consideration of the importance of your claims, out of the deepest respect and friendship for both you and Lady Doyle. I told her—and indeed she was good enough to put it in her writing, perhaps not as prominently as I would have wished, perhaps I would have wished that it would have been placed in the very first sentence of the first paragraph of her article—that I hold both you and Lady Doyle in the highest esteem. The highest esteem! These were my words exactly, and that was at the heart of my actions, the esteem in which I hold you, my most gentlemanly, most admired friend—"

"Yes, well. I understand. And as a public man I am accustomed to the cut and thrust of public battle. I am used even to seeing myself mocked in newspapers, quite accustomed to catching a few brickbats, though I admit it came as a surprise to see my wife mocked by—"

"Mocked! Now, there you go too far—I? Mocking Lady Doyle? Nothing could—"

"Perhaps the language I used was too strong. Perhaps I ought to have said—"

"Indeed it was too strong. And as for your apologies, I accept. I know, Sir Arthur, that your task is urgent, that in your eyes you are bringing the world great knowledge, but you must see that I am undertaking a no less urgent task. And you must understand that I, too, I am your most devoted friend, and would undertake any solemn oath of friendship—"

"That will not be necessary. But friendly is, you know, as friendly does—"

"And it was in the spirit of friendship, the highest friendship, that I spoke to that reporter. The supreme value here is truth. Truth, integrity, honesty. It is well known that I, Houdini, am possessed of a physical antipathy to falsehood such as some men have to filth or sickness. I can, I believe, endure physical pain as well as any man alive, better, perhaps, some would even say I endure physical pain as well as any who ever lived, but this is my weakness: The smallest falsehood wounds me. The very whiff of dishonesty, deception, or misapprehension is to me nauseous. And it was not—hear me out on this, dear Sir Arthur, please let me finish—it was not any dissimulation on the part of you or your wife that I feared, but that the public should think for a moment that I am not who I am—and I hope you will understand that this is not a concern for me, for my own reputation in the public eye, my own profit or well-being. No. It is a concern for my public and its sense of truth, of justice, of integrity—if the public should be deceived into thinking that I believe in mystifications which I do not in fact believe, then a life's work stands in ruins, a whole school, a whole line of men devoted to investigating the substantial truth in the areas of mystery stands betrayed. You see the dangers I face. You see how it was incumbent upon me to publish my views, to banish falsehood or rumor before either reared its ugly head. You see how anything less would have been an insult to you, to your wife, and to anyone who thinks deeply about life or death, a betrayal of the very substance of integrity—"

"Yes, this is all well and good, but—"

"Sir Arthur, I must ask what you demand of me. Do you wish silence? Do you wish me to refrain from speaking my beliefs? To witness Margery's performance and then to seal my lips? No. I will speak my mind, publicly and privately always, to you and the world at large. For to me in this business of belief, true belief, solemn belief, those who hold their own truths secret are as good as liars and I will not keep silent, or be kept silent, not for any man. I will not forswear my duties, and if you wish me to refrain from speaking plainly to my public—"

"My dear Houdini—"

"If so, stop the car. I will not visit your friend Margery under such circumstances. Driver—"

"There is no need—"

"Driver!" Houdini shouts through the tube.

"Please. All I require of you is an open mind. A touch of faith, of hope—"

"Hope? I am, if I may say so, the most hopeful man alive." He smiles. "Driver, carry on."

The car turns off the rough road and onto an even smaller one, and a plume of dust follows its wake. Queen Anne's lace in the high grass. A truck passes, loaded with chickens in wood and wire coops, and both vehicles slow and ease up onto the grass banks on the shoulders. The sky is blue as a jay, high clouds spread thin. About six miles from town, they pull up to a cottage.

"Can this be it?" Houdini asks.

A neat little box with two windows on either side of the

door, the house, thinks Doyle, of a man who has left the material world behind. Clapboard and two-story, its shutters painted white, the cottage sits upon a rise, while two big elm trees shade the sloping lawn. On either side, woods and bushes grow unnaturally close to the house, as if the whole thing were hiding from prying eyes. Across the way, duckweed scums a pond, cattails rise on the edges of abandoned pasture, and dragonflies patrol the reeds.

Houdini bounces out of the automobile before its motor gives its last kick. He hops off the running board and up the lawn, knocking at the door, while Doyle, with a grunt, unfolds himself from the back seat, knees stiff after the long ride. He stands his big body on skinny legs and then pauses to admire the countryside, the winding road, the swallows over the water, the birds lined up on the telephone wire. He takes off his glasses, he wipes his face.

And just as Doyle begins his way up the lawn, Sabatier appears. He pops out of the bushes at the side of the house, wearing a yellow suit and a pink ascot. He raises his fingers in the air.

"Ah," cries Doyle.

Houdini doffs his cap.

"You had a tolerable drive, I assume." Sabatier smiles. Then he beckons for them to follow him into the woods.

They do. The path is narrow. Twigs crackle under leather-soled shoes. Doyle ducks beneath the branches. Brambles catch his trousers, he slips on bulging roots. Houdini struts ahead, moving through the woods with a predator's grace. The path twists and turns. Every so often Doyle glimpses through the bracken flashes of Sabatier's suit, the professor appearing from behind a distant birch trunk. Doyle has his eyes on his feet while they manage a particularly tricky patch of schist, and then, pushing a raspberry branch out of the way, he finds himself in the sunshine.

The grass grows thick, cut short, a rich, dark, saturated green which varies only with light and shadow. The lawn is banked by hedges and brambles, before them beds of marigolds and impatiens and tall red exotic flowers Conan Doyle cannot name. About fifty yards to his right, the lawn disappears into high meadows. A low stone wall marks the boundary, but the effect from a distance is of a cliff. The cottage they had noticed from the street now sits high above, but emerging from the rocky shelf on which it sits is a kind of bungalow, seemingly built into the granite outcropping, and the roof suggests that this annex is perhaps connected through the rock to the original clapboard home. The bungalow seems Japanese in its austerity, with dark-stained wood and long screens and windows. Green grapes hang on a trellis, leaves thick and shady. Under a pagoda stands a handsome Asian valet in a waist-length jacket, carrying a tray of glasses filled with ice, and beyond the pagoda lies a pink marble swimming pool into which small fountains in the shape of pudgy naked toddlers pee. In the tinkling pool's rippling reflections of cloud and sky Doyle discerns a strange dark shape, a body which breaks the surface at the far side—Margery. She rises from the pool, striding up marble steps, wet shoulders, long back, broad behind, all of her in a dark red bathing suit.

Desire like a fist—Doyle clenches against its blow. He looks at Houdini, as much to look away from the lady as to catch his friend's eye, but Houdini seems imperturbable. Sabatier continues to smile. For an awful moment Doyle sees it all through the magician's eyes, that Margery is a whore and Sabatier her whore-master, but Doyle's reflexive sympathy explains away the problem of her appearance. It is common for mediums to be stripped before séances, to be searched, to prove there is nothing hidden on their persons, and here Margery in her beauty has sacrificed her shame and done it for them, presenting herself unprotected and at the mercy of their chivalry. He remembers how she described herself to him, as an instrument, as a tool. Doyle is relieved to find, when he looks back, that she has dressed herself in a kimono made of silk. He rests a hand on Houdini's shoulder, but the shoulder is forgiving as a rock.

Margery crosses the lawn barefoot, stepping the line where the grass meets the pink marble of the pool, her long legs easy, the kimono clinging to her chest. Her dark hair is slicked back from her forehead, she flicks a stray lock behind an ear, then smiles, her smile oblivious to the movement of her breasts. Her lipstick is unconventionally bright. Could she be as young as twenty-five or even twenty? Sabatier gestures toward the valet and the pagoda, the empty cane chairs. The beautiful boy pours blue drinks from a clear glass pitcher. Houdini holds back as his three companions seat themselves. A cluster of grackles springs up from the lawn.

"Brilliant," he says. "Absolutely brilliant. Never have I seen such an overture. Even now I feel I have advanced into the heart of mystery—the naked lady, the beautiful Oriental, the peculiar architecture, your colorful suit. Why, here among the crickets and bees I feel the very chanting, humming voices of the universe already. This is precisely the spot for it, something enigmatic in even the angle of the sun."

"I suppose that is all meant as a compliment, Mr. Houdini, but I am afraid you will find us very simple folk." Sabatier bows and extends a hand. "Forgive my silence as I led you back here, boy-ish nervousness, I assure you, though you will hardly credit it, so difficult to credit shyness in an adult. My apologies. But to have two such eminences arrive at my home—"

"I have rarely seen a home more beautiful," Doyle interjects.

"I thank you. May I interest either of you gentlemen in a drink, a simple floral infusion? Very refreshing, I assure you. And where are my manners? My wife, Margery, and I am, as you know, though we have not formally been introduced, Mr. Houdini, your servant, Dr. Hugo Sabatier, and may I say, Mr. Houdini, what a pleasure, what a daunting honor it is to entertain a celebrity such as yourself in my good home, and Sir Arthur, it can only be my deepest, sin-cerest hope that you will not be disappointed at what you find here. You both do us honor, such honor—"

"Nonsense," says Houdini.

"Thank you." Doyle smiles.

"You are both welcome," says Margery. She nods and the folds of her kimono open.

Ice clinks in the blue drinks. Margery's lips leave prints on her glass. Conversation runs the roads and journey and Sabatier describes the plan of the house. It was designed by a man who built mechanical contrivances for display in the windows of shops and hotels, little automata with windup mechanisms, men and women, dogs and ponies; quite a few of them could still be found around the house. The heirs of this mechanical genius, committed Spiritualists both, have lent the place to the Sabatiers indefinitely.

"So we are guests here," he says, "but comfortable."

After drinks he leads them into the house. The plain wood of the bungalow is elaborately worked at the corners and window frames, subtle, intricate designs in the shapes of interconnecting vines and leaves and flowers. To the left and right of the entrance lie screened porches with rattan furniture wrought in the shapes of birds and cats. On the long low tables rest abundant papers and books, but the party does not linger. Sabatier leads them through a narrow corridor, where on either wall hang Japanese prints, frothy waves, sandy shores, flower stems, and birds. Next to these are a few selected spirit photographs, nebulous forms hung in dark rooms, men gathered in circles with mediums. Margery strides above them up a flight of stairs, her bottom kissing the silk kimono. Through a wainscoted hallway, they pass a window with its curtains spread, and below Doyle can see the elms, the lawn, the black Packard, and his chauffeur reading a newspaper.

"A perfect day," says Sabatier, and he opens a heavy wooden door.

In the center of the room sits a plain wood table, no seams, no leaves, just a rectangular slab of hardwood, smooth as glass and stained mahogany, around it four chairs with cane legs and wicker seats. Sabatier moves silently, footsteps absorbed by the thick-piled carpet. When all have entered and the door shuts, he draws a velvet curtain that rings the room. Behind it, walls and windows disappear. Sabatier lights one wick in the big candelabra, and they see each other through the smoke of incense which has been gathering for some time and whose scent has grown heavy now that the curtain is drawn. By the candelabra on the table sits a small square apparatus with which both Houdini and Doyle are familiar, a wood box with a bell within, the bell inaccessible to any but spirit hands, its ring—so its defenders have it—the surest indication of etheric presences. As he and Houdini take their seats, Doyle notices that the ceiling, too, has been hung in velvet.

Margery prepares for her trance. Eyes shut and head raised, she stands between the men and the table, clad in her kimono, her hair black as the darkness around her. Sabatier passes a hand in front of Margery's face. He whispers to her. He barks. He makes as if to slap her. Margery does not flinch. She no longer smiles, her lips slightly parted, red cosmetic wax clinging at odd points. Her husband circles her twice and strips her of her robe. He invites his guests to search her body. They decline.

One hand to her neck, the other to her back, Sabatier moves his wife as if she were a clockwork mannequin. Once he seats her, he discovers in the darkness beneath the table a doctor's bag. He sets this in front of him and gets to work. From the satchel comes a long rope coil. He unravels it dramatically, cracking the free end as if it were a whip. A yard's length, he wraps it around Margery's waist, then pulls so her body jerks. He ropes the rest several times around her bare flesh, pulling each coil tight. Her breasts are pinched, her naked shoulders, her arms, her belly, her gut, and her thighs.

Sabatier invites Houdini to test the knots, but Houdini again declines.

"I want you to see this," Sabatier insists. He holds her chin and squeezes her mouth. "Stick a finger in. If you are like any number of doubters, you will want to be sure there is nothing in here." He angles her hair back. The candlelight shines up her nose. "Poke a finger in." Sabatier nods encouragingly. "She'll never know."

Houdini raises a polite hand. Sabatier shrugs, then stuffs his wife's mouth with plaster. Leaning back in his chair, away from Sabatier and Margery, Houdini has lost a shade of his arrogance. He fails in his mannered attempts at ease. Having sealed her mouth and assured his visitors that nothing is hidden anywhere on her body—since they refuse to search, he does it for them— Sabatier pulls from his bag an elastic net and fixes it over Margery's head. Black thread cuts one-inch diamonds into her face, holding down her wet hair and disfiguring her nose. At the net's base sits a collar. Sabatier pulls two strings and draws them so tight that Doyle can hear a rasp in Margery's breathing. After tying the strings, he stands back, and with a wave of his hands shows off the wicked binding of his wife.

Then Sabatier snuffs the candle. In darkness, he crosses the room and Doyle feels the shift in air as the man passes behind him, hears the chair creak as Sabatier sits. They reach for one another's hands. Margery's is delicate. Lithe cool fingers settle into his palm and he feels a chill, a tickle on the back of his neck. He can feel the energy coursing from Margery through him and to Professor Sabatier. In the silent enclosure Doyle feels the balance of nature shift. He shuts his eyes, he opens them, but though his pupils dilate to adjust, they comprehend nothing. Sabatier's hand is moist and strong and uncomfortable.

The bell box rings faintly, then stronger. And sooner than Doyle would have expected, the table begins its rise, a gentle pressure beneath his elbows. One inch, then another, the sitters are obliged to straighten their arms and strengthen their grasps.

Sabatier's fingers are oily and urgent, Margery's feminine and weak. The room grows warm. There's a tickle in his throat from the smoke. Doyle knows what pressure raises the table, knows what snakes from between her legs and levers the furniture up. The pseudopod is hers and its own, a strange serpentine force, acting out its own birth while she remains passive. This is Margery's spiritual self made physical, giving voice to the singing in the air, which Doyle hears faintly, angels. And for a moment he imagines Houdini's skepticism, a concealed phonograph somewhere, the table attached to pulleys or a hydraulic lift, but Margery's grasp convinces him otherwise. It is not the evident miracles that impress Doyle—not the singing or the bell box or the table's rise—but the room's atmosphere of hope. This is the ineffable sensation for which words and arguments are inadequate: the opening of the telescopic eye within, the lifting of the airplane of the heart, the conviction of peace, alone in his own psyche yet linked with the psychology of the universe, a sense not of divine presence but of unity with the divine. Doyle bobs in an ocean of meaning and of love: for his wives, dead and living, for his children, here and beyond, for his ancestors, and for grandchildren waiting to be born. Then the table drops and Sabatier and Margery release his hands.

There are sparks, then what seems to eyes accustomed to darkness to be an explosion. Sabatier has lit a match. Doyle shuts his eyes and against his lids sees the imprint of the flame's yellow burst. Sabatier lights a candle. Houdini's face looms in the smoke trail. Doyle turns to Margery, and then sees the thing: The size of a small potato or large mouse, it hangs outside the net covering her face, one end from a pale string that extends from her ear, the other from her right nostril. It bobs—a furry, thready, damp mass neither gelid nor solid, wet and perhaps stringy, something of the texture of a hair ball at the base of a mucky drain, gray-brown in the half-light and mottled, clearly ectoplasmic, a kind of extraneous pseudopod extending from her face. Doyle has never before witnessed this sort of manifestation, but has read about it, particularly in Dingwall Bird's pioneering work of 1908. Margery remains roped to her chair, but she has regurgitated the plaster in her mouth, and it lies in a pile on the tabletop. Under the netting, her eyes flicker so that Doyle sees their whites. No doubt about this growth: It is a newly materialized organ through which she can communicate with the dead. Doyle's knees move together. He has the same sense he did in his rooftop tea with the medium, that her pseudopod is prowling under the table, looking for something to grab.

"Reach out," Sabatier directs the sitters, "clasp my wife's hands."

Now her grasp feels limp and damp, her fingers loll in his palm. Sabatier snuffs the candle again and reaches for his guests. Minutes after they are linked, the bell box rings.

"Spirit," calls Sabatier, "are you there?"

No response. The darkness is absolute. Doyle coughs; the incense and candle smoke irritate his throat.

"Spirit, are you there?"

The bell box rings, weak clappers flailing.

"Speak, spirit, speak!"

Again, the bell box. Against the weight of their arms, the table begins its second rise. It goes upward slowly and then with a sudden bolt jumps a full half foot, pulling Doyle's hand from Margery's.

"Blast," he cries, fishing in the darkness for her. His fingers slip into something oily, then he feels the wind as a heavy object zings by his head. A muffled thump comes from Houdini's side of the room as something strikes the curtain and the wall. Another thud, a shattering, a piece of wood strikes Doyle in the chest.

"I say!"

A cool breeze sweeps the still room, coming from nowhere, as the windows are shut. The bell box rings thrice in succession and then the table falls.

"Spirit!" cries Sabatier. "Speak!"

Doyle reaches uselessly for Margery, and Sabatier calls louder still.

"Speak!"

Still no voice responds, but this time Doyle touches Margery's fingers and at the moment their hands clasp, the candle lights itself, and all their sweaty faces are visible in the gloom. The gray blob still trails from Margery's ear and nose, but her half-parted lips are now visible, and from them comes a three-toned repetitive chant that Sabatier joins, followed by Doyle, then Houdini, a simple minor arpeggio which they repeat five, ten, fifteen times. The candle flame bends, dancing to a wind no sitter can feel. The wax rises in the center, peels down the side, and drips kiss the tabletop. Margery's head droops, her chin lolling against her chest, her strange ectoplasmic attachment sliming her cheek.

Their chanting continues and the shape glistens vaguely in the half-light, as if coated in its own afterbirth. Sabatier has shut his eyes and Doyle follows suit, wondering in the darkness if Houdini's eyes are open, but soon this question is put aside in favor of more urgent concerns. A fourth voice has joined their chorus. It sings a longer, more complex melodic line, and seems to originate from the ceiling, and not from any of the three sitters. Doyle opens his eyes. Houdini stares at the medium. Her ectoplasmic blob throbs with the tempo of the chant, but Margery's half-opened mouth produces the same three tones as the other sitters; this mysterious voice is not hers. Doyle scans the room quickly, sees the objects thrown about the plush carpet: a large silver pot, a red speaking trumpet, a book open to its cover page and on that his own name beneath the title *Sir Nigel*. The high voice abandons its singing and commences a sound more like a hyena's than a human being's. Sabatier keeps chanting, so does Houdini, also Conan Doyle. He is sweating now, the room uncomfortably hot, the smoke tearing his eyes. His glasses feel ready to slip down his nose, and Doyle lifts his head up to keep them in place. An accidental glance at the ceiling and he gasps: an old woman, just her face, suspended in the candle-lit haze. The face grows, shrinks and bends, black and gray, showing tints of orange or yellow; the mouth is half opened, and it seems to smile.

"Oh, my son"—her voice distant, strangled, meek, and tired—"oh, my Harry—"

"Good God," says Conan Doyle.

And Houdini glances upward just as the specter vanishes.

"Please," says Sabatier when the figure is gone. "Remember. I must be the only one to speak."

But Doyle needs to know. "Did you see her? Did you—"

Houdini nods.

"Gentlemen." Sabatier demands their attention. "Let us once again take hands."

"What's that?" asks Doyle.

And Margery screams. The ectoplasmic organ has dropped from her face, and her face has fallen to the table. A voice comes from within her, as if from some deep hole. The words are indecipherable, but they come again, repeatedly, urgently.

And then, just as he thinks he understands her, Margery jerks up unnaturally, her face like a corpse's, her mouth open wide. The voice that comes finally is guttural, otherworldly, and not her own.

"Death to the doubter," she moans.

Margery collapses and Sabatier leaps to his feet. He parts the heavy curtain and points his guests to the door.

X

"WHAT A WONDERFUL SHOW!"

"What's that?"

"Very impressive."

"Indeed. I have never—"

"Why do you suppose the woods grow so close to the cottage?"

"Beg pardon?"

But Houdini has asked this question without interest in Doyle's reply. He steps to his right, considering the construction of the house, the way it sits on the schist outcropping. The houseboy under the pagoda refills sweating tumblers with ice and blue water. Houdini rises on his toes.

"Interesting, interesting."

"Is that all you have to say?"

"A moment, Sir Arthur, please."

So Doyle leaves him, passes the houseboy, and strolls to the pool. The fountains ripple the surface so that pockets of cloud and sky appear within his reflected arm and torso. Margery is the most remarkable woman he has ever met: her composure, her calm, her beauty, her strength in the face of torment. So vulnerable, so delicately human, so powerfully receptive to the spirits' forces, so wickedly punished by those forces, so willing to be punished again. As for Dr. Sabatier, Doyle cannot like the man, but this and chivalry argue for his further involvement in the case, and furthermore for Sabatier's authenticity. If a man so clever were a charlatan, he would not behave like one. And if Doyle were through financial investment to assist in the creation of Sabatier's retreat, he might have a say in how business would be conducted there. It ought, he thinks, to be a place both manly and vigorous, dignified and unafraid. But further investigation will be required if he is to hand over any money. Doyle imagines a séance without Houdini—he will of course hear whatever Houdini has to say, even though the magician's actions thus far indicate a commitment not to skepticism but to willful blindness, a kind of extreme faith in materialism which requires him to reject even the most obvious evidence of the world beyond, so committed is he to his public posture of contradiction. Doyle wonders whether this mad-dog contrariness evinces something worse than skepticism: a desire on Houdini's part for a monopoly on miracle-making, a monopoly he will defend at all costs. In fact, Doyle considers, the very violence of Houdini's negativism might indicate not a medium's falsehood but her power.

Doyle imagines a séance with like-minded men, serious investigators of spiritual phenomena who, unlike Houdini, do not reflexively reject everything that comes before them, but rather consider evidence in light of accepted empirical practices, men of science, not theater, perhaps even Dingwall Bird himself, a man who could share in the miracle of Margery and assist Doyle in demonstrating conclusively the reality of her power. The eminent Bird's opinions would justify Doyle's excitement, lend credence to his investments, and together they could demonstrate that, through hard work, faith, determination, and with the assistance of a powerful medium, a human being could scale the infinitely high walls that border the mortal world.

He stands at ease, hands clasped behind him, watching his reflection ripple, but feels as though the ground beneath him trembles. The conundrums of human existence seem for the moment soluble. They will rectify the theories of religion and psychology, prove with concrete evidence—photographs, recordings, perfectly observed and undeniable data—exactly the relation of spirit to body, of the soul to the universe, of humanity to life. If this means the creation of Sabatier's retreat, then so be it, but that retreat, in Doyle's vision, would have to be a scientific institute. Darwin, Freud, Edison, Einstein, their notions and inventions would seem paltry next to the truths that Margery could reveal.

The swinging of a screen door breaks his reverie. She emerges from the sunroom into the garden, followed by her husband, and appears as mysteriously radiant as she had the day he first met her. Modest, ladylike, she blushes under her veil when Houdini smiles at her. Sabatier laughs. Doyle hurries across the grass.

"Miraculous," he says. "Truly. I have seen—I have worked with—a number of mediums, you know, and never, never have I felt such a powerful presence. Never have so many spirits, so varied, never have I felt their presence so keenly—"

"Please," Sabatier interrupts. "Please sit. Come to the shade. We have had quite an afternoon."

"But the most exquisite feelings, I tell you, such pain, such power—"

"She remembers nothing."

Margery lowers her eyes as Sabatier holds a chair for her.

"Fascinating," says Doyle. "And is this always the case?"

"Certainly. And I for one was frustrated by this afternoon's experience." Settling himself down, Sabatier crosses his thin legs. "We were never able to maintain the connections for a decent interval. Terribly frustrating. But what did you think, Mr. Houdini?"

"Ah." He stands apart. "Do not put me to it."

"But we are curious." Sabatier gestures to the houseboy; he wants Houdini to sit, to drink. "It is not every day, you know, that the great Houdini comes into one's living room, and of course, while you are under no obligations to express any opinions whatsoever, as a guest in my home I ask nothing of you, and many who sit with my wife prefer silent contemplation afterward. Please, if you like, wander the woods behind, think over what you have seen—and yet, it would be disingenuous of me not to express my curiosity. At our séances we have never yet entertained anyone who might be characterized as a doubter."

"Well, doubters." Houdini grins. "Death to them."

No one laughs.

"Your mother was there," says Doyle.

"Really." Houdini clasps his hands together. "You really ought not put it to me like this. I am, you know, quite a critic of these events. I need some time to—"

"Why not simply tell us?" Conan Doyle interrupts. "Express your doubts, then let us be done with them. We are honest folk and can take your skepticism, if honestly expressed, at its word. You need not tiptoe here. We are true blue in our belief—based as it is on both private conviction and solid, scientific evidence. I know what I have seen. Nothing you can say can alter it. So, come. Out with it."

"My dear Sir Arthur," Houdini complains, "I'm not sure what you can possibly expect from me. But I do have questions for both the professor and his wife."

"Join us, have a seat," says Sabatier. "Ask me any question you like."

And so it begins. Houdini refuses a glass of blue water. Pressing his finger sometimes to his lips, sometimes to his chin, sometimes wagging it, he interrogates his host. How long have they lived in the cottage? Sabatier is vague in reply. When did they move there? He cannot be precise, but remembers the temperature of the day, the frost on the ground, the sunlight through the trees. Had any workmen been hired recently? The roof needed shingling. Did anyone else live on the grounds?

"The groundskeeper has a cottage in the meadow beyond the lawn. Would you like to meet him?"

"Quite unnecessary," says Houdini.

More personal questions follow, and Sabatier remains evasive: When and where was Margery born? Educated? Where have her travels taken her? How old is she? With a smile, Sabatier demurs. He must protect his wife above all. So Houdini turns his attention on the professor. How old is he? Where has he studied? Where has he taught? But all this, says Sabatier, is public record. Then: How did he meet his wife? When did they begin their professional association? Did it precede or follow romantic involvement?

"Please, Houdini," blurts Conan Doyle.

"No, no, it's quite all right. I enjoy your friend's pugnacity. But surely Mr. Houdini will need a pen and paper. All these questions, all these answers, you'll want to take notes."

"Not necessary," says Houdini. "I remember everything."

And he continues. Was the professor the first man to notice Margery's gifts? When and how were those gifts first discovered? When did she begin performing? Sabatier dodges the first two but attacks the last.

"My wife has never performed for anyone. Obviously, we cannot keep her gifts hidden from the world. That would be immoral, a waste. Her talents are not for herself, or even for me to experience privately—she is here on earth to help those who require it. Yet we prefer to keep a certain distance from the public eye, you know. You will never see us, like our dear friend Sir Arthur, filling the pews of Carnegie Hall. No. I will not allow the press to attack my wife's dignity; I will not have her deemed a publicity seeker. This is why we do not allow photographs of her face to be published, this is why séances are by invitation only, and why the list of those whom she has met is kept secret. As a gentleman, you understand, surely. My dream is to make her powers available to a circle wide enough to admit all those who would earnestly benefit from the experience, yet narrow enough to exclude the violence and jeering of accusing crowds—"

"But what is wrong with honest investigation?"

"I have no problem with anything honest," says Sabatier.

"Then why are you so guarded in answers to my questions? Why do you keep your wife's identity secret?"

"There are no secrets," says Sabatier. "After all, I have invited you, sir, the world's foremost skeptic of mediums—"

"But you will not tell me who she is."

Sabatier looks at her, and for the first time, Margery speaks.

"I am myself," she says. "Just me."

Doyle wants to cheer. Such grace, such simplicity. He will support her. He will invest in Margery. Her pearl-white skin, her guileless voice—if need be he will live beside her in Sabatier's spiritual mecca, and so draw others to the light.

"Of course," said Houdini. "Of course you are who you are." He smiles at her, an indulgent uncle to a schoolgirl. "But that does not mean she cannot prove it, cannot admit to it publicly. In fact, her confidence should inspire you. If you are honest, then no one can prove that she is not—"

"She is my wife," says Sabatier. "I will protect her. I will not have anyone *prove* anything about her. Would you have your wife poked and prodded by those who, before having met her, had deemed her a circus freak, a fraud? Would you have me flaunt her gifts as vaudeville amusements? No. Don't be offended. I admire your performances. But your world is not for us."

"Bravo," says Doyle.

And it is not until the car ride home that he speaks to Houdini, reminding him of all his promises made on the drive up, promises now broken. "You told me clearly that you would refrain from any outward displays of doubt or aggression, that you would be a good guest to their good hosts."

"Do you feel I was less than polite?"

The cottage recedes through the dusty rear window of the car.

"This isn't the first time this has happened, you know. I have repeatedly placed my trust in you, and repeatedly that trust has been violated—"

"But we have not even begun to discuss the evidence—"

"Hear me. Between Margery's display of power and your refusal to acknowledge—I say. If you behave with hostility to my family or to my friends, if you turn what could be reasonable discussion into a fight—"

"I have never—"

"If you do so, I must choose sides."

"And whose side do you choose?"

"Between you and the Margery? I choose what I have seen, what I know to be true. I choose her."

"And that's final?"

"Why do you smile?"

"Behold!" Houdini pulls up his pants leg, unsnaps his garter, turns down his sock, and reveals a rubber bandage wrapped around his ankle, over his Achilles tendon and partway up the fierce muscle of his calf. The skin above is red and swollen. "You see"—despite Doyle's annoyance, Houdini carries on— "I have tied this so tightly as to swell and irritate the skin of my lower leg. You see, it is red and supersensitive. Yes, there is some pain, but you know that my threshold for pain is much higher than any ordinary—"

"Houdini," Doyle groans. With a bump, the car climbs onto the wider road which leads south to the city. "I don't see how any of this can be at all relevant to what we have just—"

"Just so." Houdini unties the bandage and his pedantic finger rises. "The skin of my leg, so irritated, has become supersensitive, as I say, and so is able to feel that which ordinary legs would never—"

"Houdini—"

"And I felt her leg—"

"What? Margery's leg?"

"Her leg under the table, during the séance—"

"I don't see what that could possibly indicate other than your own bullheadedness. I am a doctor, do not lecture me on skin and nerves. And while I am sure your irritated leg felt something pass by it, whether it was an ectoplasmic force or merely one of several objects hurled about the room by spirit hands, I cannot say. Still, I remain convinced, and I can assure you that it was not Margery. I know what I saw. She fell into a trance. She was bound at the end of the séance just as she had been at the start—"

Houdini raises a hand to quiet Doyle. He maintains his showman's smile. "I felt her leg. She slipped those ropes and tucked herself back in. I know it, because I have done it myself, and I know how it's done."

"But that's not logic. Because you have played a trick, this has no bearing on Margery—"

"Ah!" Houdini, the pedant. "Let us consider. For one, the large coil of rope. Most impractical, and used by miracle-mongers and so-called magicians because of its impracticality. Had Sabatier truly wanted to fix Margery to a chair, he would have done so with several small secure bindings. One around each wrist, one around each ankle, perhaps one around the waist. Simple effective bonds, simple effective knots. A large coil is useless, but makes for a good show, and your friend Sabatier was quite magnificent in his showmanship: He drew the rope out from the bag with real razzle-dazzle, you know. But my point: The long coil, since all of its bindings communicate with one another, is the easiest to slip. Slack at any one point in the bindings can be transferred to any other. I can assure you, she slipped from the bindings just before the bell box was rung, and slipped in again once Sabatier lit the candle."

"Absurd!" Doyle is such a large man that he finds the back of even this car uncomfortable. He rearranges his legs, crosses his arms, does his best to moderate his anger. "We were in the presence of etheric forces, man, forces beyond comprehension. What you felt on your leg, to have that in the center of your consciousness, and in such an accusing way—Houdini, my friend, spirits who cross from their world to ours to tell us expressly of its comforts and to warn against doubts do so at great cost to themselves, and do so only out of love for the poor mortal souls they wish to comfort. They require love and comfort in return, and though it seems paradoxical from your perspective, one must admit to their existence before one is in any position to doubt the truth of any particular apparition. This may seem to you strange, but it is in keeping with the world of ordinary science. One cannot perform empirical experiments, cannot gather any scientific data, on any chemical, any animal, any force of nature, unless one is prepared to accept, as a first principle, the evidence in front of one's eyes, ears, and fingertips. Before one can perform an experiment, one must first admit that the subject of the experiment exists—or else, where are you? And in this case it is most essential. One must not simply believe in the possibility of the existence of spirits, one must embrace with a loving heart the spirits who come before you. Why, in this sense they are like young students, like small children: They flourish in the presence of love, and shrivel when they meet with scorn or disapprobation. Will you willfully disbelieve the evidence put in front of you? It seems absurd, almost infantile to pursue these questions about leg bindings, but I will indulge you this far: I saw her tied securely to her chair, and every time I looked that way, the bindings seemed decidedly secure—"

"Seemed," cries Houdini.

"Were," counters Doyle. "The voice of your mother spoke from the beyond."

"In English!"

"That again? I thought I had—"

"It did look like my mother, up on the dark ceiling of that smoky room. They must have cadged a photograph of her somehow. Do you know how such effects are generally achieved? I will tell you. It is really quite ingenious. A small mirror, concealed, is set to reflect a photographic image against a screen or in this case a smoky haze. By manipulating the distance between the photograph, the flame, and the mirror, one can make the image grow and shrink. And the undulations of the haze, particularly when the image is shifting in size and shape and is glimpsed obscurely, can produce the illusion that the figure is moving, almost alive."

"I saw her there as clear as day. Damn it, man, how can I help you when you will not see? What of those singing voices we heard or her strange disembodied screaming?"

"At this moment I can provide no immediate explanation." Houdini, cocksure. "But I suspect some combination of ventriloquism and mechanical contrivance. Maybe a phonograph. I must discuss this further with my man Jim Collins. But there are other evidentiary questions, conclusions which at this point we can for certain draw. For instance, the presence of an assistant to Sabatier and Margery—this could not have been done without one. Tall enough to manipulate the ceiling drapes, thin enough to hide behind the wall drapes, strong enough to send those objects flying and yet to make no noise in doing so. Possibly with the talents of a ventriloquist, but certainly an experienced illusionist. I will have to investigate further the history of their groundskeeper."

"Why, the professor invited you to interview the groundskeeper—"

"Ah, Sir Arthur, I fear I must explain the fundamentals of my trade. When a man like Professor Sabatier invites one to investigate, one can be certain that direction will not be a profitable one."

"But all this is tangled, premised on doubt. You postulate a hidden man. Why? Because you cannot believe the air was filled with spirits. You decide he is tall and thin. Why? Because that suits the dimensions of the room. And you refuse to even meet with the groundskeeper you suspect—perhaps because you fear he will be a short fat mute, incapable of any of the deviousness you—"

"We are all capable of deviousness."

"You will never be satisfied. You cannot explain and yet you are comfortable assuming they were fraudulent."

"No trick was beyond my immediate comprehension."

"Your immediate comprehension! Good Lord, man. It prophesied your doom!"

Houdini leans close to Doyle. "You believe me to have some supernatural power?" The shadows of passing trees flicker across his face. "I will make a prediction. At some point to come, in the mists of time, I see a man with a mustache accompanied by a half-naked dancing girl, asking you for money."

"Do not mock me. I will not be mocked."

By the time the car reaches Manhattan, the two men are no longer speaking, and before the sun sets both place calls to the *Radio Times* and ask for the reporter whose name they remember and in whose pages they will be allowed to speak.

XI

SOME DAYS THE CITY felt like an emperor uncle.
Clouds crossed the Flatiron, a man hailed a cab, and New
York conferred on Molly her birthright to it all. She might as
well have been a niece of Genghis Khan. In her room on Gay
Street, she had a gas ring and a percolator and a frying pan.
Butter smoked, the flame burned high, she poured batter into the
spitting pan and with a wooden spoon peeled skin from the skillet, drawing the raw and the cooked into custard. But she had no
patience for cleaning and her iron skillet rusted. Molly thought
her life in Greenwich Village should be Parisian, that she could
have her own regular café, but as soon as she chose one it
changed its menu or brought in a raucous piano. At Slocum's,
earnest lesbians shared draughts of Madden's ale, and the
spaghetti sauce came loaded with sugar. Everyone told her the
Village's moment had passed. From her room, Molly watched a
knife grinder make his way down the angled street. Cigarette

smoke rose in mystic patterns and she knew she'd been drawn into a plot.

Not yet dawn. In the Van Sievers' guest room, Molly tried to piece together the dream that had awakened her. Ocean waves had lapped at her feet. Someone sat beside her or behind her. The breakers reached her ankles, then her knees, and then the wave's caresses merged with her lover's. Molly was relaxing, becoming excited by the scratch of red beard on the back of her neck and by the waves at her hips and her breasts and over her hair, when suddenly she was drawn under, and the weight of her lover became the pull of undertow. She woke with her mouth dry and her head feeling pinched. She raised her knees under silk sheets. She had a hangover. Was it Lyden she had dreamed of? Streetlights showed through the curtains on the window that led to the balcony on which last night she and Sukey had stood and talked and kissed and stared over Central Park, their fingers entwining, tickling, at play. Molly had snuggled in the spot where Sukey's neck met her shoulder, inhaling, and Sukey had giggled, then pulled herself back, and raised her arm to the night.

"Tell me you love me!"

Molly had said, "I," and then stopped.

Now she dragged her legs out of bed. She had no right to be here, in this phony Florentine Fifth Avenue palace. It all rebuked her, the broad bed, the dark rugs, the marble floor. She bit her lip. She wanted to slip out without being seen. In Sukey's second-best nightgown, a silver sheath from Paris, she gripped the iron handle that turned the window into a door, and stepped out onto the cold tiled balcony three floors above the park. She stared down the avenue from the office buildings, to the church spires, then into the woods of the park, and the casino's light. The wind blew, carrying smells of rotting leaves, nameless garbage, car exhaust, and burnt coal. The breeze through her nightgown goose-pimpled her arms. Five in the morning, nothing moved under the streetlights except for a few blown leaves, and most of the windows of the city were dark. Molly said a prayer into the darkness. She needed a bath.

Turning from the balcony, she closed the window behind her. The taste of hangover was fur and leather, as if her mouth had been redone in cowhide. She was supposed to go with Archie Miles to Philadelphia tomorrow to see Doyle lecture on spirit photography and the mysterious Margery, and Molly could not bear the thought. Doyle would say more or less the same things he had said in Carnegie Hall, show the same pictures. How many words could a girl write about ectoplasm? And then she thought of the train and big, handsome Archie. He was insinuating and too intimate. Her hangover made her oversensitive. The air grated. Her skin felt dry. On wobbly legs, Molly crossed the big, dark room. She needed to wash herself free of entanglements.

The Van Sievers' guest bath had a marble basin and a lion's-head spout. She turned the big knobs, put a plush cloth under the flow, and mopped her cheeks and her forehead, first with cold water that had spent the night in the pipes, then soon with hot that steamed the mirrors. Molly stretched her mouth and stuck out her tongue. While the tub was filling, she went to fetch a cigarette, reached into her purse, and touched the envelope her father had given her yesterday, Lyden Silver's letter, which she had not opened yet.

"Crap."

Had she opened the note when he had given it to her, Molly would have done so without anxiety, but now her shoulders clenched. She remembered the dream, the beard on her neck. What had her father said, that Lyden's mother was dying? Poor Clarissa! Molly cursed. She had meant to read the letter at her desk at work, but there had not been a moment, and now that she had held it for a day in the attic of her consciousness, the envelope had gathered a fine smudgy layer of dread. Why was Lyden writing her? She looked at the address, her name in his earnest, aggressive, faltering hand, then shoved it back in the pocketbook and took out her cigarettes. What could he want of her?

Molly let her head slide underwater. She opened her eyes to see the light twinkling on the surface. Then she rose up, breathing. Why was she kissing Sukey? What business of it was hers? She was like her father, that explained it all, she could not control her appetites. Molly took advantage, or maybe she was just easy to seduce. In any case, it marked a weak kind of selfishness—dependence, confusion, and guilt, like her silly prayers, something she did helplessly. Molly pulled herself out of the tub, wrapped herself in a white robe that hung by the towels. She had never owned something so plush in her life.

She crossed the guest room, head ringing and heavy, and she left little, embarrassing puddles on the floor. Five-thirty, and already she felt desperate to leave, fingers anxiously tapping at her sides. Molly drew out the center drawer of the desk, which held pretty pens, some watermarked stationery, and matching cloth-woven envelopes. Her note to Sukey came in three drafts.

The first began, My *dear friend*, and attempted sober honesty, but upon rereading seemed hurtful and dull, an awful thing to give someone before breakfast. The second attempt started with *Darling!* and ended *love*, but when Molly wrote that word, she felt the same freeze that had struck her last night on the balcony. She crumpled the page into a ball. The final version was a quick, cute half lie about business, pleasure, and dashing off before dawn. Molly dropped the failed drafts in the enameled trash bin, but then collected them—didn't want anything to be found. And when she shoved the balled-up drafts in her purse, Molly saw Lyden's envelope, waiting for her, a grim suitor.

She laid it down on the desk and decided to dress. Yesterday's underpants smelled of herself, yesterday's stockings had a run. Her dress sat all wrong on her shoulders, her damp hair curled in the front, a little cowlick she had always hated. She lit a fresh cigarette. She rested that in an ashtray and grabbed her lipstick, applying it carefully in front of the mirror and tamping her mouth on a tissue. Molly shut her eyes. She put on her glasses. She would never have admitted to herself or anyone that she expected anything of Lyden. An ancient fondness, so she told herself, almost a cousin, a family friend. She just hoped this was not a love note—she could not bear that. Hungover veins throbbed in her temples. Maybe she should leave the letter for breakfast. She stood up from the desk. Oh, Carl, she prayed.

But no help came. There it was, addressed to her. Standing now, she took a deep breath and with a brass opener, sliced the envelope above the seal.

Mol—

Good to see you the other night, and good to meet your friend.

Sorry if I was at all out of line about what I said about you and your business, reporting, you know—all I meant was to leap to your defense, but I know that you're not much the type that needs defense, much less a fellow leaping. Wanted to say something then, but as soon as I spoke, you ran from the table. Here's hoping you're not upset.

You know I mean no harm. Only good things.

—L

She balled the note up, threw it into the enameled bin, took it out again—again afraid that it might be noticed—and she put it, a third crumpled page, into her pocketbook. Of course, she hadn't expected anything from Lyden—hadn't expected him to write her, but since he had written she at least expected . . . she did not know what.

Back on Gay Street, at six in the morning, Pignoli the painter was washing his terrier in the tub and singing from *Don Giovanni*. Molly kicked the bathroom door as she passed it. The dog barked. Her neighbor screamed.

"IT IS URGENT," Houdini said over the telephone. Molly dropped a story about hemlines immediately. "Absolutely urgent," he repeated, "that I talk to you, and if you promise to cooperate with me, I will talk with no one else, no other representative of the press. I have made a promise to my dear and

respected friend Sir Arthur Conan Doyle that I will not broadcast this news officially or widely or in my own name, but I
believe that I can stand well within the limits of this promise—
both of its spirit and its words—and still maintain my obligations
both to the scientific and religiously inclined public, if I tell you
the following, tell it to you honestly and confidentially, not to be
printed with attribution unless you should hear news from either
Sir Arthur Conan Doyle or Dr. Hugo Sabatier—or unless
another paper should print the story, this last possibility is highly
unlikely, as Conan Doyle has told me that you have his confidence, but I may be forced to take precautions—"

"You are calling other papers, then—"

"Miss Goodman, I am not calling you. Honesty can compel
secrecy; indeed, experience teaches us that secrecy is often bul-
wark of truth. I come to you again in difficult circumstances, as
you have proved useful in the past, and I come to you because I
must protect myself, protect my friendship, and protect the
truth. I call you because you are likely to receive a telephone
call, either from Sir Arthur Conan Doyle or from Dr. Hugo
Sabatier—there was a fourth witness, yes, she calls herself
Margery, but she is nothing but a mere performing monkey."

Molly fairly knocked her typewriter off her desk.

Houdini gave her the location of the Sabatiers' home, directions to get there, the size of the cottage, its rise from the road,
the dimensions of the extension, the quality of the lawn grass, the
putti peeing into the pool. When it came to the séance, he
became still more determined, more specific, as if quoting from a
time log, not just the acts, but the duration in minutes of each, the
reactions of Sabatier and Conan Doyle, and he offered technical

glosses, explanations for the medium's effects. Molly began her notes on a pad, but was soon scrawling on whatever was available, yanking the string of her pencil to free more lead, scribbling across the back of the women's-page article, 250 words on skirts. Fans in the corners blew smoke around the newsroom, the sun set over the dirty river, copyboys dashed down the aisles between reporters' desks, and telephones and typewriters rattled and rang.

"The last can only be interpreted as a threat against me," said Houdini, "and it is only because I have been threatened that I am speaking to you, but you must understand the delicacy of my situation. I have made promises to my dear friend Sir Arthur Conan Doyle, promises not to report to the newspapers or in any way publicize the occurrences of yesterday afternoon. However, as you can no doubt surmise, it is because of my public character, because of the importance of my position, nationally and scientifically, that I am compelled, you understand, to take action. Threats to me personally are of no account, but threats to the ideals for which I stand must be met. So personally, as a public person, I refrain from comment on this event. I am speaking to you only as a gentleman to a lady, and not so much of what has transpired to Houdini, but to reveal the nature of the forces that threaten all rational, honest, scientific men—represented here in the person of Harry Houdini, yes, but only in his philosophical, not his social character—and as you are a woman of science, I must speak to you. If you attribute a single word to me in print, I will deny that I have said it, and my denials will be vigorous and loud. However, I think you will agree that you have a professional responsibility to pursue this information, an obligation to explore, as it were, this anonymous piece of mystery. Did these so-called miracle-mongers threaten Houdini? A newsworthy question, you must admit, for a threat to Houdini, in my capacity as a debunker of mysticism, is a threat to science, and to the rational progress of man."

She was lost in it: scribbling, imagining details.

"Are you claiming that Sir Arthur Conan Doyle was party to a threat on your life?"

"I had assumed you were a reasonable woman, Miss Goodman, that is why I chose to speak to you. If you twist my words in that way, or make insinuations of that sort—"

"But you see Sir Arthur and Mrs. Sabatier as—"

"Sir Arthur Conan Doyle is among the most honest, most honorable, most manly creatures to stride the earth. Set that down. But these miraculous Sabatiers are brazen as horse thieves and cunning as snakes—"

"Can I quote you?"

"Have you not heard? You cannot quote one word. Attribute a single word to me and I will see to it that your career is ruined."

He hung up. The telephone line died. Molly was left with the voice of the operator. In the excitement of the interview she had all but forgotten the newsroom, and it came back to her slowly, its bustle and its noise. She was surprised to find Archie Miles near her desk, staring down at her, smiling. She had no idea how long he had been there. He looked to her enormous and beautifully clean. She could see his big soft chin, smell the talcum powder on his neck. He held his hat in one hand and had a leather bag of photographic equipment slung carelessly across the shoulder of his creamy suit.

"I'm at work," she said, too quickly, wishing as soon as she said it that the words had come out differently. She stood up quickly and straightened her skirt. "I mean." She tried her best to smile. "Good to see you, Miles."

"It's okay," said Archie. "Go work. I got time."

He sat on the corner of her desk, his big clean thighs right next to her and wrapped in linen, his shoes smelling of polish and leather.

Molly glanced backward around the enormous, clattering room, from the big curved copy desk at the back, to the glass box up front that housed Farquharson, hidden from view by the slats of wood blinds. Justy Vittles at the desk next to her was bent characteristically close to the keys of his typewriter, jacket off, and she could see his black suspenders loose on his sloping back. Molly sat back down at her desk. She tried to smile at him, but her smile came off awkwardly.

"You don't want me to leave?" asked Archie. "I ain't making you nervous?"

"No, no," she blurted, "I love—I mean—just a—"

Then her phone rang. She had a sudden terror that it was Sukey Van Siever, crying about last night and the letter she had left. Molly lunged for the phone. She bobbled it. The earpiece struck the table, and the wire flipped over her wrist. Archie, neat as a shortstop playing a bad hop, caught both and answered.

"Molly Goodman, star reporter."

She snatched it from him, hands grabby as her father's. The operator told her who was on the line, and Molly's heart leapt.

"Sir Arthur?"

Archie dropped his jaw. Molly wanted to kick him, to chase him away. He seemed suddenly impertinent, obnoxious, all the things she had thought before that night when they kissed. She tried to concentrate on the telephone call.

He was ringing her, Doyle explained, because his wife insisted he make some public assertions, following a spiritual premonition she had had. Scurrilous rumors were being passed—or might be passed. Lady Doyle had told Sir Arthur that the spirits had counseled he take action, that at all accounts he not remain passive as he had after the séance at Atlantic City. He had learned, Doyle said, from his passivity at that point. Had Miss Goodman not pursued that story, had she not telephoned him and allowed him to contradict Houdini's claims, why, then the only notices in the papers that even acknowledged his perspective would have been those that mocked him, for example the gossip pages of that dreadful *Graphic*.

"It was the ordinary course of business to phone you," Molly assured him.

"And it is much to your credit that you see it as such."

Doyle understood Miss Goodman as an honest reporter with an honest interest in both Spiritualism and science. Her coverage of the magicians' convention had been quite admirable and complete—both in terms of its understanding of Spiritualism and the science of film.

"Why, thank you," said Molly.

Furthermore, Doyle understood that Houdini had sought her out before, and he suspected that Houdini might seek her out again. Houdini and he had made promises, Doyle told her, not to speak to the press or public at large about certain events they had witnessed; still he had heard such promises before and precaution and discretion had warred within him until he had determined that the better part of his obligations demanded that he sound her out. Had she heard any news of a séance in Pleasant Valley?

"I think I understand," said Molly.

"Have you spoken with Harry Houdini?" Doyle asked.

She shut her eyes, tried to pretend that Archie Miles was not sitting on her desk, chipper and whistling "Alexander's Ragtime Band."

"By your silence, then," Doyle said, "I take it you have."

Her heart was thumping, she needed to say something. She bit her lip, ignored the heat that seemed to come from Archie. She reached into her bag for a cigarette, but found only crumpled letters there.

"I have heard rumors of a séance in Pleasant Valley," she admitted, breathing out. "And I'm delighted that you've called. These rumors do demand public attention, and the way that I heard them put me in a position—"

"You have not heard from Dr. Sabatier—"

"No."

"We understand each other, then."

"I think we do. The rumors come from a very powerful source," said Molly, "the kind a reporter cannot ignore. But I would feel much more comfortable running only those rumors which were confirmed. It's important, in the name of science, to keep this as accurate as possible, and I think it would be to everyone's advantage—the public's included—" said Molly, with the bright idea of fishing for an exclusive, "if the publicity surrounding these events were contained, somewhat—"

"I quite agree," said Doyle, "but can you assure me that Houdini has spoken to no reporter other than yourself?"

Molly coughed. She wanted a cigarette. Archie's big legs swung easily beside her. He was whistling a new tune. Molly closed her eyes and spoke carefully: "Houdini spoke on the condition of anonymity. He said that I could attach his name to this story only in order to contradict or confirm the words of other witnesses—"

"My word," said Doyle.

"I didn't like it, either," said Molly, "but if we work together, we can control this. I think it's fair to assume that, if he called other reporters, he made the same deal with them. I think it's fair to assume some of the big papers will ignore a deal like that, and some of the smaller ones—well, no one will really believe what they print. I don't think I'm boasting to say that I've been on top of this story in a way that other papers have not." She cleared her throat. She fumbled in her purse. The balls of paper scattered across her desk. Archie reached for one, and she slapped his hand. "It's silly for me to give advice to a gentleman like you, Sir Arthur. I hesitate even to speak. But hear me out: This is to everyone's advantage. You don't want this news to be splashed all over town, and I don't want to print anything that's not strictly aboveboard. If we work together, this is what you will get: The news will come out in just one paper—just here, nowhere else, with attribution from both you and Houdini—and I'll print nothing sensational, no outrageous claims made without contradiction. Of course, I am completely at your disposal, but I think you see the plan I suggest. . . . " She let her voice trail off.

"Killer," whispered Archie Miles. "The girl's a killer!"

"Would you agree," asked Molly, "that the spirits threatened Houdini's death?"

Archie took out one of his fancy cigarettes, lit it in his own mouth, and handed it to her.

"In a sense," said Doyle, "that could be said, but it would be a distortion."

She pulled out her reporter's notebook. Doyle explained that this was not his view on the situation, not at all. Molly began scribbling again, this time getting down Doyle's view, his sense that the words from the beyond ought never to be taken at face value, and that any sense of direct threat should be taken care-fully and mulled over. One thing one could always be certain of, when it came to presences from the beyond, was that their words should always be accepted in a spirit of openheartedness and love, never fear or confrontation.

Archie was up off the desk and stood behind her, hands on Molly's back, urging her on. His excitement drew the attention of reporters nearby, and he explained the situation to them as best he understood it: Molly was on the phone with Arthur Conan Doyle, she had sewn up an exclusive, right there in the bag, right in front of him. Doyle had threatened to kill Houdini, or something like that. Maybe it was that medium they were talking about, Margery, but 'death threat' had been the words he'd heard.

The *Radio Times* was a small paper and most of the reporters were young. Most, growing up, had idolized at least one of Conan Doyle's heros: Sir Nigel or Sherlock Holmes or Professor Challenger. All of them as boys had been in awe of Houdini. They were mostly nervous around Molly, if not contemptuous—this pretty girl who wore pants and makeup and glasses, a college girl, a rich kid, a Jew, her father a famous pink. But she was tough and they liked that, and she had gone and made her own story out of Doyle and Houdini, and they could not fail to be impressed. They got her a new pad when she filled her last page. They lit her cigarettes. They cheered her.

Cool as her own gray eyes, Molly went through the séance with Conan Doyle, moment by moment, reading Houdini's account, leaving off only his rational explanations of the otherworldly phenomena, Doyle never contradicting but sometimes augmenting or developing a point. The boys gathered around her desk listened. They whispered "death threat" to the green eyeshades at copy, and even more enthusiastically the famous names involved, and then the word "exclusive" was passed. They liked the way Molly handled Doyle—no-nonsense, polite, straight, not a grilling but not high tea either. Operators had opened other lines, and four men stood at Justy Vittles's desk, gathered around the telephone earpiece so they looked like a barbershop quartet.

And Archie Miles stood above her like a proud papa, his hat on her desk, and by the time Molly hung up the phone, there was applause. Farquharson opened the door of his office to see what the fuss was. The wood slats of his blinds clattered with the swing of the door. He crossed the newsroom, arms cocked stiffly, and by the time he'd gotten to Molly's desk he had a sense of the situation and the story. Reading glasses hung from a string around his neck. He smoothed down some long gray strands of hair. Farquharson laid down two nut-brown hands on her desk and smiled at her, his smile unpleasantly spreading his white beard and showing the big teeth underneath.

"Tell me what you got."

"I need a minute to put it together," she said.

"Tell me what you're putting together, dear. There's some excitement here. Tell Daddy what you know."

Molly took off her glasses and set her eyes on his. "That story you assigned me," she said, "of course. Mrs. Astor? Hemlines? Wasn't that what you had me working on? I've got that, if you want it," and she began rolling the page out of her typewriter. "You weren't interested in the first Doyle piece, right? I was supposed to pay my way to Atlantic City—"

"Don't be like this, honey." Farquharson was originally from Tennessee, and he still had a trace of a drawl. "We're all part of a team here. We're all on the same side. I know you can make news from this Doyle thing, always said you could make news."

Molly smiled. "But you said there wasn't a story there, didn't you? Old farts on the beach—"

"You want a pay raise, don't you?" Farquharson leered at the boys gathered around. He put his hands to his suspenders. "Little Jewess got my balls in a vise."

"You and I ought to talk in your office," Molly told him. "Because I do have a big story here, and I don't want to take this story to another paper. I really don't. I think this is something that's got to be printed tonight. And in the *Radio Times*, but—"

"Forty dollars a week," said Farquharson. Sweat made yellow arcs around his armpits.

"Fifty," said Molly. "And never put me on cosmetics, never again."

"Shit." His beard parted and he gave her his hideous smile.

Skinny Justy Vittles unbent his back. He was looking up from his typewriter goggle-eyed at Molly, and what she saw when he

looked at her was a vision of her reflected success. She saw it in
the way they all looked at her. Archie Miles stood by her desk, a
little bigger than the rest, his face a little pinker and more handsome, his smile a little broader; it was his clothes, too, he was
the richest man there. His grin simultaneously was full of envy
and lust.

The newsroom at the *Radio Times* was big and airy. Naked
bulbs hung from the ceiling, the windows were all on the eastern
wall, and three columns stood spaced regularly in the center.
The concrete floor was covered in cheap carpet, and electrical
and telephone wires hung from the ceiling like vines. The big
desks were aligned in rows, but still there was a sense of temporary residence, also of the building's industrial past, and this last
was accentuated when the presses ran below. The reporters
themselves were a motley bunch, pimply, overweight, young or
second-rate, men who had taken a low salary hoping to make a
mark with the newest paper in town. Still, Molly felt glamour as
she faced them. She was glamorous in their eyes, and she felt
imbued with the glamour that they saw in her. From his bag,
Archie pulled out a pretty leatherette camera, which opened
with a neat modern bellows attached. He snapped a few shots of
her under the harsh light of the room, and she smiled.

THE NEXT night in Pleasant Valley, Margery lies lashed to her
bed, all her husband's drugs failing her. However he treats her or
wants to use her, the reckless voices come calling, and her visions
of the future are real. Black men hang in bunches like cherries
from boughs of Southern trees. Four children are lashed to their

mother, one to each limb, and the family is pitched into an African lake big as a sea. She hears the buzz of airplanes, the impact of the bombs, the families fleeing across the desert. Downstairs, two men drink coffee. The one in the groundskeeper's outfit punches a copy of the *Radio Times*.

"He says 'tall,' he says, 'thin,' he says, 'practiced in ventriloquism and prestidigitation'—"

"There's no need to get excited, Diggs."

"He's seen me. He knows me." Diggs rises from the couch. Red hair, a heavy jaw, traces of a beard, skin that's seen too much weather. They're in the sunroom, the strange furniture wrought in the shapes of beasts, the low tables cluttered with books and papers. Diggs's head almost touches the low ceiling. "He's got to be chased away."

"I have no idea what you're suggesting." Sabatier, seated in an armchair, swings one leg above the other.

"You know your business," Diggs whispers. "I know mine. We've got to embarrass him. Shame him and he'll stay away."

"Well." Sabatier smiles. "How does one embarrass that sort of a man?"

"Listen, will you? He's going to jump in the river tomorrow. And when he does, you and me are going to be there."

"We are?" asks Sabatier. "I don't plan on embarrassing myself, mind you."

"Something wrong, now? Scared of a fight?"

"Not in the least."

Screams come from upstairs, but they ignore her.

XII

HOUDINI'S FILM *The Man from Beyond* opens with the Bible, John 5:28, and closes with words from Conan Doyle's *The Vital Message*. Howard Hillary, seal hunter a century dead, is found shirtless and preserved in a block of Arctic ice. Revived and returned to civilization, he attends a wedding and recognizes the bride-to-be as the reincarnation of his lost love. Hillary explodes from the congregation, confounding his host, interrupting the ceremony, and he is carted off to a mental hospital, where, bound in a straitjacket, he escapes. Nita Naldi performs a snaky dance, and Hillary fights his enemy on the edge of a cliff. He seems about to tumble, but his adversary falls. Meanwhile, his reincarnated love rides a boat straight for the mouth of Niagara Falls. Eight cameras film the sequence as Hillary swims right out into the torrent to rescue her. Finally, in hazy double exposure, the soul of his lost love enters the body of his new bride, and the words of Doyle are superimposed on the wedding. The schedule for publicity sends Houdini across the continent. In Chicago, he will hang upside down in chains before the crowd at the base of the Tribune Building. In Los Angeles, he will disappear an elephant downtown. But first, New York—the river jump, his most dangerous stunt, no chance that the weather will postpone it.

A STORM is moving up the coast and westward, toward the city. A train rumbles down from the suburbs, tossing gray steam behind it. The steam rises over the hobos who sleep in the mudflats by the New York Central's tracks, over the wall that separates the wasteland from the promenade, caking soot onto the windows of the apartments of Riverside Drive. Under the elms of the promenade at 86th Street, a dog-walker and a nurse notice the commotion at the Columbia Yacht Club, a three-story building on the other side of the tracks. They stand yards from each other, leaning on the cool stone wall and peering downward, while their respective charges, a white poodle and a pink infant, yip and mewl. Movie lights hang by the docks. A camera operator works from a crane attached to a barge. Sailors take out cutters against the weather to come. Hearing of the river jump, some linger in the club's gardens and grounds, but some head indoors, to be out of the storm when it hits. Outside the club's fence, boys cluster on the rocks where sometimes they hunt crabs. Irish kids from Hell's Kitchen, black kids from San Juan Hill, oblivious to the weather, they throw bottles and shout at the tops of their voices. Each gang performs for the other, each pretends the other isn't there. They've seen the movie lights, they've heard the name Houdini, they're not leaving.

The camera pans the assembled faces. Jim Collins, the magician's chief assistant, lean, distracted, and smoking. He's got a
high professorial forehead, the face of a stern preacher, and long
spidery limbs. Across from him, reporters gather: chubby Dewey
Baedeker of the *World*, hunched Alton Grimm from the *Graphic*.
Photographers, too, there's Archie Miles. The wire service boys
share an umbrella and chew gum not far from the man with the
Times. The camera lingers on pretty Molly. It catches her in profile, bobbed and stylish. No rain right now, but there's expectant
electricity in the air, the wind gone dead, and thunder rumbling
in the distance. A solitary mustached figure hurries over the
bridge that links the marina to the park. Sabatier swings his
umbrella and checks his watch.

The back door of the yacht club opens. The camera expects
Houdini, but it gets the smiling, bearded president of the club,
and then Houdini's wife Bess. She's a small woman, a former circus trouper with enormous eyes and a mouth that runs across her
face. Another train passes, heading north. The kids start throwing rocks. On the docks, the clubmen and reporters mingle sepa-
rately. Jim Collins stands apart, and Bess Houdini exchanges
pleasantries with the president. The sense among the press is
that the jump will be rescheduled, but Houdini's representatives
are reassuring. He has survived the stormy North Sea and a
frozen river in Detroit. His skill remains undiminished. A hurri-
cane would not deter him. Reporters scribble. They look over a
crane designed specially by Collins, built to drop a man into the
sea. And Collins, arms long and thin in his stiff black suit, shows
off the handcuffs, the long heavy chains that will wrap Houdini's
body, the burlap sack he will be sewn into, the pine box that will

be nailed shut. Sabatier appears at the edge of the crowd just as this demonstration is concluded, wiping sweat from his forehead, catching his breath. A few reporters notice him—not just Molly but also Grimm from the *Graphic* and Baedeker from the *World*—but there is no time for questions. Just as Sabatier appears, Houdini emerges from the boathouse.

They cannot see him in the park above the tracks. Still, people gather by the wall that edges the promenade, his mystical name drawing them. The wall is built of enormous rectangular blocks of granite, rough-hewn at the edges, dark gray, with mica glints. In its crevices live ants and beetles, rats and even raccoons. The wall at the top is cool to the touch and damp. Men loosen the knots of ties. Children strain and point but no one sees a thing.

"Is that his boat? Is it that one?" Umbrellas open.

In the mudflats below, in that wasteland by the tracks and nasty fences, lie sinkholes and coal bins and greasy puddles, clumps of bushes and the occasional weedy tree. Here and there a glimpse of a shanty, barrels and boxes made into homes. The kids on the rocks have trespassed experimentally near the boats and docks, and when no one chases them away, they come closer. They're disappointed when they see Houdini, his middle-aged hairline, his droopy jowls. He is short and pudgy, a slope-shouldered Jewish businessman in a robe. Even his intensity seems a joke, those crazy eyes whose glare gives the lie to his smile.

Houdini shakes hands with the stiffness of a politician. As he bends forward to listen, he coils to spring back. His eyes fix on each face, but there is a practiced rhythm to his glances. His wave is broad as semaphore, hand held in the air to be photographed. He points at Molly as if to an unexpected friend. He whispers conspiratorially with the club's president. When he sees Sabatier, Houdini pauses, but stretches his arms wide in greeting, Houdini as a boxer before a fight. He laughs and poses, then invites Sabatier to be a member of the committee that will cuff and chain and bind and box him. Sabatier declines, but Houdini insists, and when Sabatier declines a third time (later, his defenders will point to this as evidence of his innocence), Houdini suggests that the professor at least select the committee.

"Who could be better guarantor of my integrity than a man who has threatened my life?"

"Dear me!" Sabatier exclaims.

He is there to watch, nothing more. He wants to take no part, cast no doubt. But Houdini continues to insist, even as the first rain begins to fall. The camera refocuses and captures this nicely, both men's overbroad, gentlemanly theatricality. With a bow, Sabatier relents. He will select a few onlookers, randomly. The rain presses time and Sabatier makes his first two choices quickly, the yacht club president, whose name is Percival Hastings, and Molly Goodman of the *Radio Times*.

"But I can't," says Molly. "I can't write about this and take part in it."

"Of course you can, my dear," says Percival Hastings with a bow. He wears a blue serge suit with a small silver nautical pin, an anchor on its lapel, insignia of the Columbia Yacht Club.

"We have no time to dicker," Sabatier reminds her.

Houdini says, "Don't be shy."

And with Dewey Baedeker and Alton Grimm nudging her, Molly relents. The camera catches her anxiety as she moves from the dock to Houdini's boat. Jim Collins pulls her across, holding her upper arm. Molly, thrust onstage, arranges her glasses and tucks her hair behind her ears. She stands in a line with Sabatier and the club president. It is time now for the final selection of a committee member and Sabatier demurs.

"Why don't you choose?" he asks Molly.

"Why should I?"

"Because I cannot choose everyone. It makes me feel responsible for the thing."

"I don't want to be responsible."

And this makes Houdini laugh. "Won't someone take responsibility, please?"

Impatiently, Molly looks around her, from Jim Collins to the kids on the rocks by the river's edge. Then, following Sabatier's gaze, her eyes settle on a sailor who is cleating home the lines of his little gray skiff.

"How about him?"

Sabatier raises his eyebrows. Houdini nods. Jim Collins calls to the man, who seems not to notice, and it takes a few other sailors, pointing and smiling—"Is this the one? Him?"—to draw the man's attention to Houdini and the stunt. His legs are spread, one on his boat, the other on the docks. There's a cigar stub pinched in his lips and his big hands work the ropes like second nature. He's a tall, thin, rawboned fellow, bareheaded, sleeves rolled, suspenders holding up canvas pants. Done with the rope, he tosses his butt in the Hudson, settles his long skinny legs on the dock, and squints while he talks with the clubmen, who give him the news that he's just been selected to handcuff Houdini.

"Who?" He shrugs. They point.

His hair is red and close-cropped. His eyes are hollow. Wrinkles cascade across his face with each grimace and squint. A beard grows as if accidentally across his big jaw. He grabs a red jacket from the bottom of his little boat and asks how much he'll get paid to participate. Then he lights a wooden match with his thumb and breathes in a little on his new cigar before agreeing to take part, so long as he'll have time to avoid the rain. He saunters through the press, looking up tolerantly at the movie camera. Collins asks for his name and the man says, "Johnson. No, write Stevenson. Why would that be your business anyhow?" His crustiness gets a laugh from Houdini.

Who is he? No one knows. He doesn't act like a member of the club, but does as instructed, gets in line next to Sabatier and Percival Hastings and Molly, hops easily from dock to boat. He's a foot taller than she is, and beside him she looks like a small girl. Houdini strips down to his trunks and climbs on board. He raises his hands to the small crowd and lightning strikes New Jersey.

"Quickly," says Houdini.

Jim Collins gives the handcuffs to Percival Hastings, who fixes Houdini's arms behind his back.

"That's right!" says Houdini. "You've got me now."

Jim Collins asks for the key back. Then he tosses it into the water, an understated showman's joke, which gets laughs even from the big gruff sailor next to Molly.

Next come the chains, and Sabatier tells the sailor to step forward. In the context of the event, it does not seem strange that he should direct the man. After all, Houdini has put him in charge of the committee, but later it will arise as a question: What business of it was his? Collins takes the chains from a sack and snakes out the line of them to the big redheaded man. This, too, plays as comedy, as three, then four, then five, then six, then nine feet of heavy links are passed like an absurdly long string of sausages, the big redheaded man passing them on to Molly, Molly passing them on to the club president. The reporters and onlookers laugh, but then there's lightning again, and again thunder, and though the storm has not broken in earnest over the river, everyone knows they must hurry. The big man wraps Houdini in chains.

He's good at it. He follows Jim Collins's directions well. He makes loops of the links and wraps them around the magician, his legs, his middle, his arms. He pulls tight and tests parts while Houdini jokes.

"Thinking of a career as a jailor?"

Sabatier asks if he can look over the chains, too. Houdini assents and Jim Collins steps close, to watch the professor. Meanwhile, the sailor tugs hopelessly on the handcuffs.

"Be gentle with me," says Houdini.

Collins asks for Sabatier's help and they hold on to the sack, Houdini, making comical faces, hops in. It's burlap, heavy and rough cloth, a bag made for hauling potatoes. Molly is given a needle and thread and she sews hastily. She sticks her thumb as she works. Another train passes, the rain falls in mild diagonals, and Molly lets out her breath when she is done. Then Houdini is hefted into the wood box, so much like a coffin. The lid is laid on top and Percival Hastings nails it home. The dramatic roll of thunder, and even up on the wall of the promenade where bystanders now share opera glasses there is a premonition of death. And because it is Houdini, they don't have to deny the pleasure of it. Morbid titillation is part of the show, the set of inversions that makes Houdini's seeming torturers—those who would bind him and box him and toss him in a stormy river— into his dupes. They are all, like those who come to see a hanging, accomplices, partners in the show. They are also all fools, but happy because they come to be fooled, to have their morbid pleasures made into the trick of miracle. He will survive this.

The committee climbs back to the dock. Collins hooks the crate to its crane, and boxed and bound Houdini is hoisted above the waves. The boat's motor rumbles, and as the rain comes down they edge out into the river, Collins wiping water from his hands, the yacht club receding, the box visible now to even those on the promenade. The kids on the rocks stop throwing stones.

Collins knocks on the crate. He signals to the boat pilot. And then, with a sudden throw of a lever, the chains of the crane release, the box falls into the river, and Houdini is gone. The camera sees it happen: the sudden drop of the box so that frame by frame its outlines melt, the spume and froth in black and white, then the sinking as the water foams and eddies and reconstitutes itself. Thunder booms and the rain comes down.

HANDCUFFS ARE temporary restraints built mostly to hold a man while he's watched or caged, and they are not—as are safes or even ordinary door locks—designed against the attacks of lockpickers. The drama of escape lies not in the difficulty of the lock but in the body, the binding, the vision of the man restrained. An amateur committee likewise makes a nice show, and the vision of the community gathering to torture carries faint echos of witch trials, but in the end the amateurs, like the easy lock, assure the magician's safety: The volunteers are overmatched. They have no idea what they're doing. Tight as they pull the chains, the magician can slack them. Similarly with the sack: The audience member hoisted onstage makes for a nervous seamstress, her sewing is rushed and sloppy, and she creates the weakest point in an otherwise strong trap. After that, the box is nailed shut on the wrong side, all that hammering does is distract from the crate's bottom, where cut screws cling to a false base. The smack of the crate against water is enough to dislodge the flimsy lower lid. Meanwhile, the loud motor of the boat and the creaking winch of the crane distract the audience from any noise the magician might make as he struggles to free himself. Generally, by the time Jim Collins knocks on the side of the wooden crate, Houdini is sitting comfortably in his bathing suit, the locks and chains and handcuffs sewn neatly back in the potato sack, Houdini by feel in the darkness following his volunteer's crude stitches. But this time, as the thunder cracks and the rain beats down, the handcuffs are still on him. He probes them in the darkness with his thin metal pick. Something jams the lock, or gunks the teeth of the bracelets, or both. And there is crud in the space where his pick would enter.

The winch grinds, the crane lifts, the crate hangs above the gray Hudson. Jim Collins knocks and Houdini considers. The chains lie in the sack at his feet. He's picking the gunk out furiously, and calculates a minute or two to break the cuffs underwater. Houdini counts seconds between the lightning flashes that

light the crate's slats and the low booms of thunder that follow.
He decides he can manage it and knocks back. Jim Collins
throws a lever. Leather straps slip free. The crate plunges,
Houdini braces himself, and in a minute he is falling through the
gray filthy Hudson, abandoning himself to the current, working
calmly with the pick in his right hand, knees bent, hair rising.

The crowd wants him drowned, it wants him to live. They are
excited and frightened, and the effect is visceral, felt on their
bodies as sure as their skin feels the shift in the air pressure with
the storm's release. Freight cars pull north, a passenger south.
The flags of the yacht club ripple in the wind and rain. Black
umbrellas open on the docks. They can see it: the storm front
crossing the Hudson, riling the water and the waves, a white-
gray tidal monster moving from Jersey to Manhattan. The sailor
who bound Houdini squints so the crow's-feet blossom at the
sides of his face. He takes a pull on his cigar, turns his collar up,
and heads for the club. This is the last anyone sees of him.
Dewey Baedeker's umbrella inverts, caught in a crazy gust of
wind, and the rainwater splashes Molly's glasses.

Houdini underwater drives the pick deep in the cuff. His fingers furious, his body limp, he squats at the bottom of the river,
settling into the accumulated shit and rusting barrels, and the
fetid silt stings as its level rises, ankles, knees, waist, chest. Only
when it comes to his chin does he kick and drive himself toward
the surface. The gunk in the lock is getting grittier, less cohesive.
He needs a minute more. Borne by the current, he hits a skeleton of rusted machinery, and then swims against the river. He
must emerge by his boat, right in front of the crowd, or the show
is for nothing. A lightning flash illuminates the world under-

water. His lungs burn. His legs kick. Still he works the pick, jam-
ming it, yanking it, bending it.

He has been down three minutes. The rain is ripping hard.

"Has he no sympathy for us?" asks Alton Grimm, with his evil
long-toothed smile. His collar is up, the rain rakes his cheek.

"It's too long," says the yacht club's president.

And underwater, Houdini has ruined his first pick. He reaches
to his heel, where a second small piece of metal is hidden in a
callus developed for just this contingency. His plan is to emerge
from the water on the other side of Collins's boat, where no one
will see him. He will gulp one more large breath, plunge under
for a minute, and then emerge, cuffs in hands, before the storm's
next strike.

Bess Houdini nervously steps to the edge of the dock, wind
blowing her skirt, rain drenching her. Jim Collins checks his watch.

The current runs fiercely, the wind blows hard. In a flash of
lightning, Houdini makes out the bottom of Collins's boat and
gains confidence. Whatever has gunked his handcuffs is dissolving, the water working in tandem with his pick, and in a minute
he'll be free.

He is swimming under, kicking hard, when the storm gives
the boat a jerk. It rolls, and from underwater Houdini can't see or
guess at the keel's sudden heave. He has no clearance, it's aimed
at the edge of his head, and clips him with all the force of the
boat's pitching, tearing skin and hair from his scalp. Another
man might have died then, short of air, losing consciousness, but
Houdini's legs keep kicking, he pops to the surface, bloody-faced,
gulping air. From the docks, no one can see him, though Bess
Houdini clutches her skirt and peers desperately into the murk

and rain. Houdini has lost his pick and his hands are limp. A wave crests and he swallows dirty water. He is borne with the current, helpless but alive.

"Christ," says Baedeker. "He's a goner."

"How long do you think it's possible?" asks the man from the *Times*. "How long can a fellow stay under?"

Jim Collins curses. Fifteen minutes now, an eternity. The rain, which seemed for a moment to have slackened, redoubles in its intensity. The thunder comes only seconds after the lightning's burst. Another train whistle hoots, the single light on the locomotive illuminating a cone of torrid rain. Collins grips Bess Houdini's shoulder. The youngest kids on the riverbank cry, the oldest seem exultant.

Houdini half recovers himself, still handcuffed, kicking with fury and form. He has given up on his handcuffs. He's losing blood and energy. There is no point in struggling against the current. He can't make it back to the yacht club. He looks up from the whitecaps and the rain, seeking the closest route to shore. In the murk, he makes out a small boat, yards ahead of him, abandoned at anchor. Thunder resolves his calculations. He prays to his mother and remembers his wife.

Then he rolls on his stomach and swims for it. With the current driving him, Houdini soon reaches the barnacled, black side of the tub. He finds its anchor line with his cuffed hands, then, powerful as any acrobat, swings his legs from the water. He's nearly up when lightning strikes. Then he falls to the waves, hanging by his handcuffs, and his vision is nothing, just black.

XIII

THE MORNING OF THE JUMP, Doyle rides north from Philadelphia, flipping through newspaper clippings in his compartment in a Pennsylvania Railroad train. He fidgets in the leather banquette, scratches at his pants leg, tugs at his ear. "Margery Genuine, Doyle Claims," says a headline out of Hartford, "Author Scores Houdini." Doyle wonders about that verb. A misprint, an Americanism? The *New York American* mentions the river jump, but it's an item in the *Sun* that annoys him most. Doyle goes back to it, fixes it on top of his pile. Shadows from the window tremble on the page, little dust flakes making elongated dashes, while shadows of telephone poles swing rhythmically past. Houdini's name runs in the byline, and his words set out to destroy if not Doyle then at least their friendship.

Doyle breathes deeply. He reads it again. "Sir Arthur is one of the great literary geniuses of our time," the second paragraph begins, "but in matters like these he demonstrates the credulousness of a five-year-old boy." *Credulousness*, Doyle suspects a ghostwriter. He's received too many misspelled letters, has a good sense of the limits of the man's style. But whatever help Houdini has received, the motive is personal, the mind behind the rhetoric his own—the high-flown pronouncements, the arrogance, the absolute, willful, egomaniacal blindness to any moderating point of view. "It is my intention," Houdini concludes, after setting out his case against Margery, "to challenge this woman, to draw her out, and to prove to the satisfaction of the most gullible believer that she is nothing but a sham, a kind of temptress of the soul, a charlatan practicing on the weak-minded and the innocent. If she takes up my challenge I will destroy her, and if she declines, she will henceforth be known as a shirker and a coward." Houdini has built a box for Margery, a case to keep her in, from which he says it will be impossible for her to perform her tricks.

Doyle folds the paper twice, removes his glasses, and shuts his eyes. When the train pulls out of Princeton, he heads to the dining car, takes a table in the corner, and orders tea and soft-boiled eggs. A schoolboy approaches, a copy of a Sherlock Holmes book in hand, and Doyle signs without smiling.

He wets his fingers on the condensation outside his glass of ice and water. He dries them on his folded white napkin. His eyes are set on the window, but he sees neither his reflection nor the cornfields and pastures as they pass. Beneath his mustache, his lips move slightly, composing his opening thrust. Doyle will refrain from personal attacks. He will not defend himself. The subject here is Margery, and nothing Houdini has said or written will shake Doyle's faith in her. The thing to be ridiculed is this idea of a box, this mad challenge, an idiot demonstration of the limits of Houdini's doubts. The doubts themselves are a box, and Houdini is trapped in it.

"You're Sir Arthur Conan Doyle, ain't you?"

"Sorry?" Doyle looks up.

He had taken the group at the table across the way for raucous salesmen, but this one is a boy. He wears an orange and black tie, his hair is slicked back with water, his grin sets his baby-fat cheeks cockeyed—a university man, thinks Doyle, and his four friends at the table all drunk before lunchtime, students, not salesmen.

"You don't have a minute, do you, for a kind of moment of spiritual talk?" The boy's lips trick, trying to hide a smile. "My friend Oaksey has a problem."

"Your friend Oaksey?"

The table of college kids spasms with hilarity. One of them drops his curly head on folded arms.

"Another time," says Doyle. "At the moment—"

But the boy will not be put off. He rambles, leaning toward Doyle when waiters pass, tripping on his words, losing his balance with the bumps of the train. It's something very tired and very silly—something about a pig farm and slaughtered pigs and the fear of pigs in the afterlife. The boy wants to talk, if he can, to a dead pig, just so he can be sure there's no hard feelings between Oaksey and the porcine beyond.

"You'll want to see a reincarnated hog, then."

"Reincarnated," says the boy. "That'd be swell."

"Here's what to do." Doyle sighs. "Sit by the window, very close, shut your eyes, and when we pass through a tunnel, open them."

"Great! Then I'll see the—but in the dark I'll be looking at—"

"Your own reflection," says Doyle. "Quite."

He reaches Pennsylvania Station before noon, when Houdini's boat is only just arriving at the docks of the Columbia Yacht Club, and the storm is blowing in over the beaches of southern New Jersey. A driver meets Doyle on the platform, under the huge, curving I-beams and the plates of filthy glass. Doyle arranges to be dropped at the service entrance of his hotel. He wants to avoid reporters in the lobby. His wife and the children have not yet returned from an afternoon at the Museum of Natural History, so when Doyle arrives at his suite he takes off his jacket and calls down to the lobby for a sandwich of rare roast beef, which arrives with a mysterious, complimentary, illegal bottle of beer. Doyle thanks God, drinks, kicks his shoes off, and settles in bed.

Why the beer, he wonders, a gift of the house, or some other order mixed up with his own? He smiles at his luck, but on the cusp of unconsciousness worries. He tries to recall the exact words of the letter he has sent off to the *Sun*. "Misguided," had he written that? "Fool"? He can't be sure. Did he call Houdini his "enemy" or was that a word Houdini used against him? And as his dreams overtake his worries, Doyle imagines himself talking to Houdini, friendly enough at the start, but soon his hands are on the magician. He grabs him by the lapels. He shakes him. He screams.

And he wakes up with an echo of that screaming in his head. Four o'clock, just as Houdini's crate sinks, Doyle drinks club soda in the apartment of his U.S. editor. The windows look out over Gramercy Park, the apartment's lights flicker with the explosions of thunder. It feels unreal here, twelve stories above the earth and the afternoon gone dark, the warm September air turned dangerous, this room full of laughing women, men drinking wine, rampant violations of the laws of nature and of man. Doyle stays close to his wife, protectively. She's uncomfortable here, and soon two eager fellows in glasses have the Doyles pinned between a blue chair and a bookshelf. One goes on about the death of the heroic ideal, while the other smiles and titters.

Jews, thinks Doyle, considering how a nose emerges from glasses. One spreads his arms and waves, selling the notion of depressed alienation like it's a pair of trousers. Meanwhile, his partner giggles.

"Young people can't be idealistic anymore," says the enthusiast, pointing at Doyle's chest, "and it's not just the horrors of war, it's more than that—a failure of society, a failure of the nation-state. Don't you think, Sir Arthur, that the idea of heroism is connected somehow to national pride, wrapped up in it—we have to believe in heroes and nations both at once?"

"I couldn't say." Doyle smiles sleepily.

The tittering man coughs. Homosexuals, Doyle decides. He takes his wife's arm and looks for firmer conversational turf—this at the moment the keel whacks Houdini's head.

BARTENDERS IN Harlem turn their backs on practicing musicians to watch the rain beat the hell out of Lenox Avenue. On 135th Street, the stables of a laundry company, horses whinny and stomp. The marquees of Times Square flicker in the sudden darkness, and El trains list in the wind. In coffee shops men wave cups for refills, set their hats on booth benches, light cigars or order pie. Immigrants out of work at garment shops and cigar-rolling factories huddle in doorways, where girls laugh and old women mutter. Wall Street brokers flap wet newspapers at passing cabs. And when the rain breaks past sundown, the streets smell clean and steamy. Sidewalks get busy, the throng emerging now that the storm has passed. The Doyles' car pulls up in front of the Plaza, wheels shooting waves from the flooded gutter into the sidewalk.

Doormen with umbrellas trot down the hotel steps. There's a bit of drizzle in the air. The back door of the cab opens, and Sir Arthur hauls himself out and up, grimacing at the pain in his knees. He pulls up his collar, squares his hat, and steps from the running board as the doormen arrive. He helps his wife across a puddle. The doormen shelter her, while the driver, dressed in oilskins, runs to the trunk. Newsboys are shouting, "Extra!" but Doyle pays no attention, his mind fixed on his wife's slow progress up the stairs. The boy with the camera surprises him.

A flash explodes. Doyle's world goes yellow. He blinks. Lady Doyle misses a step.

A doorman lowers his umbrella to help, the cameraman reaches in his pocket for a new bulb, Doyle's temporary blindness eases, and he sees before him an apparition: the ugliest man in the world.

"Alton Grimm"—slouching and fawning and green-toothed— "from the *Graphic*."

"I say—"

"Any comment on Houdini's murder?"

"You dreadful man," Lady Doyle shouts.

"What—what?" Doyle keeps the doorman from shoving Grimm down the steps. "What's this you say—"

"You mean to tell me you don't know?" Grimm, wheedling. "Haven't you heard? Houdini's drowned."

"Good God!"

Lady Doyle covers her mouth.

"Just this evening," continues Grimm. "At the river. Dreadful, yes, as she says. Your friend Dr. Sabatier is in custody. We're reporting it as murder."

"You say you're from the newspapers?"

"The *Graphic*." Grimm smiles. "But as you're a friend of Houdini's and an expert on crime, I thought—"

"Horrid!" shouts Lady Doyle.

"Now then," says Sir Arthur. "I have nothing to say, nor will I, save that this is most distressing. Dr. Sabatier is—what did you say?"

"May I quote—"

"No, you may not," Lady Doyle interrupts. She comes out from the doorman's umbrella. "Arthur, please. This is beastly—"

But Doyle is going nowhere. His big, liver-spotted hand grips Grimm's trenchcoat. "You must come into the lobby and tell me what you know." He speaks quietly, bending over the reporter. "You must be precise. This is urgent. I must know exactly what has passed."

"Deepest apologies," says Grimm. "If I had time, I'd explain—"

The camera flashes again, this time catching Doyle as he looms above Grimm. Doyle lets loose the reporter and points at the boy with the flash.

"You, there! You! Come here right now."

But the photographer is a jackrabbit skipping toward the curb, discarding his burnt bulb and loading another.

"We've got a hell of a busy night." Grimm shrugs and backs away. "We've got to talk to cops, experts. Apologies."

Doyle follows stiffly, but slips. The wind gusts as he catches himself. His hat lofts off his head, bouncing down, across the sidewalk, and into traffic.

"Look here, look here," he cries. "This is my friend. This is my friend who has—who—"

"That's exactly it," Grimm snaps. "I'll quote you. But in this evening's *Sun*, you know, you call him your enemy."

The photographer steps into the driver's seat of an old gray Ford, turns the ignition, and the engine rumbles. Grimm, nimble in his rubbers, skips down the last few steps and crosses the sidewalk, Doyle lumbering after.

"Now, see here, you're not going to have me calling him that now that he's—"

"Apologies," calls Grimm with a wave from the running board. "But if you care to make a statement . . ."

"How can I when I haven't the foggiest—"

"That'll do." And the car begins to move.

In the lobby, Lady Doyle tries to comfort her husband, but her words are to his distress as her hand to his back, too small to cover any of it.

"Dear, dear, Arthur," she says, "what shall we tell the children?" And in the elevator, she is circumspect. "It has passed as Margery predicted."

"Scant comfort in that." Doyle's face is pale, wet, and slack. In the long carpeted hallway he wanders past an enormous flower-pot and has to be called back by his brisk-stepping wife. He fumbles for his keys in several pockets. "Yes, yes," he says when his wife reminds him to check his jacket. They call for tea, and for the extra editions of the papers that are available even now in the lobby.

The *World* is persuasive and important: Dewey Baedeker has miraculously produced a quick history of Houdini's river jumps. The photographs of the committee are crude, most focused on pretty Molly Goodman and on mustached Sabatier. Percival Hastings beams at the camera, but the mysterious sailor, Stevenson or Johnson, seems to disappear into the shadows in every shot. Doyle turns to the *Graphic*, where the pictographs are eye-catching but useless: old shots of Houdini, the photographs framed in solemn wreaths, and one close-up of Molly's pretty face. Her two articles in the flimsy four-sheeted extra of the *Radio Times* master the story. The first piece is news, "Houdini Drowns," and it hews close to the facts. The clarity of her prose convinces Doyle of her accuracy. She never once uses the word "murder," but she confirms the essential facts: Houdini is gone, and Sabatier is in custody, along with Jim Collins, Houdini's chief assistant. Molly's second article, an account of her role in the stunt, runs under the headline "I Saw Him Die." Doyle reads it quickly and then goes to the phone. He puts the operator through her paces, placing calls to the Houdini residence, to the police, to the *Radio Times*, and to his own lawyer.

Then he slumps in one of the hotel chairs and imagines the scene again. His hard, fat finger runs under his chin. He needs to envision this man, variously referred to as "Stevenson," "Johnson," "the mystery boatsman," or "the sailor." The *World* calls him "thin-faced," and the *Radio Times*, "hollow-eyed." The *Daily News* describes his "lantern jaw." Doyle flips through the pages again, but none of the photographs are satisfactory. Collins is clearly innocent and Sabatier, he decides, likewise. Unable to arrest this mystery man, the police have picked up whomever they can. Doyle needs to visit the scene, speak to the principals, imagine it all. He takes off his glasses and throws back his head.

Later, they draw the blinds and place a candle on the table. Doyle strikes a match. A siren runs the avenue. Hotel guests wander the hall. Wind from the street riles the candle flame. Lady Doyle marks her cross at the top of the page and lays her pen tip to the paper. It scratches a small line, a single groove, which it will not leave. Ink flows outward from her mark, saturating the paper. Doyle stares impatiently and tries to relax, not to demand anything of the spirits, to let explanation come from where it will, but he hopes—he knows—that if the body of Houdini is gone, the magician's truer self remains, and will come and manipulate the pen in Lady Doyle's hand. His mind needs to leave off its urgings, its aggravation; he must let it go blank as his wife's. He tries to fix his attention on the candle flame. He tries to name the shades of color, the yellows and oranges as it burns; he thinks of the flame's flow and of the shape of fire, then the shape of water, Houdini in the water, drowned, Margery in her pool, spirit forms, the shapes of faces in the shapes of clouds. The candle burns down, wet wax runs the candlestick. His wife drops her pen, looks at him, and shakes her head.

Later she sits at her dressing table drawing pins from her hair. She inspects her chin in the mirror. Her husband paces behind her.

"He did not come to me," she says, "therefore, he is alive."

"Lord knows what's afoot," says Doyle.

Then he hears a sound in the hall. A knock at the door, Doyle gets up to answer. A flash of a badge, a quick introduction. Detective Abel Combs of the New York City police has come to question Sir Arthur Conan Doyle. The detective's foot is wrapped in a plaster cast. Resting on his crutches, he removes his fedora and reveals a shining, bulbous forehead.

XIV

"THE ADVICE IS FREE sweetheart: Don't try and play hard with me."

"Don't worry, Detective, I'll be very gentle."

Combs blinked. He had come into the room and seen a sweet little half-drowned kitten, a pale-faced pretty girl he would never have taken for a Jew or a female reporter. There she was, soaked through to the bone. She had seen a man die, had been made to take part in it, had gone to work right afterward, filing her story, and Detective Combs like so many of the cops in the place had taken pity on her. They had set her up in this cozy parlor with its memorabilia and plaques on the wall, its model ships on the mantel. She was in one of the hard leather armchairs, her shoes and jacket drying by the fire, a blanket wrapped around her shoulders, and a cup of tea sweetened with a bit of rum on the table by her side. Combs had come at her easy, hoping to open her up, get her to talk about death threats and mystics and the whole crazy cabal, but then she had put on her glasses and turned into a nasty little college girl.

He asked his questions and she turned snooty. She was going to protect her sources, she would not tell him a thing, and Detective Combs, rocking above her on his crutches, had overplayed his hand.

"What I want to know, sister, is how come you ignored your boss. He sent you to Philadelphia, but you didn't go. The next day you showed up here."

But Molly seemed unfazed. "I knew what was going to happen in Philadelphia." She pulled her blanket over her wet blouse. "I had no idea what was going to happen here. All I was trying to do was my job. I couldn't guess I'd be dragged in for questioning."

"And we let you do your job, didn't we?" Combs had a pinched, ugly face. "Listen. No one is accusing you of nothing. No one is dragging you. You got to call in your story. All we want is a little cooperation. We want to know who you been talking to. Did you talk to this Sabatier about that death-threat séance you wrote about the other day? Did he describe it to you? Did you know he was going to be here?"

"I didn't know he was going to be here." She wanted to pick up her tea, but restrained herself. "But as to the rest—whether I've talked to him, and what he's said . . . listen, Detective, you know I can't tell you that."

"Hate to see a pretty girl get herself in trouble."

"I'll take my chances." Her heart was thumping, but her face stayed calm.

"We could make a whole lot of trouble for you."

"So throw me in jail, Detective." She leaned forward. "It'll make you famous in all the wrong ways."

Her face was white, her lips tinted blue, and her teeth set to keep them from chattering. Likewise her hands, she kept them clenched so the fingers would not tremble. Her anger was her guide. She glared with dull gray eyes, tough as her older brother Carl. The performance did not seem her own.

It had been like that since Houdini's box struck the water. They let her have a phone and she had read her notes slowly: "The greatest magician of our time has vanished, comma, never to appear again, stop." She had the facts in front of her, and the shape of the story was clear, and out of that shape words seemed to assemble themselves. Molly's mouth was working and she had one piece of the phone to her mouth and the other to her ear, and she could hear the satisfying clackety-clack of the typewriter across town in copy. Each succeeding paragraph surprised her in its fullness, as if the piece were driving itself onward, as if the clackety-clacking of the typewriter she heard over the wire were not the sound of the words of her sentences being committed to type, but rather the sound of her next sentence, in code, coming like inspiration.

She had hung up, dizzy with cold and exhaustion. The cops had led her to this room and its cozy fire, which burned but did not warm her. They had given her a blanket, and the cup of spiked tea, and then this skinny man on crutches had appeared in his cheap suit. Molly placed him at about fifty years old, and had not thought him entirely repulsive until he removed his hat and showed that big round protruding forehead, so at odds with the

clipped features of his face. She hadn't realized he was a policeman until his third question, and then it seemed absurd to her to
call this murder. An old man had jumped into a river, chained,
bound, bagged, and boxed—whose fault was it if he had drowned?

"Listen, you little tart." Detective Combs puffed his chest.
"You and me could be on the same team, getting to the bottom
of this."

"If you want to be my teammate," said Molly, "you'd better
leave off calling me names."

Fifteen minutes later, she was limping through the club's front
hall. Her left shoe wobbled, a strap had come loose. Her stocking
and skirt were damp, her shirt clung to her, and her jacket,
despite its time by the fire, was still cold and useless. Her hair lay
plastered to her scalp and her little cloche cap was ruined. Still, a
cop let out a low whistle as she passed. Molly kept her eyes deter-
minedly in front of her. Where the hell was Archie Miles? she
wondered. If he were a gentleman, he would have stuck around
to walk her out of this place, but he was nowhere and Molly
hated him. She reached into her bag for a cigarette, managed to
find the case, and put one in her mouth, but didn't dare light it
for fear of showing her trembling fingers. A sergeant nearby
reached out with a match. Molly accepted his gallantry without
thanking him. The big room had a chandelier made from a
pilot's wheel and on its wood-paneled walls were portraits of
yacht club presidents next to famous admirals: Nelson on one
wall, Dewey across. The cops lounged carelessly in the sofas and
tramped the carpets brown with mud. Chin up, Molly might
have passed for triumphant as she paraded past them, but she
stumbled by the door and almost fell into an umbrella stand.

A bright-looking cop with freckles reached to help, but Molly jerked her arm away.

"Officer Bendix," he introduced himself as he held open the door. "I'm supposed to escort you over to the park, give you a ride home."

Molly opened her mouth, lips shaking above white teeth. But she could not get out a word, so dashed out into the darkness. Officer Bendix followed.

Mist was coming down evenly. The smell of the river was strong, the gutters of the city overflowing with rain. The lights at the entryway gave shape to the shadowy hedges by the path, but just beyond the world drifted into darkness. The grounds of the club were black, mosquitoes swarmed, and yachts and cutters and sailboats bobbed, clinking on the tide. The sky was starless, and the buildings above—so familiar to Molly, just blocks from her parents' home—showed little lives, high up in the distance. The rain fell, and Molly's tears began to run. Bendix followed, and she shut her eyes. Soaked and cold, she shivered but tried to repress that and stepped confidently as she could with her broken shoe on the uneven gravel of the path. A dozen yards away from the door, she turned back to see the police boats churning the water, lights probing for the drowned magician. Bendix was right behind her, his smile in the darkness menacing.

"I'm all right," Molly said. "I can make it back—" but before she finished that sentence she stumbled.

Bendix was quick to grab her arm. His face came close. She wanted to kick him.

On her feet again she tugged her arm free and struggled on toward the gates at the limit of the club's one-acre grounds, trying to escape the shelter of the policeman's umbrella. Her throat burned. The muscles ached. There were compressed sobs there; it had been awful to see a man die. And then that damned police detective, skinny and condescending and by turns saccharine and threatening. The wind picked up and cut through her wet jacket and Molly shivered from her teeth on down. A prayer reached out from in her to someone—her brother, maybe—but it was incomplete, as if the wiring were broken either on her end or his. Anyway she had no words for Carl. The prayers were a spasm like the jerking in her throat, involuntary as the tears in her eyes or her need to get away from the policeman. Molly was a windup toy gone haywire, all kinds of jerks in the mechanism, and she tried to keep her mind to simple tasks: landing her shoe so it wouldn't twist her ankle, hewing to the path in the increasing darkness, getting away from Bendix. He had taken out a big flashlight and was pointing its beam in front of her, so she could see the gravel path and the low rope fence that separated them from the club's soft lawns. She wiped her eyes and tried to hide the gesture. Vaguely, vision adjusting to the dark, she could make out the shape of the distant bridge that climbed over the train tracks. Behind and illuminating the nasty fence of the New York Central, hoboes' fires burned in old steel drums. A howling whistle and a commuter train roared north, its big front headlight defining a hard cone of rain. For a moment in that light the bridge became visible in all its intricacies and shadows. The train came around the gentle curve, and some ugly scrub trees were lit outside the yacht club grounds, shadows stretching long and then snapping short, and for only a moment the path in front of her was clear. Then the locomotive passed, and in the windows of the train she could see the passengers and their evening papers, businessmen heading home. Soon she was watching the taillights from the last car, and again the world around her was dark and creepy. Officer Bendix said something that was lost in the rattle of the wheels, and Molly was frightened: the train and the cop and the night and the weird landscape that was in the city but not of it. Exhaustion rendered her hypersensitive. Emotion grabbed her in its fist: first anger, then fear, now an acute, rending sorrow. Oh, God, she thought, oh, God. That was her parents' building up there to her left, the lights maybe from the Silvers' apartment. Those were police boats scanning the water back there, searching for the corpse of Houdini. All she could do was go forward, feet unhesitating into the unseen. In the intermittent glow of Bendix's flashlight, she saw the scrub bush, her own shadow, a dead lamppost, and then the shape of a man standing beneath it.

"Hey," he said, startling both Molly and the cop.

"Who's there?" Bendix called.

A big man in a hat and an overcoat, he held a closed umbrella and a lit cigarette.

"Goodman." His voice was familiar. "You poor, soaked little mouse."

"Miles!"

The word exploded from her, as the policeman's flashlight lit his face. He laughed at the way she leapt for him, and caught Molly neatly in his arms. She dived in: his soft expensive raincoat, his clean face smelling of powder, and if not for the comical way he patted her, Molly might have let go the burden of her tears.

"Christ," she said with a sniff. "I could use a drink."

"You're a mess, kid," Archie said with a laugh. And then, opening his umbrella, he called to Bendix, "All right if I take her home?"

Molly came under. A silver flask appeared when the cop was gone, and she took a warming swig. Then, guiding her with one hand and holding the umbrella with the other, Archie told her how wonderfully she had done. Her two stories both ran on the front page of the evening extra. Heck, he said, what did he know about newspaper writing, but he was there again on the dock reading it, and he even teared up a little over old Houdini. From below them in the marshy ground by the train tracks came the stink and smoke of the vagrants' fires, also the mingled trash and sewage smell of the river. They walked as quickly as Molly could with her broken shoe and soon reached the steps to the park. Away from the world of vanishing magicians and threatening policemen, Molly realized as Archie spoke that she was seeing the day all wrong: What a bore to think it terrifying and tragic when it could be an adventure, and one in which she, as Archie had it, came out triumphant. Her hands were still shaking but she put up a smile, and before long they emerged into the street-lights and promenade of her childhood.

"Listen," Miles said as he gave her a new cigarette. "You're soaked. Come up to my place, it's not far. I'll give you something warm to drink, get you out of those wet clothes—"

"Archie." She was exhausted. She had planned on going home. "Now's not the time to get me out of my clothes."

He laughed, ducked his head a bit, giving her his boyish, ingenuous grin. "I'm just trying to take care of you, kid."

"Call me a cab, then," she said. "It's been an exhausting night."

"Oh, baby," said Archie. "We ought to celebrate." Cabs were zipping along the wet blacktop. From an awning across the drive came two men in top hats accompanied by women in gowns. A doorman led the party with his umbrella, a chauffeur opened the limousine door. "Bad night? You're the envy of every newspaperman in town. You got the big story, Goodman. He said, Go to Philadelphia, you said, No, I'm staying here, and when Houdini went down in the waves, you were on the boat, part of his—what does he call it?—committee. Heck, our little newspaper should rechristen itself the *Molly Goodman Times*."

"That'd boost circulation."

"It's cause to celebrate. Think it over, at least. Walk with me as far as West End Avenue."

His whiskey flask came out again. She was so tired. They stepped into the street. The pair had to scamper to get out of the way of a rolling bus, and Molly lost her shoe. She glanced back to see it thrown by the bus's tire, and Archie dodged to get it. She hopped for the curb. A truck came close and honked, and then Archie came rushing like a fullback and scooped her up in his arms, carrying her the last few yards with his umbrella gripped beneath her. His tongue hung out, Archie making comedy of his strength and athleticism, and Molly was still laughing when he set her down on the sidewalk. With a grand false chivalry, he pulled her busted filthy shoe from his raincoat pocket.

"So you're coming to my place, now that I've saved your life?"

Molly pulled away from him, wiping her eyes.

"Hey?"

"Listen," she said, tapping him on the chest. "I'm a mess. I'm

in no condition—" Her throat constricted. "The cops were terrible. And then. . . ." She couldn't finish.

"Yo comprendo." He nodded. "You been through the mill. But
don't go home alone and wet and shivering. That's not right.
Come up to my place. You'll get sick if you stay in those clothes."

"And what will happen to me if I get out of them?"

"Nothing bad." He held up his hands. "We'll catch a cab on
West End. I'm a dozen blocks from here. I'll fix you a drink—tea.
I'll put you in slippers and warm pajamas. You trust me, don't you?"

Molly shook her head, but when he extended his hand, she
took it. A voice in her head whispered that bad things would
happen if she went in with Archie, but she felt it was time maybe
to ignore that voice, which belonged to a different life when as a
college girl she didn't have to cope with drownings and interro-
gations and there were no handsome men inviting her up to
hotel rooms. Across the street from Archie's hotel was the high
fence of the lordly Schwab mansion, the building's Francophilic
spires rising into the night, and nighttime birds clustering in the
bushes and pear trees that hid the lawns from passersby. It had
been so nice of him to come and pick her up from the yacht club.
No one else had come. As she hobbled into his foyer on one
good shoe, out of the cold and into the warmth, she had an
unaccountable feeling, as though she had left a piece of baggage
on the curb, a sense of being unburdened and of having lost
something. She was so tired. It had been awful to see Houdini go.
In the lobby mirror, she barely recognized herself. There was
Archie, large and substantial in his gleaming black raincoat with
its belts and straps and epaulets, his big black hat and his long
umbrella, and there was she, one shoe off and one shoe on, with

a skirt that stuck to her thighs, a ruined cap in one hand, a useless soaked jacket, and a blouse almost transparent with rain. Her
hair was flat and thick and ugly. But the doorman was too well
paid to make any face or comment.

Molly came out of Miles's bathroom in ridiculous clothes.
Archie's slippers stuck out in front of her like clown shoes. The
legs and sleeves of his pajamas were rolled, but to no avail; his
big blue bathrobe trailed on the floor. She was like a little girl in
grown-up clothes, her short hair brushed back, her face pink and
warm. He had fixed toast with anchovies and hot buttered rum.

"I called down for some bread and chili," he said, "hope
you've got an appetite."

"How am I going to go home dressed like this?"

"You're not."

His Victrola played tepid romantic piano music. Archie had
taken off his coat, hat, gloves, scarf, and rubbers. The brogues he
wore were shining, his taupe slacks matched his jacket and shirt.
What was left of his hair was combed close to his head and oiled
so it shone. He might have been more handsome, but his baldness and pudginess gave him the hint of comedy that was at the
heart of his attractiveness, the sense that he was a boy—a child
like herself—who had had some ridiculous trick of aging played
on him, and who had the grace to laugh along with the joke. She
was struck by the dark colors of the room, the books in glass-
fronted cases. A hunting rifle wouldn't have been out of place, or
the head of a moose. But it smelled good, of toast and rum, cigar
smoke and leather. His cheeks looked very pink.

She took the offered cup in two hands and the porcelain was
just right—cozy, but comfortable to touch. She sat on the couch,

and he stood above her. Molly thought of other women who might have sat on Archie's couch. She remembered that bathing beauty she had seen with him in August in the Atlantic City hotel, and she recalled what Alton Grimm had said at the time, that he could tell by Archie's smile that he hadn't fucked the girl yet. Now Archie's smile was very warm. He was adjusting a piece of toast on a plate, getting ready to give it to her. She sipped her drink, and its warm creamy sweetness went right to her head. When Archie sat beside her it was the most natural thing in the world. Her teeth sank into the crust of the toast and the salty taste filled her mouth.

"Ooo," she said.

Archie laughed. "You want to try something fun?"

"This is fun." She took another bite of toast.

"It might be more fun."

Her head felt at once very clear and very light. Archie pulled out some papers and an envelope of green sticky herbs.

"A cigarette?"

"Oh, silly," he said. "It's not tobacco."

Molly started—her mother would not like this. But then she thought of Sukey, not as a rival to Archie, but what Sukey would have done, and the answer was clear: Sukey would have smoked whatever Archie had to offer. Her throat still hurt, her eyes felt dry and used up, even though she had never really let go and cried. She shivered, just once, some odd, dislocated, physical recollection of the cold. Then she sipped her hot drink and shut her eyes.

"What is it I'm trying here?" she asked. "And are you one of those dangerous men who drug innocent girls and then drop them in the river?"

"Oh, absolutely. Look, you don't do it like a cigarette. You suck the smoke deep in your lungs and hold it."

"If you want to get dropped in the river, that is."

"Absolutely. Watch."

She slipped her feet out of the slippers and rested them on the coffee-table top. Then he passed his skinny cigarette to her, and she had the feeling again that she had left some piece of luggage on the street. She worried. Then, Lose it, she thought. And because she was drunk and tired and happy to find herself doing something so uncharacteristic, she laughed. Archie didn't seem to need to know why she was laughing, but it made him smile. Molly followed directions: She sucked in the smoke and held it in her lungs. She kept her lips shut and opened her eyes so wide he laughed.

"You can breathe now," said Archie, and she laughed with him, smoke exploding.

"Nothing happened," she complained.

And he laughed again.

It was a long laugh, and her laugh sounded weird as it came from her, broken up somehow into strange pieces, and the pieces seemed to surround her like waves, and the waves echoed against the invisible bubble of her personality. What an exhausting thing it is, she thought then, to have a personality. What a burden to maintain it all one's life. She hoped suddenly that was what she had left on the sidewalk, the big awkward portmanteau of her self.

Molly tasted another one of his toasts and she had never tasted anything so salty. Another puff on his magic cigarette and she was listening to the music differently, as if it were segmented not just in harmony but also in time, and she felt curiously aware of the intricate parts that the piano was playing, as if she had rare comprehension of the way those parts fit together. She reached for the cigarette again.

"No, no, darling," said Archie. "We've had enough."

"Or what?" groaned Molly. "I end up on the bottom of the river?"

"Very likely."

And he laughed, and she laughed with him, but then worried he was laughing at her, and this frustrated her, and she looked at him crossly, which only made him laugh more. Her lips were tingling from the salt and the alcohol and the cigarettes and the marijuana. His lips looked very comfortable.

Oh, hell, thought Molly.

And giving up entirely on that big suitcase she had left on the street, she lunged across the sofa to kiss him.

"My God," Archie cried. And he gathered her in his arms.

Molly felt she was sacrificing something as she lay beneath him, and as if she were not quite getting enough in return. Sometimes it felt good, and sometimes it was uncomfortable, and when he started rutting like a big beast, it shocked her. She had been shocked by so much of it. It really was obscene: the size of his penis, its uncircumsized shape, the hairiness of his chest and back and buttocks. She didn't like it. It hurt. And before she really figured out where the sex was going, it was over, disappointingly so. Archie groaned and gasped and then rolled over to the other side of the bed, his forehead glowing with sweat. Her heart was thumping. The thumping didn't seem to ease. Five minutes later, she tried to say something to him—she was worried that the drugs or the sex might hurt her—but he was fast asleep and snoring.

Molly looked at the complex gilded molding on the ceiling, the thick drapes that hid the windows and the light from the street. She reached out for Archie's face, his glasses, his beard, but then remembered that he didn't have glasses or beard, that was Lyden, but why think of Lyden? With a start, she remembered the suitcase she had left on the street, but then she remembered that it was only an imaginary suitcase. Still, it worried her. How humiliating it would be to be pregnant.

She shut her eyes and tried to pray: Please God don't let that happen. But it did no good. It was as if God couldn't contact her here as easily as he could in her room on Gay Street. This was not a sense of sin on Molly's part, just dislocation. She prayed to Carl, but she could not reach Carl, either. Nor could she sleep. She wrapped herself in Archie's big robe. He had not answered the delivery's knock a half hour ago, and the chili was still there outside the door. Molly brought it in, and ate savagely, using dinner rolls in place of a fork. The food was cold and glutinous and oversalted, but she sat on his couch and ate.

I should go home, thought Molly. But then she thought, Wearing what?

And so she crept to the bedroom and slid into the sheets by the big, snoring, naked man, staring at the ceiling, wide awake.

XV

THE CLOUDS CLEAR. The waxing moon, a golden coin, gleams against the velvet backing of the sky. He sees none of this. Face down on a deck slick with rain, algae, and oil, he lies breathing shallowly, wrists skinned and manacled, fingers swollen, feet torn from climbing the barnacled hull. His head aches as if the wound there were burning. He touches it, and without a wince pulls himself to standing. But the boat rocks on a swell and he slips again, and would go crashing into the water if not for physical genius and the memory of reflex. He catches the rusted balustrade, swings out over the Hudson and back, landing on his feet.

His gut spasms. He coughs, grabs the railing, and retches.

On the riverbank, a train chugs past, the top of its steam cloud a single black shape with the elms of the nighttime park, and the low mansions of Riverside Drive. Houdini tastes the bile in his mouth and tries to gauge his position. He is blocks downtown, past the garbage heaps and scows of 79th Street—how could he have missed them in the river and the storm?—and well offshore from the park. He can glimpse the silhouetted turrets of the Schwab mansion. Houdini knows nothing of boats, but catches the smell of coal and of alcohol. He sees the stubby smokestack and figures he is on some tramp steamer that found quick harbor against the storm. His fingers feel weak and fudgy. There's a ringing in his ears. His stomach swells and heaves.

A needle-thin lockpick rests in the callus of his left heel. He lifts his wrists to examine the handcuffs. And even though he is feverish and weak, the task brings his mind to focus. All that remains in the lock are some coarse grains of sand, no longer the cement that he had worked against in the water. His adversary used some kind of semi-soluble paste. Very clever, for had he drowned it would have dissolved, and on his recovered corpse the manacles would show no sign of tampering. But now he can flick the last grit out easily, even as he struggles against the urge to vomit. Poisoned by the river water but working steadily, Houdini feels the rusted guardrail for an uncorroded point. A jerk, a smack, metal against metal, a deliberate flexing of the muscles, and he is free.

But the work makes him woozy. His bowels heave. He barely has time to pull down his shorts, when the shit leaves his guts as if propelled through a spigot. His stomach clenches. He doubles over, forehead pressed against the cold, slimy deck.

Death to the doubter. The words echo in his head.

He will destroy whoever did this to him. Sabatier, Margery, the weird sailor, whoever they are, whatever their motive. He thinks of Bess. The humiliation galls him. That she should think him defeated and drowned, that his wife should mourn Houdini, that the world should think he failed. He replays the scene as though he were the camera that filmed it, and from this godly perspective of perfect memory, he comprehends the entire act, in which his corporeal self, whom he sees strutting foolishly on the deck and performing, plays the fool and is played upon by a villain. He understands now the misdirection that he missed on account of his anxiety about the storm: how Sabatier maneuvered Molly Goodman through glances and smiles and the cock of his head, how he made her select that sailor. And was the sailor's name Stevenson or Johnson or did he give both? Useless aliases. Miss Goodman was not part of the plot, she had to have been played, and when, like idiots, he and Jim Collins had their eyes on Sabatier, who was inspecting the chains, Stevenson-Johnson had fixed the handcuffs. Houdini thinks of the strange dangling ectoplasmic thing that hung from Margery's ear at the séance, the kitchen-counter chemistry involved in Spiritualist tricks. They could have used anything, a teaspoon of fine sand, some viscous adhesive, a dab on each thumb, and the handcuffs would be inoperable. He pulls up his trunks, mouth gone dry, but no sooner is he staggering to his feet than he feels it coming on again. He tries to aim the diarrhea into the Hudson but it spits wildly, hot against his ankles. Houdini squats, clinging exhausted to the rusty post of the guardrail, letting it all run out of him. A breeze against his nakedness and he shudders. His teeth chatter. He feels his fever rise. His arms want to tremble, but Houdini makes them stop.

When the lightning struck the river, it knocked him senseless. He began to sink, but the taste of the Hudson woke him. Panic struck underwater. Houdini tried to breathe, felt the water coming in, and his body worked like a miracle machine, breathed out when he was breathless, kicked his furious legs, shot upward, broke the surface, coughed, spat, and gulped air. The rain hit hard, but he kept on swimming. Dark of night, he remembered the boat. Hands in cuffs, head bleeding, skin on fire with pain, he went against the current, and before he knew who or where or why he was, he had scrambled up the side, vomiting, chest heaving, hands and feet chafed raw, skin electric. Now he walks stiffly across the deck toward the boat's little cabin, where he thinks he might find some shelter against the wind, if not the cold. His teeth chatter, his head pulses, his hearing is strange and dull.

On jelly legs he works the cabin door, breathing deep before moving, but the entrance fools him. Houdini misses a step, stumbles, and pitches into darkness. Falling, he reaches to his right, grabs a shelf, but this time his strength and reflexes play against him. The shelf he grabs pulls free. It whacks his back as he falls. A thought at the speed of blinking: bootleggers walloping him. But the blow to his gut is a stool, and with a crack a paint can nails him at the point where his neck meets his skull. He lies where he falls and his unconscious bowels let loose.

Dawn finds him hallucinating, his body tiny, his head overlarge, his injuries glowing. He has a third arm, but has somehow misplaced it. Where did he put that arm? He lies in his shit, surrounded by the rum-runner's ragtag equipment. A filthy wool blanket, a hammer, a wrench, a coil of rope, pitch, paint, and grease, the shelf itself, a clasp knife, an old shirt, a raincoat, some empty bottles, and old magazines. He opens his eyes and feels the cold shit on his thighs. He spots the blanket and bundles himself in it, never mind the smell. The cabin has a small cracked window, its bottom pane gone. Houdini chatters and sweats. His tongue probes his mouth, a chipped tooth, a loose tooth. His hands shake and he wills them still. Someone wants to kill Houdini, he reasons, therefore Houdini will triumph.

He wipes himself with an old rag. He rinses his trunks in a slimy bucket. The old raincoat itches. The blanket is stiff. He spots the clasp knife on the floor and drops it in the pocket of the coat. Again, he needs to shit.

The man who emerges from the cabin is unrecognizable as the great magician. The grubby clothes, the slight stoop, the shuffling, his hair matted with shit and blood, his face disfigured, black and blue, feverish, sweating, off-kilter, but strong. Dawn spreads behind the buildings of Manhattan, a jagged line of mansions and apartment houses and steeples. Their shadows lie across the gray water. The weather has turned cool, as though the storm swept out summer and introduced the autumn chill. Beyond the garbage scows he can make out the marina, and on its docks the armature of lights that had been rigged overnight to help divers search for his body. A few bustling uniformed figures haunt the piers. Houdini moves to the far side of the cabin so no detective with binoculars will spot him. He leaves the blanket on deck, drops the handcuffs in the raincoat's pocket along with his knife. Then, bundle in hand and wearing his filthy, soaking swim trunks, Houdini makes a perfect dive into the Hudson. Sick, beaten, feverish, and exhausted, he retains the lung capacity of a small whale.

Over the greasy rocks he climbs, dry-mouthed, thirsty, barefoot, his head throbbing. Momentum overrules the urge to col-
lapse, and he passes into the brambles and ailanthus trees, filthy
with bottles, rusted cans, and mossy women's underwear.
Houdini shakes out the raincoat and pulls it on, his shoulder
muscles jerking with the cold. A commuter train passes, heading
south to the city. Houdini watches through the rusty fence.
Bankers, ad men, and insurance agents drift by. In the wasteland
between the river and the wall of Olmstead's park live a hundred
drunks and drifters. The ground is soft, riddled with sinkholes.
Houdini follows the track north, sticking close to coal bins,
bushes, and piles of trash, anything that might indicate solid
footing. Something rustles in the underbrush, the dash of a tail,
and there are two of them, rats up on their haunches. Uphill, he
sees a crate on its side, a makeshift hovel. Everywhere, the smell
of urine. Grunts and groans come from a stand of weedy trees
across the tracks. Houdini glimpses a man shitting or masturbat-
ing, and he looks away.

He keeps by the riverbank. The shantytown lies on the other
side of the tracks and the raw wire fencing: little huts of discarded
wood, sometimes with a sheet-metal roof. Hoboes huddle for
warmth, old men curled like pairs of nestling boys. Fever makes
Houdini sweat. His jacket itches as though it crawls with tiny
bugs. His vision focuses and blurs. Before long he comes to the
mountains of trash at 79th Street. Seagulls whirl and caw above
the heaping rubbish, enormous rats prowl the periphery. The big
scows are huddled close to the shore against yesterday's storms,
and the hauling machines are parked by a bridge that runs over

the railroad tracks. Houdini looks over it all, the impassable brown green pile of food and clothing and glass and metal. The reek is unbearable. He gathers himself, climbs the slack fence, crosses the southbound tracks, then the north, and again, nimble and deft, makes the next rusty barrier and lands on his feet. He flexes his raw, sore hands. There's a narrow space between the New York Central's fence and the eastern wall of the garbage-men's bridge. Houdini makes it through, bent and barely breath-ing, stepping carefully between the sleeping bodies packed close in the dark. He emerges from the fetid air into shadow that feels like sunlight. Houdini stands on a rock and watches the police-men work near the yacht club. He does not have to worry about being spotted, his broken body is an impenetrable disguise.

Through the scrub grass and brambles he goes, stepping once on a sharp long needle of glass which drives deep into the sole of his foot. He curses, draws out most of the green broken bottle, and trudges forward, heading for home. At 96th Street there's another huge pile of waste, also a pipe that pumps sewage into the river. The passable land narrows and Houdini trudges close by a passenger train heading south. Soot and dust attack his eyes, but he habituates himself to that also, and marches stoically past the long line of clanking cars. Puddles and mud and more sink-holes. He crosses the tracks at a hole in the fence and follows them until another train convinces him to walk by the river-bank, on the rocks exposed by the lowering tide, his muddy, bloody feet slipping on the moss and green algae.

"Mother," Houdini groans.

Then he lifts his head to see a shorebird, not ten yards away, staring at him. Not a gull, something magnificent, white and long-legged, an egret. The bird is thin as paper, then turns again into long profile and regards him steadily. Houdini studies its beautiful neck.

"Mother?"

The bird keeps its eye on him.

"Help."

And it takes off, upriver. He watches the way its big wings work. Ponderously at first, but then magically they render the creature weightless, and it soars.

Somewhere around 100th Street, he sees a pair of ragpickers eating breakfast by a stream of runoff that's a couple of yards wide and brown as mud. Houdini runs his hand across his mouth and then crosses the stream carefully, making his plans with his approach. Up the rise from the men sits their cart; hanging from one handle is a pair of leather shoes. The water of the stream rises higher than he had expected, over his knees, and when at one point his foot drops in the mud, his swim trunks are wetted all over again. But he makes it to the other side feeling only once for the clasp knife, whose weight in the pocket of his raincoat he finds comforting.

"Hello," he calls. "Good morning."

The men regard him with the indifference all city dwellers affect on the approach of potential danger. They pretend not to have heard him, and the shorter of the two—a dumpling of a middle-aged man—grunts at the taller, who laughs even as he chews his morning bread. They have lit a small fire. Houdini can smell their breakfast.

"Good morning," he says again.

The little dumpling waves his hand as though shooing away a dog.

"Friends—" Houdini says, but his throat is dry and his voice cracks. "I only wish you good morning."

"And we wish you to get lost, eh?" The dumpling has a cauliflowered ear, short, matted dark gray hair, and an accent that might be Russian or Greek.

Houdini laughs. "I want to trade with you."

"Do we do trading?" the dumpling asks his taller, thinner companion. They sit on their haunches, neither facing Houdini. "I don't think so. Not with the stumblebums."

At this point the thin man stands. He is even taller and lankier than he seemed while squatting, and unfolds upright like a stork. His beard is so pale as to be nearly translucent and hangs like plant growth down his skinny neck.

"I want those shoes," says Houdini, pointing toward the cart. "I have a knife." And it appears in his left hand. "And I will trade it for those shoes over there."

"A knife?" The short man stands, hiking his pants. "I never trade shoes for lousy knife," he says. "But," he continues with a sigh, "you should let me see."

Houdini flicks open the blade, spins the handle in his clever hands. The dumpling backs away. The knife vanishes.

"I only want the shoes," says Houdini.

"I have take good look at knife. Maybe I give pants for it." The dumpling extends a filthy palm. "You want deal, I have to see knife."

Shorter and wider than Houdini, with a grubby cap on his head, he turns the weapon over in his hands and then points its blade at Houdini.

"Now you scat, hey," he threatens. "I got knife and you scat." He pokes the air with his blade.

Houdini looks beyond the men. "I want those shoes," he says.

"Funny." But the dumpling does not smile. "I kill you, funny guy, okay?"

Houdini squats, heels in the mud by the stream of runoff, eyes still on the cart. Despite the battered face and matted hair, his eyes retain their hypnotic power. The tall, bearded crane steps forward, ready for a fight. Houdini picks up a handful of pebbles.

"Buddy, funny buddy. I kill you, hey. Go home."

"No trade," says the crane. "We already got knife."

"Bye-bye, funny buddy."

Houdini tosses the pebbles in the air: one, two, three, four, five. They rise in a line, and seem to hang in the sky, then in formation they drop into his open hand. He closes his fist, opens it, and the pebbles vanish.

"No funny business, buddy," says the dumpling, but he and his partner back off when Houdini claps.

He holds a black rock the size of a baseball. He claps his hands again and it's gone.

The dumpling stares. The stupid crane smiles. Houdini puts his hand to his mouth and spits out pebbles: one, two, three, four, five, and then, miraculously, opens his jaws wider than they would have thought possible to produce the round black rock.

"Ach," says the dumpling.

Houdini approaches. He shows his stone to one ragman, then

to the other. Then he tosses it in the air. They lift their chins to watch. It arcs into the sky, the puffy clouds moving in the path of the northbound storm. The black rock pauses at the peak of its rise—high as an apartment building—then, with a thump, it lands between the dumpling's feet. No magic there, except that Houdini now holds the clasp knife and its point is at the fat man's belly.

"The shoes," he says. "The ones you're wearing. And a hat and a shirt and a decent pair of pants."

XVI

LEANING OVER THE STEAMING BATH, Bess
puts her mouth to her husband's foot and sucks. The glass
slips free. After the curved green shard comes pus and mud and
then bleeding. Bess spits the glass into a rattling bowl and pro-
ceeds to the right foot. Thick calluses reveal themselves under
the dirt. On his heel and the ball, layers of skin flap like fish gills.
Through their years of the knockabout circus life, she nursed
him. Now the practice comes back to her. Careful with her husband's scalp, she soaps and wipes and breaks the crusted blood to
clean the filth within. From a kettle, she pours hot water on her
cloth and presses it to the wound. Then she trims the hair above
the mess and shaves in quick bold strokes. Blood mingles with
foam above the discolored follicles. Houdini does not flinch. She
lights a match to clean a needle, and Doyle sits three miles
downtown at a table at the center of his suite. He works in black
ink and a stiff piece of paper while his wife and children sleep.

His sketch begins at the border. Little naked cherubs frame the page. He scribbles their bottoms with quick curves like commas and their bellies with overblown quotation marks. The early reports already set out possibilities: a hoax, an accident, or a murder. Doyle rejects all three. Houdini would not pretend, could not fail, and no ordinary man could kill him. Doyle gives his cherubs O's for mouths, periods for eyes, wisps of hair around their skulls. As the infant angels look on, he plants three figures across the page in a diagonal. Possibilities darker than murder run through his mind, considerations bound to render the police unmanned and the newspapers baffled. The mystery sailor, for instance, Stevenson or Johnson: Perhaps like Houdini he keeps one foot in the material world and another in the etheric, per-haps he uses to cruel purposes the resources of the beyond.

The central figure in Doyle's sketch emerges in three lines from concentric circles, the circles become waves, the shapes two arms and a head. He inks the hair, cuffs the hands, and it is Houdini, struggling in water. Fearless, Doyle resolves to press the investigation whoever his enemy is, to draw the mystery man out. Whoever the man really is, this Johnson or Stevenson must maintain a serious interest in the science of escape. How else could he foil Houdini? Perhaps he could be tempted by a fine set of manacles. This morning he will call the newspapers, place a notice in the *Radio Times* and also the *World*, a rare pair of antique handcuffs for sale; among those who come to buy will be the mystery sailor. Doyle decides to ask Bess Houdini to loan him a valuable set from her husband's collection.

He works the large figure at the top of the page. It appears in outline as a tilted windmill, but he makes its base a bell, which flowers into a skirt, and then the swirl on top becomes a mass of dark, flowing hair. A face drawn in a dozen lines, and it is Margery, reaching toward the water. The police, Doyle decides, are worse than useless. They declared the death an accident, they arrested Sabatier, and this Detective Combs who showed up at his door last night had raised the possibility that this drowning was a publicity stunt, Houdini and Sabatier working in cahoots. These actions were contradictory, and the only reason to speak with the police department would be to encourage them to moderate their incompetence. Still, to rescue Houdini—and he believes, as his wife does, that Houdini is alive—Doyle will need assistance, particularly if he is struggling against, as he suspects, dark forces from beyond, and no assistance could be more valuable than Margery's. Poor woman—what will she do, he wonders, while her husband is in jail? It will be his to protect her, and hers to assist him, for the search for Houdini must take place on two planes: the material and the etheric. In the former, he would have to work alone, but in the latter he could have no better guide than Margery. Inking and shading, he smiles. Houdini is alive, he feels certain. With Margery's help, he will be rescued. Success in this search will be success all around, because after being saved by her, Houdini will have no choice but to acknowledge and celebrate Margery. He will come perforce to the side of truth, and they will gather their energies together—Margery, Conan Doyle, and Houdini—to build Sabatier's dreamland and there to light a blaze of searing wisdom to scorch the earth to purity. He sketches a final figure, bigger than the other two, a two-armed hulk which soon grows glasses and a mustache, a cartoon of himself that is, like the figure of Margery, reaching toward the water.

Doyle puts his pen to his lips. The distances are off. The hands do not reach. He tries to stretch the arms of the outer figures, but his corrections muddle the sketch. It is impossible to tell if Doyle and Margery are trying to save Houdini or to drown him.

MORNING BREAKS and he is at the yacht club, scene of the crime. Police cars linger under the yellowing elms of Riverside Park, and police boats trawl the water. No one stops him as he crosses the bridge over the railroad tracks, but when Doyle reaches the gate at the yacht club grounds a big, uniformed patrolman holds up a hand. He stands about Doyle's height, might be a few years younger, and wears a heavy mustache above his fighter's chin. The double-breasted buttons of his uniform gleam above the lumps and rolls of his middle.

"Lord be," he says at the sight of Doyle, "Mr. Sherlock Holmes." And he trots off to fetch his superior.

Three men on a barge haul a diver from the river. Water courses off his complicated suit, and to Doyle the man resembles a knight in futuristic armor, his helmet a bubble, its visor glass, the collar decorated in metal bolts—a man from the future plunked into the muck of the present. Assistants on the barge unfasten his helmet, while with his enormous gloves the diver gestures hopelessly. Useless, Doyle knows; the body will not be recovered. Even if it were a human corpse, without the magic of Houdini, even then, between the current, the storm, and the size and murkiness of the river, it would take a miracle to find a recognizable body.

Doyle tries to imagine it: late afternoon, the storm, the darkness, and Houdini going down. The ground around reeks of rot and decay. Gulls swoop and swirl a half mile upriver, where the sewage pours into the Hudson. Uptown and down, Doyle sees the mounds of garbage, the birds fighting above. He contemplates the buildings behind him, and thinks of all the lives, all the toilets, all the way up to Harlem fouling the river. A man who swallowed that would be sick; the onset would be quick and awful. Doyle sighs, draws a leather-bound pad from his breast pocket, and makes a quick sketch of the area—trying to get the docks right and the shape of the shore. As he finishes the big square that will be the club, its front door opens and out comes the big mustached patrolman accompanied by a thin gray man in a gray hat and shining suit, swinging forward on crutches, Abel Combs.

Doyle touches his hand to his hat.

The detective does not return his greeting. "I told you last night." He lights a cigarette. "There's nothing here to see."

"Still, I thought I'd have a look about."

"Why would you want to do that?"

"Well." Doyle laughs. "You've come, haven't you?"

"I get paid to do it. I'm overseeing the investigation. What's your angle?"

"Angle?" Doyle keeps up his smile. "I'm not certain I can say. But might I ask what you have so far, as you put it, overseen?"

"That's police business," Combs says. "Not like your books. Look—I know you're an important man where you come from, but over here in New York we keep police business to ourselves. Murder's not for literature, not in my book."

"Your book?" Doyle leans forward, a half foot taller than Combs, almost twice as wide, patient and immovable. They hear the cawing of gulls and the chatter of police on the dock, one of whom murmurs Doyle's famous name. "One good friend of mine is gone," says Doyle, "another is in prison. It's hardly strange that I should come here, that I should make this business my own. And as I said last night, it might be the case that I could be of some assistance to you—"

"It ain't like writing a mystery story." Combs lets off smoke. "And if you ask me, there's not much mystery. An old man in handcuffs jumps in a river. Nobody ought to be shocked when he don't come up."

"If there is no mystery, if you presume this was an accident, then may I ask—"

"It ain't my line to go presuming. And like I said to you before, Sir Conan Doyle, you're lucky we didn't haul you in for questioning, too."

"Very well," Doyle presses on. "But if an accident befell Houdini, and, as you haven't seen fit to, as you say, haul me in, may I ask why you have arrested Dr. Hugo Sabatier?"

Combs grins. His smile cuts a dozen lines in his cheeks. "You're an early riser, you know that, Sir Conan Doyle? I sent a man to your hotel room just after dawn, but he called and told me you was already out. I thought I'd have to run the city. But then you show up here."

"Then I take it you will be freeing Dr. Sabatier—"

"Why would you take it like that?"

"I should warn you, sir, that I have made appeals to my solicitors. We are prepared to go before a magistrate—"

"We call them judges here in New York."

"May we go into the club, sir, and speak more comfortably?"

"I like it out here."

Doyle wipes his brow.

"Look. Your friend the professor made some threats to Houdini, and not long before this accident. And that's the sort of thing we look into. You yourself were maybe a party to those threats. Let me explain. It's not deductive or fancy. I'm no Sherlock. But your friend had motive: Houdini called him a crook. He had opportunity: He was here when the man went down. And he made threats. Look, he broke the law. They had no permit for the show they put on here, and I can jail him for that. I know my business, Sir Conan Doyle. I can hold that man."

"When you speak of threats," says Doyle evenly, "you are referring to the séance, I presume. There was no threat. Nor was it in any sense made by Dr. Sabatier—the words were spoken by a spirit, and accurately reported in the article written in the *Radio Times*, though I believe that paper's headlines distorted the fact, and it seemed to be the headline that the other newspapers took up—"

"Take a step back, sir. This is private property, there's the line."

"Look here," says Doyle, "there was no motive to kill. Because Houdini doubted the truth of Margery's séance—"

"I said, take a step back."

"Hear me out," says Doyle. "Answer me. How could an ordinary professor outfox Houdini?"

"Just the sort of question we're asking."

"But a moment ago you said it was an—"

"We look at all the angles. That's the job."

"How can I explain to you—the words 'Death to the doubter' were spoken by a spirit—"

"I'd like to speak to that spirit."

"I could arrange that, sir, on the condition that you release Dr. Sabatier."

Combs throws down his cigarette. "Don't make me conditions, Sir Conan Doyle."

"For God's sake, man, let us talk. Have you any information about that sailor who bound Houdini in chains? Have you discovered the man's name or—"

"We're not looking into that right now. We've got other—"

"Not looking? You astound me—"

Combs laughs again. "Don't you start giving me advice, Sir Conan Doyle. This is my line of work and—"

"But you have a photograph of him, do you not? The whole event was filmed by a motion picture camera. I have some interest in phrenology, in physiognomy, I am sure that if I saw the man's face—"

"I don't need to answer your questions." Combs holds up his hand. "And I don't know that physics is the business we need here. But sure, I'll tell you: I haven't looked at the picture show."

"Then may I have a look at it?"

"That's police property. And anyway, where were you yesterday afternoon? Why weren't you here, then, if you're so interested?"

"Traveling from Philadelphia, sir," says Doyle. "Then at the home of my American editor. It was all reported in the newspapers. Do you read the newspapers?"

"I'd love to answer your questions—"

"My questions are done."

"So are mine, Sir Doyle."

And the detective turns back to the yacht club. Doyle tries to follow, but the big mustached cop blocks his way.

"May I at least—may I go on to the docks and see where it was that Houdini jumped?"

"Keep him out," says Combs over one shoulder.

"Then I'll walk by the riverbank, if I may."

The detective doesn't answer. The patrolman gives Doyle a sympathetic squint.

That bloodless skin, that vicious grin, the man seems an idiot. Not look at the film, not pursue the strange sailor—that Sabatier was in prison because of the supposed threatening nature of a spirit's remark, it galls him. How can he explain a thing to this sort of man, let alone that the gnomic imprecations of a spirit, rich with subtlety, are to be pondered and never swallowed whole? Doyle has moved to the rocks by the water. A train chugs past, newsprint and stray papers flying. He has to dodge a flapping broadsheet. Who comes to a séance to hear threats? How can revelation be prelude to murder?

Words in the spirit realm, Doyle knows, do not carry the same meaning as they do in the human. Death, for instance, from the point of view of a spirit, would never mean what it did to a man, for death in that world was as natural as breath in this—the very element the spirits inhabited. And to assume that the doubter in question was Houdini, to read the pronouncement as in any way a threat—it stemmed from a deep misunderstanding about presence and absence, this realm and beyond. A sitter at the séance may have seen Houdini as the only doubter there, yet for a spirit the ether was teeming with forces and light—and the doubter in question may have been felt in the material world as nothing but a lingering tension, a historical fact. The river is busy with ferries and cutters and barges and tugboats.

A threat—not at all. The voice that Margery had brought from beyond had spoken what was, on reflection, a profound and optimistic thought. "Death to the doubter," Doyle thinks: Given proper consideration, the words blossom and come clear. *Doubter* would refer not to an individual but to a generic force, one present at that séance and in perhaps all human events, that force of false belief and skepticism that had dominated material and social circumstance for eons, a force against which Abraham, Moses, Christ, Buddha, and Mohammad had all fought. It was *that* doubter to whom death was wished, but not death as a fool like Combs would understand it. Wishing death, in the sense meant by the spirit, was a wish not for an ending, but for transmutation, to wish for doubt's arrival in the spirit realm, and for the resolution of skepticism in the blessed clarity of the beyond.

Doyle scans the muck at the bank of the river, the rusted sardine cans and the stained old pants. Foolishness and ignorance. He shakes his head. The spirit's words could as well have been "Life to all doubters," for if the generic force of skepticism were to undergo the great transformation—the passage to the beyond that was the future inevitably of every well-meaning skeptic— then *in life* all such skeptics would be released from their skepticism—even a man like Combs—and faced with the vision of hope, light, and beauty. But how is Doyle to express this to the detective?

He leaves the rocks for the scrubby land by the fence near the tracks. Mosquitoes swarm above the bushes. Foolishness! The police are not even looking here, where Houdini, if he had sur-

vived, was most likely to have come ashore. And alone, Doyle
has neither the skills nor the resources to find the clues he
needs—footprints, handprints, gravel that might have been dis-
turbed—to see if there is a spot where a man might have risen
from the water. And in a couple of tides, he knows, all such
traces will vanish.

Downriver and twenty yards out, a beat-up, barnacled steamer
hoists anchor, starts its engine, and heads out to harbor. The water
kicks up, bubbling in its wake. Nothing to see here, just as the
detective said. Doyle resolves to call Molly Goodman when he gets
back to the hotel, and tell her about his interview with the policeman. If he can reveal some of the investigation's inadequacy and
induce Miss Goodman to publish it, then perhaps through public
pressure he might be able to force the police to conduct this investigation more reasonably, to at the very least attempt to discover
the identity of the mystery sailor, and to release Sabatier from
prison. Doyle feels he can trust the reporter this far: that she will
report his words accurately, and that she will understand him. He
intuits her sympathy with the Spiritualist cause.

The ground is wet and mucky, odd trash everywhere: clothes,
machine parts, the brown drying corpse of a gull. *Watch your
step*—that detective had better watch his, Doyle thinks, because
as soon as the word was out in the press, all eyes would be on
Abel Combs, making sure he did his job properly. Doyle laughs,
then slips.

The sinkhole goes to his knee, and he draws his foot out,
shoeless.

XVII

THE AUTUMN CHILL SETTLED in the shadows of
the buildings, but summer lingered where the sun sliced
down 75th Street to warm a parallelogram of park. Molly looked
from the promenade to the train tracks below. Barges lay on the
river. Gulls swooped and circled. Uptown, police boats sent jets
of curling water off their hulls, and mica shone in the cliffs of the
distant palisades. Molly heard the train before she saw it, and
rested her arms on the wide damp fieldstone wall. The chugging
of the locomotive, the clank of the couplings, the train and its
white smoking column stretched back as far as she could see. A
dull exhausted throb settled in her temples. She felt stupid from
the residue of marijuana, at a distance from perception and with
her brain slowed. She noticed a squirrel with a nut, then a run in
her stocking, and she touched her short, damp hair. No idea why
she went up to his apartment last night—because she was fraz-
zled, maybe, or because he was handsome, or because the force of

expectations had carried the night. Archie seemed so sure of everything. She had put herself in his trust, as if it would have been rude to do otherwise. At what point had she acceded? Right away, she decided, when she ran into his arms in the rain.

The train clanked by. Molly hobbled uptown on her broken shoe. She lit a cigarette. Worry played hopscotch in her head. Always, when she was tired, anxiety attacked. Had she gone too far with Archie? He had said that silk handkerchief would do the trick (oh, God, she prayed, let's not get pregnant), but what would he expect from her tomorrow? The train ran below, freight cars and tank cars, open gondolas carrying brick and pig iron. Red, rust, blue. The names of the railroad companies stamped all over, NEW YORK CENTRAL, NEW YORK CENTRAL, the long column of steam and smoke rising and drifting inland like the airborne crest of a long slow wave, breaking up against the scrub trees, the elms and sycamores, and the high stone wall. She was in the cloud, then it was gone, dispersing skyward. Shapes moved and shifted in the brush below. Molly made out the shanties. Men waking, men smoking, piles of rags, rusted barrels, planks, junk, wood. Near the boggy edge of the river someone had lit a morning fire, and she could glimpse a crowd of muddy figures now and then through the spaces between the empty cattle cars, all of this familiar from her childhood. Memories like ghosts: on these cobbles, by these benches, under the shade of these elms, Molly had played with her nurse, had watched Carl throw rocks at sparrows, had seen lonely Lyden Silver learn to bicycle. Archie slept with another woman every month, she figured. It couldn't mean that much to him. Hadn't she seen him in Atlantic City with that buxom farm girl, hadn't he been prac-

ticed in his seductions? She didn't want to owe anything, not to
Archie, not to anyone, Molly as usual scrupulous about debt.
But she didn't want to see him at work, Archie slinging his cap
on her lamp, Archie making himself at home on the corner of
her desk. A black bus labored up the drive, its upper deck empty.
The sun shone above the town houses and Molly squinted. The
salmon-colored granite and the curlicues carved around the
window frames, these had been the ordinary filigree of her
youth, but now seemed extravagant reminders of college art history class, some romantic revival. Fragonard, was it Fragonard?
Not Fragonard. Her mouth felt furry, her tongue swollen, her
head throbbed. A houseboy walked small dogs. His poodle
approached, sniffed the hem of her skirt, and Molly bent to greet
the little thing, but its walker yanked its chain. She would have
loved to talk over last night with Sukey, who understood so
much more about sex than she, but of course she couldn't. Then,
along with Sukey's green eyes and humorous grin, she saw a dis-
approving face examining her, this one not so forgiving, red-
haired and bearded—Lyden Silver came to mind and panic hit.
But it didn't matter. She had no obligations, she told herself, to
him. Seventy-ninth Street, the stink of garbage. Already she was
exhausted from walking, and eased herself down on a bench. She
wanted coffee. The remnants of the locomotive's steam broke
above the wall behind her.

Last night, after she had eaten Archie's chili and drunk his
wine and sat fretfully beside him in bed, Molly had barely slept.
In the middle of the night after she had stared at the ceiling and
had failed in her attempts at prayer, she worked the possibilities
of her story, where it was going next, the ramifications of this dis-

astrous river jump. She thought about Margery. Molly didn't believe that Sabatier killed Houdini, couldn't think he was capable of it, figured this drowning was the logical consequence of an old man's leaping into a big river during a lightning storm. But Sabatier's arrest provoked interest in the story. Who was this man, and who was Margery?—and lying there in Archie's bed, Molly had figured she could take advantage. The conversation at her parents'—Clarissa Silver and Sukey Van Siever competing to tell outrageous stories about Mary Twist—it had all come back to her vaguely at three A.M., and she had sat up on the edge of Archie's bed, fetched her soaking notebook from her ruined purse, then scribbled notes on the back of an *American Mercury* on the night table. So long as Sabatier was in jail, it was a story to pursue; she would have to put it together, then present it to Farquharson. He wouldn't go for it, she guessed, unless Molly had something solid—she couldn't just say, I'm going to look into Margery's past; he'd want more than that—but when she did find her story, he'd have to run it: The Real Life of Margery. She had gotten antsy in Archie's room, and before dawn she had washed her face and dressed. Molly left his apartment in her cold damp clothes without leaving so much as a note. Archie was still snoring when she closed his door.

Now she had lost some of that energetic spark. A fool to get going without coffee, but she trudged toward the yacht club, better to look there first. That would be expected of her. She had a job to do. The ground rose slowly and curved as she limped from 74th to 86th Street. The strapless left shoe flapped against her heel, and her toes hurt from the effort to keep the shoe from slipping. Her jacket was clammy. By 80th Street, the pain in her toes had spread to her calf muscles, her foot making odd contortions as she strode uphill. Vaguely, she was concerned about her work. She thought perhaps she ought to head to the office, or at least call, but it was not yet eight A.M., she was only blocks from the yacht club, and the only reasonable thing to do was investigate. Her legs itched in her damp stockings and she began to sweat.

The park was mostly empty save for a few bird feeders and dog walkers and morning strollers. Delivery trucks and taxis ran the drive. Ahead she saw the line of black police cars parked diagonally to the curb, and the small bustling cluster of onlookers and reporters. She still had her notebook in her purse, though its pages rippled with rain, and she had the torn green cover of Archie's magazine. The service road entered at 85th Street, winding in a low arc down the embankment, over the bridge, and to the yacht club, and the cops were moving equipment downhill. Fat patrolmen in double-breasted uniforms spread their arms to keep pedestrians back. Molly tried to count them. A thin old woman waved her hand dramatically, and it took Molly a second look to realize the woman was not so old and was waving at her. She squinted through her glasses, and again felt that sense of magic. Too much for coincidence: It was Clarissa Silver, who on seeing Molly marched in front of an oncoming police car, her confidence causing the cop to brake, and her bearing leading the patrolman on duty to reverse his job entirely. Instead of stopping her, he guided Clarissa right past the department vehicle. Then her arms were open and she sailed, tall thin woman, toward Molly.

"Why, you're damp, darling." After she had hugged her. "And I had no idea you were in the neighborhood. I suppose you've come to see the show. Well, I read your paper last night, and I had to see it. Just had to. You wrote so beautifully—of course, Lyden brought the extra home. I think it's wonderful even though it's so awful. How brave of you to be there—Molly Goodman, intrepid reporter! Oh, and more wonderful to see you. Lyden will be jealous." She rubbed Molly's shoulder. "Oh, so damp. Dear, were you out all night? Did they make you work like that? Oh, and your shoe! Can we sit and talk, or are you terribly busy? A tragedy about Houdini, isn't it? Such a young man, and I felt that I knew him. Michael is terribly distraught, Lyden of course rather grumpy, but then I thought, well, I had to go out and see, and I was hoping I would catch you—I had a funny dream you would be here—but don't let me distract you, I'm sure you have plenty of work to do, I shouldn't bother—"

"No." Molly smiled. "You're not bothering me. On the contrary."

She liked Clarissa's face: long, aristocratic, the space between eyes and mouth, the dignity of each feature. And some damp anxiety fidgeted in her slow, smoky mind: Clarissa's heart, what had her father said about it? Nothing, nothing, it was fine, her father had said, but of course what he had said had run in several directions.

"Do you need to run down to the yacht club?"

"No, not at all. I'm so—it's wonderful to see you. But you're out so early." Molly tried for as bright a tone as she could. "Are you well?"

"I'm well." Clarissa spoke too quickly. "I'm well. Oh, you're so beautiful, Molly. I love these short haircuts." Clarissa reached to touch her hair and Molly laughed. "Do you have a minute for an old woman? Or, silly me, I've caught you at work, of course, and we can't sit here and chat. You're not a woman of leisure—"

"I would love to—"

"Really?" Clarissa's smile got brighter. "All the benches are wet, but I don't mind. Lyden will be delighted to hear that I've seen you."

"He will?" Molly asked. Then, "We should sit." And she felt she might as well admit it. "The truth is, Clarissa, I'm lucky to see you. If I hadn't, I would have telephoned."

"Me? About what on earth could you need to—" But she didn't quite finish that question. "Look," she said, taking Molly by the hand. "I can see it in your face. Don't bring it up. I'm quite well, or as well as anyone my age has a right to expect to be. Who was it who said anything to you, and what?"

Molly would not answer.

"Was it your mother? Of course not. I can see that." Clarissa squinted slightly and with one long finger touched Molly's chin. "Listen. Your father is a silly man sometimes and he talks too much, and I'm sure that he's talked too much to you. I'm well. I got your note. I don't know why he put you up to it."

"I just. . . ." Molly didn't know quite what to say. "We're all concerned." She looked over Clarissa's shoulder. "I won't say a thing more." Pigeons scattered and regrouped themselves. "But I do need to talk to you," said Molly. "And not about that." A police car heaved its wheels gently onto the curb, over the cobbles of the promenade, and down the service road. "I need to gossip."

"How delicious."

"You really don't mind the bench?"

They wiped one down with handkerchiefs and settled in,

watching the policemen work. Molly glimpsed out of the corner of her eye pudgy Dewey Baedeker hustling past, his overcoat pockets stuffed with papers and notebooks. There were other faces she recognized, boys from the news services, occasional photographers, traveling in, traveling out. But she pulled out her wrecked notebook and the things she had written last night on the back of Archie's *American Mercury*, and she spoke quietly with Clarissa.

Conversation from the dinner at her parents' came back to her, and Molly tried to remember the names and fates of Margery's—or Mary Twist's—family: which one had been a doctor, which a suicide, which a lunatic, which a genius. *Doctor Omicron Twist*, she wrote, and took down other names and notes, and Clarissa spoke conspiratorially, sometimes lowering her voice to a whisper, sometimes opening her eyes wide, sometimes nodding her chin for emphasis. Molly had the odd sense of Alton Grimm, whorish and bent, staring fish-eyed from behind an elm tree, and suggested she and Clarissa walk away from the policemen and newspaper writers and their hangers-on. As they stood she saw bent, bespectacled Justy Vittles of the *Radio Times* climbing up the road to street level.

"What are you doing here?" asked Molly.

"Your job," he said with a laugh.

"I'm doing that," Molly called back, but he trotted busily across the street, paying little attention to her. She would call Farquharson, she decided, she would find out about this.

"What did he say?" asked Clarissa, looking after stooped, hustling Vittles.

"I have no idea."

"Are you sure you should be talking to me?"

"Absolutely."

There were only a few more details she needed about Mary Twist's childhood in Europe and Boston, and as they headed toward West End Avenue, Molly calculated how to confirm and expand the details of this story. At the same time she thought about the woman at the center of it all, Margery. Her memories of Mary Twist at college were vague; the name was familiar but she had no face with which to join it. She would need to talk to Sukey to flesh out the story. She decided to call Sukey first thing when she got to her office.

"Are you sure you can afford to do this?"

"I can't afford not to," said Molly. "I'm desperate for coffee."

"Poor girl!"

"Anyway, it looks like the paper sent someone else down to cover the scene—"

Clarissa smiled. "I know just the place."

It was on Broadway, a steaming cafeteria full of old men and students, the sort of place in which Molly would never expect to find Clarissa Silver, but it turned out to be one of her secret pleasures to drink the weak coffee and eat the sugary pastries and watch the squabbles and sad faces. She paid for Molly's toast and eggs and they spoke about the fall, Clarissa's favorite time of year.

"I don't know if it's because my parents were university people, or because everyone returns to the city, but whenever I put on that first sweater I feel life is coming back to usual again. Do you want to know a secret? I hate summers in the country, really. Oh, there was a charm to it when you and Carl and Lyden were children, taking those rattling motorcars—Michael was such an anxious driver, always! And when we would get there he would exult upon the trees and air. Then, of course, he would run back to the city, leaving me with Belle and our nurses and the children, and nothing to do but plan the next outing, the next meal. I used to envy Abe and Michael each Sunday when they would leave! You'll think I'm terrible," said Clarissa, but Molly just laughed.

She had always thought that the Silvers were preferable parents to her own, and now she wondered, over eggs fried hard and tasting vaguely of metal, whether it was the distance she admired. While her parents anxiously hovered over their children's existence, Michael and Clarissa seemed to hang back, Clarissa slightly superior to the duties of motherhood. They kissed farewell on a street corner, and Molly felt the thump-thump-thumping of Clarissa's heart. Clarissa looked healthy and happy, and Molly turned once as she walked away, to see her tall and dignified from behind, walking quickly, and looking not half so old as she had when Molly had spotted her in the park.

On the subway platform she thought of Lyden. Eighty-sixth Street, it was his stop, but now probably a little late to see him. The clock on the station wall read almost nine, and though the platform was heavy with men carrying briefcases and newspapers, many of these were checking their watches and staring nervously down the tunnel. It must have been lonely, she thought, being an only child with kind but distant parents, Michael consumed with his work and Clarissa with herself. Maybe they ought to have swapped parents. Lyden would have done well with Abe, who would have gone with him to the gym to practice boxing; Lyden would never have run from Abe, not the way Carl had.

The crowd changed as the subway made its way southward,

Negroes mixing with the richer Jews, and then at 34th Street the Pennsylvania Station commuters piled on, and they stood out, somehow, their complexions differed and so did their physiognomies: the suburban crowd as obvious as the immigrants. An Italian family stalled the train, the husband holding the door while the mother and three children piled on, laughing as they made it—the magic and novelty of public transportation turning their ordinary life into a game. Someone near her muttered about the smell of garlic.

Molly had three papers she had picked up, and in all of them she read the Houdini story. He led the news in each paper, and as usual Molly started with the *World*, where Baedeker had produced some handsome neutral work so deeply professional and stylish she thought she would never compete with it. Her own prose by contrast felt hurried and amateurish—she could see herself nervously phoning it in from the yacht club, stammering over her notes. Meanwhile, Baedeker had hurried back to the office, composed on a typewriter, and it showed. The sentences were elegant, and he had worked with the paper's staff and library—he must have reviewed all the Houdini clips on hand, every jump. What it must be like to work for a paper like that— Molly felt chastened by it. She had beat him in the extra editions last night, but his work this morning was vastly more polished, more comprehensive than her own.

IT RUNS from him for seven days in tea-colored bursts, Houdini sweating, trembling, parched, and powerless. Bess scrubs his face, changes his sheets and dirty underwear. She feeds him water from a sponge. Hallucinating, he calls for his mother. Then, ten days after taking to his bed, he rises. Stomach limp, forehead cold, knees jiggly, he leans against walls and makes it to the bathroom. What he sees in the mirror is the perfect disguise, not Houdini at all, his skin gaunt, his unfinished beard. Broken teeth, swollen gums, dried lips. He eats sparingly at first: toast, tea, and boiled chicken. But his appetite grows. He practices standing, extending his arms. He raises one leg, then the other. He stands on one foot for fifteen minutes, then the next day twenty. He walks a balance beam, then hops it, later cartwheels. After a week, he balances on his hands with his knees pumping in and out of his armpits. A coin rolls through his fingers, then disappears, then multiplies. The beard grows full and he hangs upside down in his basement. He sticks his feet in buckets of rice and turns them, exercising every toe. A thick rubber bandage across his back, he extends his arms and touches hands together ten, fifteen, fifty, two hundred times. He runs through a great gross of locks, stopwatch in front of him, pick in hand, until he can open all in half an hour. In his beard and cap he crosses under the flashing shadows of the El train. Houdini rides the subways uptown and down. He walks through thick crowds of Grand Central Station, never touching a soul, invisible.

XVIII

HOUDINI'S MOTION PICTURE ENDS its run, and on September 17 a murder in New Brunswick steals the front page: The Reverend John Edward Wheeler Hall is discovered shot to death, his corpse laid side by side with that of Mrs. James Mills, the married choir leader of his church. Sex, violence, and sin are unearthed beneath the middle-class respectability in New Jersey, and the papers run off to see. While in the middle pages of the papers remembrances of Houdini alternate with accounts of eccentrics unreconciled to his end, the front pages tout the big story. At every news kiosk, the shocking first scene is replayed compulsively. The married Reverend Hall, the upright Mrs. Mills, the *Graphic* leads with a suggestive composite of the pair and Hearst's *American* throws half its staff at New Jersey. They trawl and catch a load of suspects: first Mrs. Mills's jealous husband, then Reverend Hall's jealous wife, and third (but not lastly) Mrs. Mills's brothers

Henry and Willie, one of whom seems mentally off-key. Speculation abounds: a tragic, romantic suicide pact, a middle-aged Romeo and Juliet of the suburbs. Reporters dig for hints of corruption, rum-running or rackets. Mass production demands new celebrities. The whole world meets the pig woman next door, and the crabapple tree on DeRussey's Lane, site of the putative lovers' tryst, adorns every front page. It's compulsive. The mode is hysteria: spastic repetition of words and of images, desperate dreams written in the timbre of solemn fact. The many-headed hydra of the American press yips like an excited poodle. When the police free Jim Collins and Sabatier, only the personality pages cover it.

Doyle stands on the courthouse steps with the doctor, beaming and hearty as a few cameras flash, but then in the limousine, away from the glare of the press, Sabatier seems distracted, the investigation into Houdini's end far from his mind. "Of course we are as anxious as you are to get to the bottom of this business." He smiles and crosses his legs. "More anxious, if possible. My reputation is at stake, after all. But at the moment, I tell you, I don't see at all what I can do about it." And when Doyle suggests that Margery is the best tool to get to the bottom of the mystery, Sabatier winces. "Not so much of a mystery, is it? Horrible, yes, but I suppose it was an accident—just as the police say—and the time is not right for Margery's powers to be taxed. Look, there's no crime here; the man jumped. Oh, don't be disappointed. Like you, I've always dreamed, Sir Arthur, that her powers could be put to use for practical good—just as you suggest, we are of like minds, I assure you—but this whole business, particularly my being imprisoned, has been an enormous burden on her. You cannot imagine. I dare not force her to stare at the world through such a terrible lens. You know she's not a tool, she cannot be used for any purpose one chooses. I don't have to tell you that one can't predict the results of a séance. And then, I have so much to attend to, urgent business; nothing like prison for letting work pile up. I tell you, all this commotion has drawn such attention to our cause, such sympathy—declaring me a murderer, can you imagine? You have no idea how my correspondence has grown. How many have become interested in supporting our cause." Doyle bites his mustache.

His scheme to catch the mystery man fails. Black-bordered notices run in the newspapers, fine antique manacles for sale, but to no effect. There are a half dozen phone calls, including a humiliating one from Detective Abel Combs ("I thought it might be you, Sir Conan Doyle"), and before September's end, his wife and the children leave for England. At the docks, Joanna does her best to cheer him. "If he has gone to the other side," she says, "then we shall see him in good time. Just as you said about our dear departed Kingsley, nothing worse than as if he took a trip to the Antipodes." Then Doyle stands and waves a handkerchief, cheering as the boat leaves harbor, watching the white spume where the motor churns.

Leaves turn. Trees in Central Park perform their annual show, nightsticks knock the heads of Bolsheviks, and the stock market revs for its decade-long boom. There are lectures to give and dinners to attend and lunches with editors and press agents. He has several manuscripts to complete—*Our Second American Journey, The New Revelation*, and a series of stories he is plotting about a policeman with telepathic powers—but Doyle sits at his desk in his empty hotel suite, drawing in the margins of his notebooks. Without the company of his family, his mind wanders; he yearns for home; he feels helpless. By telegram Lady Doyle assures him that Houdini is alive and that the investigation must continue, but Doyle no longer knows what he is investigating. He drinks cold tea. He walks to the window, stares down at Fifth Avenue, sees the traffic, smells the exhaust, and sympathizes suddenly with godless existential despair: the sense that as we live we do not send our highest selves into the universe, but only fumes and smoke and noxious gases.

October turns to November. He cannot mope. His constitution demands action. And so, on a chill fall morning, he puts aside the manuscripts that have stumped him, and then with pen and ink on monogrammed paper, he makes a single, clear, final offer. He will deliver £20,000, sufficient funds to endow whatever Spiritualist facility Sabatier might dream, but on two conditions: first, that Margery submit at last to testing, to the well-known Bird Protocols, which Doyle proposes they undertake in a single afternoon with, if possible, the assistance of Professor Bird himself, and, second, that at a time and place of their choosing, the Sabatiers conduct a séance in which Margery allows Doyle to cross to the other side and to contact Houdini. He folds the letter, licks the envelope, and throws his pen as if it were a dart across the length of the hotel room, where it hits the wall and sticks.

One week later, he stands by the chairs in the hotel lobby, while businessmen and bellhops jostle along the red carpet behind him. His first finger stiff as metal, Doyle slices the blue envelope open. Standing in a dripping macintosh, he reads the short note, whose scrawl is almost calligraphic, the *f*'s splitting words above and below, the *g*'s swooping wildly, the capital *T*'s strutting.

My Dear Sir Arthur,

Trust is paramount in this business of ours! You have mine entirely, yet I fear I have lost yours somehow. The considerable funds you offer make me blush, I cannot tell you what they would mean to our cause, or perhaps I need not tell you. No one understands the business of religion better than you. However, the contingencies of your offer, what another man might call "strings attached," bring me a chill. My first reaction upon reading your letter was to decline the proposition entirely. I have often expressed to you my reservations, my determination, I say, to protect my dear Margery from the "slings and arrows" as it were, of those who would doubt her. I have said to you, and I believe that you have concurred wholeheartedly with my thoughts, that to put a gifted medium like my wife through the "hoops" of these examinations, these protocols of Dr. Bird's, would be a bit like admiring a sculptor's work with the aid of a tape measure and calipers.

So it was that after receiving your letter, I put it in my drawer for several days, devoting hours of my time to contemplation of the difficult position in which I had found myself. My dear Sir Arthur, I have never once asked you for a penny, and yet you must know how your offer dangles before me, a bitter fruit that, once tasted, might allow me not knowledge or power—but the ability to bring to fruition my dearest dreams. I will not burden you with my difficulties, how I watched my wife's beautiful face each morning over breakfast, and each evening as I put her to bed. Of course, I did not speak to her a word of my dilemma, her innocence must not be sullied, she is too delicate an instrument to take such hard playing, and too self-sacrificing, too. It is my scruples, not hers, that stand between my desire and my reluctance. And so it was, on realizing this—that it was in the end my selfishness that stalled me—that I determined to accept your kind but firm and businesslike proposition. To your conditions—should you insist upon them—I sacrifice my wife's dignity, because in the end, as you say, it is all for the betterment of the Spiritualist cause.

Oh, Sir Arthur, how I regret that it has come to this! I can see from your letter how doubt wars with faith in your heart! But I see that faith in the end will reign triumphant, as the very goodness of your heart—as the generosity of your offer testifies—is infinite. My only reservation is this: You have suggested that members of the press be present at the séance itself; we will have to determine who those members might be. But one thing is certain: I will undertake the protocols with no one but Dr. Bird himself supervising, and on the condition that the tests be undertaken in the strictest secrecy. I am making an exception to the one rule I swore to abide by, never to sully my wife's talents with the paws of these scientific scrubs. Dr. Bird I can countenance, but I will not have other so-called "Technicians of Faith" clambering for the opportunities to scrutinize my Margery.

I trust you will agree to these conditions, and I remain,
Sir Arthur,
Your humble servant,
G. Hugo Sabatier

Doyle balls the letter in his fist. In his hotel room, he telephones Dingwall Bird, and the next day rides out to Brooklyn to
the chemist's home laboratory.

The car makes its way through the crowded streets downtown,
below the massive white buildings, alongside the El train, and
onto the cathedral bridge. Coffee roasts in warehouses below, the
El train passes, and Doyle sees the expanse of slums uptown, the
lighted sign of the *Daily Forward*, the busy river, the shipyards on
the Brooklyn side. Through the web of suspension cables he
watches a barge and tugboat pressing out to harbor and the
Statue of Liberty. A cold wind off the river comes through the
cracks in the door, and soon they arrive in Brooklyn.

Dutch stoops and curved windows, muted brickwork and quiet
gardens, with the clouds so low the sidewalks feel like a London
suburb's. A uniformed gardener clips a hedge. Doyle checks the
address against a note in his pocket: the only wood house on the
block, wider and older than the rest, set back from the street with
a handsome flagstone walk leading to the porch. He knocks, a
maid greets him silently, and Doyle is shown to a dusty parlor
whose furniture and wallpaper match only in the extent of their
decay. Cats crouch on bookshelves whose glass fronts are clouded
with dust. One mews from underneath a tall unwound clock.

Fifteen minutes later, Bird enters in a long white lab coat. His
skin carries a pale blue tint, his head shakes with a slight palsy, his

beard dangles into another century, but Bird's grasp is firm. "How do?" The two men have not seen each other for years, but Bird avoids small talk. "I have something to show you, Sir Arthur."

The old chemist leads Doyle down a narrow hall, pictures on the wall invisible in the darkness, only the shine of their square glass frames. Bird walks slowly and deliberately. Doyle can see the dandruff on his scalp and shoulders, the thinness of his neck and legs. They head to the back of the house and under a flight of stairs. At the door to the laboratory, Bird presents a long white coat to Doyle. They wash hands in a zinc basin.

Through a door then and into the long, windowless laboratory. Here the smell of cat urine is stronger still, but the mewing much more faint. Cages line the left side of the room, six high and twelve long, each with its own dying animal: vomiting cats, hairless cats, exhausted cats, and cats with lumpy tumors. Between the door and the cages stands a cluttered battery of lights and cameras, all facing an apparatus at the far end of the room, a strange machine the size of a household furnace, whose central glass column is being polished by a smart blond youth. Like Bird, the young man wears a lab coat. A stethoscope hangs around his neck.

"Dieter," says Bird. "Meet Arthur Conan Doyle."

Bird's assistant leaps across the room, and a tall lamp wobbles in his wake.

"We kill none of them," Bird declares. "They die. So difficult to catch the moment." He shakes his head so his beard wags. "Deliveries come daily. I have a man who patrols alleyways, who petitions household vets. If they seem well enough and clean

enough, I have them live upstairs. When their cases turn termi-
nal, we move them here. Never help, never hurt. That's the
credo. They get their food, they get their drink. If a cat wants to
starve itself, we will not interfere. How many deaths a week—
what's the average, Dieter?"

"One hundred and seven, sir."

"Half of that at night, things like to die at night. Dieter comes
in the morning, he finds a lot of stiffs. So many opportunities slip
away. So many frustrations. They die in bunches. People don't
understand death. You're watching one as it seems sure to fade,
then another who has escaped your attention kicks it. But we
have one here, it's been on its last legs all morning. I'm so glad
you came just now."

As he spoke, Dieter moved toward the large glass apparatus in
the corner, and through a window in the tall column leaned with
his stethoscope, briefly interrupting the flow of a white cloud
that rose from the square steel base.

"I make no guarantee, mind you. That's half the game in science, patience. We've been watching this one for hours, all this
still watchfulness, but when the moment comes you've got to be
quick. In a typical adult feline, we estimate, the soul leaves the
body on average some six to one-hundred-and-thirty-seven seconds after the final breath drawn. Hence the number of cameras.
They attach to the control panel and a single switch fires the
entire sequence of exposures. We experiment with different
shades of light. We have red bulbs, yellow bulbs, blue—"

"Dr. Bird," says Dieter, interrupting. "The pulse is growing
quite thin."

Bird grabs Doyle by the sleeve. Again, his thin hand works powerfully. He leads Sir Arthur over to the large strange machine, where his assistant is bent carefully, his stethoscope pressed to the bald, laboring chest of an emaciated tabby.

"Examine the bed where we lay the cat," says Bird, quietly, in Doyle's ear. "See how it's got a mesh hammock. That allows the vapor to rise all around. Nothing fancy, just water, we find it draws out the shape of the soul. The rate is specified, as is the tempera- ture. Anima. Life force. Fascinating stuff. The hammock is a scale, of course, and we try to capture the differential, weight before and after death. And then we chart that weight against the size of the image we capture. The results so far are suggestive, yet complex."

"Pulse continues variable and thready," says Dieter. With his brush-cut hair and bright pink cheeks, he looks like a boy play- ing doctor. "Sir, I think it's time."

Bird moves to the photographic apparatus, checking bulbs and wires and film. "Conan Doyle," he rumbles, "you are a lucky man indeed."

Dieter arranges himself on a stool, stethoscope pressed to the animal's weak chest. The wires run in tangles across the floor, all leading to a panel of plugs and buttons, where Bird stands, squinting like a ship's captain into a fog. He exiles Doyle to a corner of the room, and the only sounds now come from the fan's whirring engine and the occasional wails of dying cats. The mist swirls and rises in its column. The lights in the back of the labo- ratory are dimmed.

"Ready one," says Bird, and his assistant pulls a lever on the big machine's side.

Then, with a finger in the air, Dieter marks the unsteady beats of the dying animal's heart. "There," he says. "There." And, after a pause, "There."

"Ready two," cries Bird.

Dieter puts a fist in the air, and then releases four fingers slowly, from pinkie to pointer. "Done," he says at last, and raises his thumb.

A silence follows, and then a mad flurry. Camera flashes cast weird uninterpretable shadows on the steam column, and the room is thrown into darkness between bursts of light. Doyle blinks, wipes his eyes, and then the shooting is done. He sees strange shapes burned onto his retina, glows in green and yellow and red. Bird's withered skull gleams.

It is only as he is leaving that Doyle broaches the subject. "I have a proposition for you," he says, "concerning a medium you may have heard of. Her name is Margery. She is married to a Professor Hugo Sabatier."

"Of course." Bird nods. "The murderer."

THAT NIGHT in wicked dreams she stands on his bed straddling him, her skirts encircling his pillow so that Doyle has a clear view of her pubic thatch, from which ectoplasm drips. Meanwhile, in Pleasant Valley, Margery thrashes in her bed while Sabatier stands above with a syringe. "Hold her," he cries, "sit on her legs! Get that arm still!" The man he screams at— long-boned, with a lantern jaw and sunken eyes, Bartholomew Diggs—snatches Margery as she bounces off the mattress. He clamps her elbows to her side, hurls her back down, and sits on her. Sabatier drives the needle home.

Downtown, Doyle wakes and splashes water on his face. His eyelashes drip, as does his mustache, and as he passes through the central room of his suite he discovers a hat on his desk, dead center of the green felt blotter. He tries it on. It's too small. Revolving it around in his hands, Doyle recognizes Houdini's derby, and the hat feels to him like a message written in the magician's familiar hand.

XIX

SUKEY VAN SIEVER REFUSED to discuss Margery.

"You leave my house before dawn, alarming the servants, baffling my aunt, embarrassing me." She had talked to Dr. Capoulosse. "I told him all about you. I know you have other lovers, Molly. I told him that your romantic tendencies run—run towards members of your own sex. I did not tell him that you were a woman—I couldn't—but I told him about your racial—oh, Molly, you have played me for a fool!"

And Molly's temper exploded: the selfishness, she told herself, the fear, the unkindness that lay beneath Sukey's sleek exterior. Molly hated that sleek front, then hated herself for having been attracted to it, hated her own bobbed hair and short dress. Late September, she walked across Houston Street, the air clean and cold. Cheese on strings in the windows of the latticini shops, the smell of basil at the fruit sellers' stands. Kids home from school played in the streets. Mothers watched from stoops, windows, and fire escapes. On Bleecker, the secondhand shops were closing. A barber swept his store. Men in rumpled suits headed home. Bins of apples stood in front of the grocers' shops, alongside potatoes and onions and squash and flowers. Bohemians bloomed, young men in sailors' sweaters, women in slouch hats appraising Molly. A couple approached, he with his beard styled like Trotsky's, she heavyset and wide-faced and not particularly pretty, but with a radiant smile. She was irresistible to him and she knew it and it showed in her laughter as she passed, and her laughter ruined Molly. Archie Miles leaned over the desk of Thelma George, the redhead who answered Farquharson's phone, and on Thelma's face Molly saw the mask of pleasure and distrust that must once have been her own.

In cold October Molly climbed the steps of the Sixth Avenue El, too early in the season for the stove on the platform to be lit. Brooklyn commuters carried evening papers. She squeezed near a door and watched the passing city, the lighted apartments, other people's lives. The train wobbled as it ran, and she felt the warm complexity of the bodies around her, the press of strangers, intimate and anonymous. In her apartment she poured herself a drink, and listened to Pignoli's dog yap on the other side of the partition, and she prayed to Carl, and cursed herself for praying, and thought: How can you be such a fool?

She traveled uptown to 89th Street and in her parents' living room, even before the first drink was poured, Abe attacked.

"Don't be an asshole," he said. "I've seen too many in my years in the business, and I can see the direction of this paper of yours. Hall-Mills. The minister schtupping the lady. It plays like comedy, but it's shit. And my daughter, in the back pages, writing about—what, the psychology of dancing? You know what you're turning into—"

"Abe!" Belle rushed in from the kitchen.

"It's all right." Molly lit a cigarette and smoothed back her hair. It was Carl's gesture, absolutely. "He doesn't bother me."

"Like her brother," said Abe, turning his back.

"What your father means," Belle explained, as she put a hand on Molly's shoulder, "is that we're worried. You think I'm a terrible person. Maybe I am a terrible person, but that's not the point, darling. Look, you'll be twenty-three in December. I'm not saying you need to get married, God help me I'm not, not this year. But what happens in three years, in five—"

Molly held up her hand, a bracelet gliding from her slim wrist to her elbow. "Mother." She looked out the window, trying to see past their reflections to the dark park and the river.

In her old bedroom she dug through her desk for relevant notebooks, but with no luck: three papers she had written on Shakespearean tragedy, her freshman philology textbook (why?), and a journal which she had kept for seven days of her last year at college. Nor could she find a captioned photograph of Mary Twist in the old yearbooks; no senior girl between Trubek and Unger. But then, in the pictures of the Christmas concert, she saw a soprano she thought might be right: a thin, pretty girl with dark hair and a pale face, mouth open wide, eyes terrified.

Molly rode the train to Poughkeepsie and lied to the dean and the alumnae office. She claimed to be writing an article on women in the sciences, but when left alone among the big steel cabinets, she ransacked the records of former students and stole Mary Twist's file. Engaging a former literature professor over coffee and cookies, she came at the story obliquely and then yanked the thread. Mary Twist was notorious, a beautiful, brilliant, troubled girl. She had never graduated, and rumors were plentiful: After Vassar, she had traveled either south or west, at her family's insistence or against their will. Back home, Molly wrote and telephoned former classmates, fishing for gossip and compiling a notebook full of innuendo. Mary Twist was a prostitute, she was in jail, she had joined a circus, she robbed banks, she was in Los Angeles in the movies or modeling underwear. Molly borrowed a Ford and drove the long route Houdini had described so carefully after he had visited the Sabatiers' home. She knocked on the door of the cottage, but the houseboy said Dr. Sabatier was indisposed. She had phoned several times, Molly explained. She had information that needed to be confirmed or denied. She presented a card from the *Radio Times* and the houseboy only smiled and nodded. His complexion was unvaried and smooth, no sign of blood beneath the skin. The bones of his face were sculptural, his lips echoed his cheekbones' curves. His smile was like a uniform, as were his eyes, which revealed as little emotion as the buttons on his shirt. Dr. Sabatier would not see her.

So she parked in the dark by a pasture wet with rain, and in an overcoat made her way through brambles and mud puddles through the woods by the quaint blue cottage. Sitting on a half-rotten stump, she drank coffee from a canteen, mosquitoes and moths fluttering. Molly stifled the urge to smoke, she did not want to show any light that a stranger might see. Alone and shivering, she prayed desperately to Carl, and just when she was about to give up, she saw it: that gorgeous face, the same one she had seen singing in her college yearbook and in newspaper stories

about Boston debutantes. She was framed by the window and
backed by pale blue wallpaper, wore a robe, and her dark hair was
drawn back. There was a mustached man with her, Sabatier, and
in the background—but she couldn't be sure of this—another figure. Then a door slammed in the farmhouse across the way, and
Molly got frightened. She drove back to the city, the central fact
of her story confirmed: Mary Twist was Margery.

October turned toward November, Molly filed stories on
housewives and radio, on office girls and shopping, on flappers
and petting. She got stuck in an elevator at work with Archie
Miles, and he coughed and bent his head.

She pushed her way through the two volumes of Doyle's *The
History of Spiritualism*. Molly read about the Knox sisters and the
Davenport brothers, girls tied up in cabinets from which came
strange clicks and raps. Eva C., the famous medium, had been
photographed with a pseudopod peeking out from her skirt, and
the afterlife was described like a seaside town, leisurely and
pleasant, spirits busily decorating homes in which loved ones,
when they arrived, could rest in peace. Molly drained a second
glass of rye. Late in the night, words seemed to drift, spoken in
Doyle's accent and rhythms, then (exhausted hallucination) the
voice that read the page was her father's. Whole sentences,
whole passages went by without comprehension. Molly's mind
was elsewhere, full of regrets. Who was she anyway, and what
was she interested in? Abe Goodman's voice stopped reading
Conan Doyle and instead berated Molly for her caution and her
fears. What kind of crazy girl believes in ghosts? She remembered
the way she had looked the night of Houdini's drowning, the
vision of herself in the lobby mirror of Miles's place, drowned

and ugly, and she shivered with an unaccountable spasm of grief. ("We don't want to make a scene about it, do we, champ?" That's what he had said in the office, later. "You and me, we play the same game, right?") Why didn't she do something useful with her life? Molly shook her head as if a fly had settled on her nose, as if by shaking the head she might get her doubts to flee. She stepped to her window to light a cigarette. She poured herself another glass of rye.

In her rickety armchair, she went back to her book, but Molly had no sense of what page she might have been reading. A dog barked, a car horn blared. She started her chapter again. A girl in a lunatic asylum heard schizophrenic voices that reported truths she had no business knowing. These voices spoke about the future, about the past, predictions that ranged from the stock market to the weather, and she knew details of other patients' childhoods. This girl—Doyle cited articles that hid her name— had been born to a prominent family in the northeastern United States, a family with an unfortunate history of madness, genius, and suicide. She had moved from Boston to attend a women's college in New York. There were just two paragraphs about her. Molly read them twice, and then dropped her drink. She got her coat. It was Mary Twist. It was Margery.

She hailed a cab, and with the second volume of *The History of Spiritualism* in her purse, went to the offices of the *Radio Times*. One A.M., but the elevator operator was hardly shocked. Reporters kept odd hours. Molly made her way through the dark newsroom, flicked on her desk lamp, and opened the drawer where she kept her files on Sabatier, Margery, Houdini, and Doyle. After circling paragraphs and crossing out others, she rolled a sheet of paper into the barrel of her typewriter and with Doyle's book on one side and her notes on the other rattled out a set of sentence fragments, one to a line. Still in her overcoat, Molly used a letter opener to jimmy the lock to the paper's library. She pulled down four boxes full of clippings cross-indexed to date, publication, and subject. Then, notes in her fist and a pencil between her teeth, she got to work, found three articles, two from *Scientific American* and one from a gossip columnist in Boston. She had the name of the doctor at Harlem River Hospital, Herman Paulson, and from the phone book his West End Avenue address. Also, she found reference to an article Paulson had published in the *Journal of Psychical Research,* "On the Phenomenon of the Visionary Delusional." Like the section in Doyle's history, the articles in *Scientific American* maintained the anonymity of the talented young patient, but Molly grew more and more certain it was Mary Twist. Here were references to her education, to her grandfather's profession, and at the very end of the second article, the mention of her late Californian husband, who went by the name of Bartholomew Diggs. Molly put away the boxes and went out to breakfast, feeling all the while that she was being led, or perhaps trailed, by beckoning hands. Her brother's? Houdini's?

In the public library, she found volumes of the *Journal for the Society of Psychical Research* and read through six. Later, she placed phone calls to San Francisco and Los Angeles, requesting police records and old newspapers. Two weeks of spending her nights poring over these, and she had a shadow history of Bartholomew Diggs. Incarcerated twice for kiting checks and defrauding war widows, he had a reputation for vanity and card tricks, billed himself as the Houdini of the fifty-two-card deck, and had died in a fuel explosion that investigators called arson. His body was burnt beyond recognition, and his young wife had left Reno two years ago by train for New York. Diggs, Molly learned, had once published a pamphlet on manual dexterity. She got this in the mail from a West Coast dealer in magician's books and ephemera, and it came to her desk in a plain brown envelope on the afternoon of November 6. To maintain the finger's suppleness, the magician advised, a man ought to wash his hands in urine every morning and night. That was a fact from the inside of the pamphlet, and on the back was the author's photograph. She sat at her desk at the *Radio Times* and admired it, feeling not at all surprised, because what she discovered fit perfectly with the world as she had imagined and dreamed it: the lantern jaw, the deep-set eyes, the slightly disfigured nose. She had identified her mystery sailor, but was not sure whether the plot was thickening or resolving itself. Molly set down what she had learned, and sent it in a letter to Arthur Conan Doyle.

SHE DREAMED she rode an elevator up a half-finished building, so that to the tenth floor it rose through the steel-girdered skeleton of the skyscraper and after that in the space the building only planned to occupy.

Champagne bubbles rose and elevators rose. In a place with white tablecloths and a hot jazz band, Texas Guinan greeted her crowd. "Hello, suckers!" Waiters glided by, trays heavy with liquor, the room alive with smoke, perfume, and gay complicity. Cameras flashed, minks wrapped necks, cops shouted: "Move along!" Long Island: The bar was in full swing, the air alive with innuendo. One cab spun around and found Sixth Avenue, another downtown hit a peddler's cart, and Delancey Street filled with melons. Food was everywhere, bread in windows, cheese in buckets, fish in barrels, food in garbage bins, and on the sidewalk, fish heads, fruit peels, apple cores, old tins. On the busy side streets, fire escapes loomed. Conan Doyle sat alone in his hotel room: his fragile glasses, his huge face, his misted-over genius. Sukcy Van Siever arranged her stockings and skirt as she left her psychoanalyst's office near midnight, checking her smudged lipstick in the lobby mirror. On the Staten Island Ferry, passengers raised their arms to Liberty, trying to exult à la Edna St. Vincent Millay. Two men passed, trenchcoats flapping, and one invoked the name of Edward Bernays. Down by the river, trucks rumbled by. "SHOULDERS, BELLIES, SPLITS, STRIPS, AND OFFAL," read a sign. Sailors in peacoats shared cigarette butts while boats whistled in the harbor. A young man with a stained hat crossed St. Mark's Place. He passed the second-floor gin shops, the basement clip joints, and a theater with a big marquee, but when he came to a fortune-teller's sign he stopped to look; it showed a black hand with a crescent moon and four stars in its palm. In Harlem, the air was filled with incense, lines of candles burned on walls, and a middle-aged man, bald, with a neat mustache, sat nervously in his milkman's uniform, his family fortune—small bills taped in bundles—all laid out in a row.

"Welcome," said the fortune-teller, Princess Marie.

And in the sixth floor of a building on 89th Street and Riverside Drive, as she lay in bed beside her husband, Clarissa Silver's fifty-three-year-old heart played its last trick. The strange mysterious dendrons that run from atria to ventricles confused themselves. The beat's impulse left the sinus node for someplace unconventional. It got there and panicked, ran like a rabbit, 180 beats in the first minute, and Clarissa rose, her mouth tasting of nickels. Tachycardia: impossible for her to distinguish between the panic in her body and the panic in her mind. Clarissa swung her legs out of bed and decided to do what the doctors told her: put her face in ice, strain her bowels. Wasn't there some other trick? Michael snored, and she went to the bathroom. In the mirror she saw her gray face as her heart's panic ascended. The heart's big chambers flipped, sped, and flapped, the walls beating like a hummingbird's wings, three hundred times in her final minute, which gave the ventricles no time to fill, no blood to pump, and she collapsed, out to inward, her mind and feet and hands denied oxygen, then her bowels and lights and lungs, and finally, her heart itself was starved.

She fell. Her head struck the sink and then the toilet and then the tiled floor. The glass that kept toothbrushes shattered. Michael woke, coming out of a dream of his parents' apartment on the Lower East Side, and as consciousness seized him he reconciled himself to his surroundings: his life now as a grown man on the other side of town. His wife wasn't screaming, but she wasn't in bed, and there had been a crash. He ran down the hallway and saw Lyden running toward him—his son, he had a son, his son was a grown man—and together they turned to see under the only light in the apartment, sprawled in an impossible contortion, the corpse of the woman each of them loved most in the world.

XX

THE RAIN CAME DOWN in a sullen mist. On the corners of upper Broadway, newsprint and horse manure caught in the bars of rain gutters, dissolving slowly. Trolley cars splashed. The sycamores in the promenade looked sick and blotchy, the elms undignified with their branches hanging down.

Neither the Maltese doorman nor the elevator operator recognized Molly; neither had worked in the building when she was a child. When she said she was going to Silver, they nodded solemnly, and she felt a guest in her parents' home. Molly dropped her umbrella in a stand in the eighth-floor lobby and pressed a button on the familiar front door. There were no sounds within, and for a moment Molly lost her sense of propriety—maybe she ought to have waited, not rushed uptown. Then she heard the turning of the lock, expected the face of the maid, but there in the little hallway was Michael Silver, in socks and without a jacket, his face drained of its usual pink.

"Oh," he said. "Oh, Molly. We didn't expect."

She threw her arms around him and Michael received her embrace with a weak hand on her back.

"Lyden has gone for a walk," he said. "Your father is in here."

She could hear Abe heft himself from the living room couch.

"Your mother's downstairs," he said when he reached the narrow foyer. "You should go down and see her."

"Have you had breakfast?" Molly asked Michael, who shrugged.

Mathilde, the Silvers' maid, was shopping and had left the men alone. Molly rushed to the kitchen. She warmed the coffee and found a carton of eggs, a brick of butter, and a bottle of milk, the cream floating up on top. In the living room, there was no conversation, the two old friends in quiet communion. Molly imagined Lyden in the park, walking through the miserable drizzle. Distracted, she burned the eggs and brought them to the living room on salad plates, silver forks clutched in her hand.

"Do you take sugar?" she asked Michael Silver.

He looked up at her, but didn't speak.

Then the telephone rang and Molly ran to answer it. At the other end was an alderman with questions. When would the Silvers be receiving guests? Molly knew nothing, told him to call back in an hour. Clarissa had tended to the Goodmans after Carl's death, had pulled things together and opened the apartment and laid out good things to eat. But Belle was downstairs now, and Molly was furious, imagined her mother too overtaken by her own grief to tend to another's. And where the hell was Mathilde? Molly called the *Radio Times* and told them not to expect her. There was a key in the door, the turn of the lock's tumbler, and Lyden came home without a hat or umbrella, his beard and hair dripping.

Molly rushed to get his coat off him. "Lyden," she said. It was soaked like a sponge, the fabric letting go water where she squeezed it.

He went to the kitchen, his shoes squishing as he stepped. Molly followed, got a towel for his hair, put a steaming mug in front of him, and said, "Can I help?" But he didn't answer, just sat and stared, and Molly knelt to untie his shoes.

"Do you know where Mathilde's got to?" she asked.

Lyden opened his mouth, but then the phone rang again, and before he could speak Molly ran to answer it. Then she went to his room to fetch him dry socks, poor Lyden grieving and barefoot in the kitchen.

Molly had not been in his room since she was a child, and was surprised by how small it was, how brown, and how neat. There were shelves of books, a maroon rug, and a solid desk with rows of files and notebooks. His bureau was varnished wood, and his bed narrow. He had framed and hung a picture of himself and Carl and Molly, all dressed in white one summer in the Bronx. And he had a poster on the wall of Houdini, the same one that had hung in Carl's room downstairs. But the room was not at all childish. His cedar drawers smelled like a man's, of tobacco, wool, and shaving soap. She found his socks, all black and brown and neatly balled, and when she closed the drawer she noticed the medal on the wall, champion prep school boxing. A muscled man posed bare-chested with his fists up, and with a flutter, Molly remembered naked Lyden kneeling on her brother's floor, playing Escape as a kid.

She cursed her mother for being gone, cursed the maid, too, for being absent when needed, and rushed through the living room where Abe and Michael smoked. The eggs had gone untouched, but the coffee cups were empty, and Molly returned to the kitchen with these in one hand and the socks in the other.

Lyden was bent over the stove, trying to light a wet cigarette from the gas flame. His glasses, which had fogged, sat behind him on a countertop. His eyes were red, but in front of her he would not cry. Still, without those glasses, Molly saw him clearly, past the beard and the broken nose. He no longer frightened her. And as she approached, Lyden reached for Molly. He grabbed. Then she grabbed back. And Molly could not deny that she loved him. Tears fell from her face; she dropped the brown socks that she had brought for him. And the two swayed in the kitchen, touching and sobbing like lost children, like shy lovers.

Then the doorbell rang. It was Belle. She arrived with a dripping umbrella and three stacked boxes of pastries. "What, you thought I would be sleeping?" Eyebrows up, incredulous. The truth? She was on top of everything. Two chickens were in the oven downstairs, Mathilde looking over them, but could you trust her? Deliveries would be arriving soon, and at three o'clock people. Lydens from Connecticut and Massachusetts had boarded trains bound for Grand Central. There was too much to do. Molly squeezed Lyden's hand and got to work.

Belle handed over the pastries. Molly served plump cuts which Michael ate gratefully. To Abe, Belle said, "Go downstairs, take a schvitz, change your shirt, and get a car ready to go to the station." The phone rang, and this time when Molly answered, she knew what to say. Freshly laundered black suits came through the front door, and at her mother's orders Molly drew baths for Lyden and Michael. The water splashed the basin and her eyes burned with tears.

Just past three and the city was still gray, the rain falling in a dreary mist, the crap in the gutters accumulating. No sunshine in the Silvers' living room, no lights lit. Mathilde had cleaned like a whirlwind, but somehow the old New England furniture felt bereft and dusty, and the wall paintings hid themselves in gloom. By four o'clock, half the Reds in New York were crammed into the high-ceilinged rooms. Actors, writers, assemblymen, union organizers, people who owed their lives to Michael Silver, who otherwise would have been jailed or deported. They drank and laughed and smoked.

"Mike was always a lot tougher than me," Molly heard her father say. An Episcopalian with a priestly collar spoke with a Baptist minister from Harlem.

And in a corner by a sofa stood pale Michael Silver. He played host as best he could, accepting embraces, offering thanks. Even in a crowd of well-wishers, he seemed not to want to impose himself, and Molly could not fail to be moved. Lyden stood apart from his father, with his back to the window. He nodded graciously at gray-haired women. A judge approached and gravely shook hands. An older man in an ill-fitting suit bowed and simpered, and Lyden did his best to smile. He shook hands, he shut his eyes behind his glasses, he even laughed. Molly thought of what Clarissa would have made of him now, the depths of her satisfaction; she knew how proud of Lyden her brother would have been, and again Molly felt she would cry. She loved him, unaccountably.

She stayed there with her parents until the bitter end, after the sunset and the spare-parts dinner, the whiskey late at night. Molly helped the maid clean. Around midnight, Michael Silver raised his arms.

"Enough of you good people. It's time we went to bed."

At the door Lyden looked at her directly for the first time since that moment in the kitchen, and it felt intimate as a kiss. Molly let go of herself. She hugged him, and he returned the embrace with savage loyalty, aknowledging what had always been true. In the taxi home, her cheek tingled where his beard had touched it. Lights in the cab windows blurred, and soon she was bawling.

"WE SEEK not proof but documentation." Bird wipes spittle from the hairy corners of his mouth. "Precautions are taken only to preserve the integrity of the evidence. Nurse Handy, you have searched the major cavities?"

The nurse nods, and the chemist makes his way to the lecture hall, where the folded wooden chairs are empty save one, far to the right, occupied by Sir Arthur Conan Doyle. Onstage, Bird's assistant, Dieter Braun, sorts equipment: cameras, lights, scales, tubes, a bell box, and a slant-topped crate large enough to transport a mastiff. At the scientist's entry, Dieter leaps from the stage, clipboard in hand, white coat flapping, pale hair shining under the lights. Bird salutes him, thin wrist making folds in the sleeve of his lab coat.

Margery is led in through the door that opens stage left, preceded by a tall gray nurse and followed by Sabatier. The clothes she arrived in have been hung in the room in which she was searched. She wears only a loose brown frock and her wet hair bears the marks of the inspecting comb. Sabatier seats himself in the front row of chairs, but across the auditorium from Conan Doyle, alone, and near the door. Dieter helps Bird up the three steps to the stage, and then seats the great man across the table from Margery. Questions follow.

Professor Bird addresses these to the nurse and, because he is hard of hearing, shouts. He wants Margery's age, height, weight, blood temperature, blood pressure, diet, the measurements of her bust, her waist, and her hips, and he reviews all these, taking down his own notes in long pauses. Doyle keeps his pen close to his lips. From his vantage, he can see the back of Bird's balding white head, then tendons of his neck beneath parchment skin, and the beautiful angles of Margery's jaw. Sabatier, on the other side of the room, sits with his legs crossed easily at the ankles, and he fingers his mustache.

From cardboard crates, Dieter removes wood and metal stands, tall iron rods, and long glass pipes and arches. He connects these tubes to more parts than seem possible or necessary: valves, extensions, and gauges, and as his piece comes together it makes for a strange instrument, first resembling a whiskey still, then a strange translucent woodwind with two mouthpieces and one horn. The effect in outline is a butterfly, its long sap-sucking feeder pointing up at the sky, its wings composed of whirling glass curlicues. At the chemist's directions, Margery puts her mouth to one end of the apparatus. Then Bird puts his to the opposite side. The two are to blow against each other regularly but not simultaneously, so that a superlight ball will hover in the central tube.

Bird puffs and the ball rises. It begins to drop, but then Margery exhales. Up it floats, and Bird blows out to keep it there. Soon they have timed their breathing so the ball hovers nearly motionless. They reach across the table to clasp hands, and the lights of the auditorium are dimmed. Doyle feels the chill—not magic, he knows, but truth, the telltale sign of spirit presence. The Delucca-Forsman Respiratory Sensor is calculated to foil even the most gifted ventriloquist. A lapse on either side, and the ball will drop, proof that someone has stopped breathing into the mechanism. All breath must be focused deliberately on the floating ball, so the test's validity depends entirely on the tester's integrity, and Dingwall Bird's is unimpeachable. The ball hovers. The room grows cold. After what seems a nearly intolerable stretch of silence, there comes from the back of the room a screeching, first quiet, then louder, and moving toward the stage, gaining volume and momentum as it crosses the big room, sounding like an airplane about to take flight. The sound hits the stage at an inhuman holler and as it climaxes, Dieter's flashbulbs blow, a blinding explosion in the dark.

Light returns. The ball has fallen. Margery lies on the floor, and strange-colored shapes dance in Doyle's eyes. He removes his spectacles, and wipes his forehead with his handkerchief. Outside, the weather has turned chilly. The windows rattle. The steam pipes clank. Bird, winded from his long turn at the breathing apparatus, takes a drink of water. Meanwhile, the nurse revives Margery, wiping her wrists with alcohol, patting her face with a cold cloth. Sabatier watches impassively, his ankles still crossed, fingers at his mustache, the same easy attitude. While Dieter disassembles the Delucca-Forsman machine, Bird amends the notes in his clipboard.

The next test involves a simple scale and four coins. Two additional chairs are drawn up to the central table. Dieter signals, and Doyle and Sabatier come up and sit. Sir Arthur approaches solemnly, adjusting his vest and jacket. Sabatier smiles, amused to find himself onstage. Dieter changes the plate in the camera. The nurse straps Margery to her seat. Her legs are fixed to the chair's legs, her arms to the chair's arms, her back to the chair's back. The nurse works with leather like horse tack, each strap a half inch wide, each pulled tight, buckled, and knotted, then tested with a solid yank. With an effort and a grunt and the help of his cane, Dr. Bird stands and arranges himself, moving to Margery's right. Doyle sits at her left. They clasp hands, with Sabatier directly across from his wife. The nurse withdraws, Dieter brings out lamps designed for this purpose, and they sit, the four of them in a circle illuminated green.

The scale is brass and from its bowed top hang thin chains supporting bowls. The coins are divided, two on each side, and after a few gentle sways—it's a sensitive instrument—the scale achieves equilibrium. After a period of quiet stillness, it appears as if it has become fixed, as if the measuring arm has been fused to its base, the whole thing, coins included, a solid unwavering mass. Then the room chills. A cold wind seems to fill it. The table buzzes, imperceptibly at first—it might be some movement in the basement of the chemistry building, it might be a pseudopod, an ectoplasmic arm. Then it shakes. Soon, like a tree's boughs tossed in the wind, the arms of the scale sway, back and forth, the well-oiled hinge never squeaking. The green light comes and goes. Doyle's face begins to sweat despite the room's coolness. Margery's small passive fingers feel cold as death in his hand. The table rattles as the scale's sway increases and the scale's arms gesture like human arms, the coins hopping in their swaying bowls. A camera flashes, then a second, Dieter capturing the scale's upset. But these disruptions seem to weaken the spirit's grip on the room, and the table stops hopping. The scale's sway slows. Doyle looks back at Margery, whose face is covered in ectoplasmic goo. The last test requires two trays of paraffin.

S NOW FALLS AND WITH IT Houdini, past windows and into dreams. Hugo Sabatier in his pajamas while
anointing his mustache before bed catches the specter, a crazy
glimpse in the corner of his mirror, the magician in a tuxedo,
raising up his hands. And poor Margery, bound and drugged but
not quite sleeping, inches her head from her pillow only to see
Houdini overlarge in her window, speaking words that strike her
like flashes of light. Standing in the yard Bartholomew Diggs
fires a pistol, across the frozen pool a glass shatters, and a flickering, recognizable face appears behind the lantern lights in low
branches of leafless trees.

Snow that morning: a crisp inch, no wind, balancing evenly
on twigs and branches, on stoops and roofs, on windshields, running boards, and hood ornaments, on signs and awnings, on the
dirty banks of the East River. It lay, a melting blanket on the beds
of the trash-packed scows. Plows worked the streets, crews spread

sand on pavement. Shovels scraped sidewalks in Chinatown and Finntown, out front of Harlem apartment buildings and the tenements of poor Jews. Uptown doormen brushed uniforms, and dogs padded by their masters' beds. Newspaper trucks pulled out from garages. On top of the Plaza Hotel, the German chef had his wait staff jumping in the roof's white crust, one, two, three. Nighttime patrolmen made their way on ferries to Queens, and garbage trucks cruised the numbered avenues, open backs steaming.

Molly climbed sluggishly from bed, glad for the day. Three oranges in a bowl and she grabbed the closest, broke its skin with a butter knife, and let the juice roll down to her thumb. The smell of bacon from across the partition, also the yapping of Pignoli's dog. Her shoulders were tight, her hands jittery, she couldn't peel the orange without mauling it.

Molly washed her fingers in the tap, dried them on her nightgown, ground her coffee until her wrist hurt, then put the percolator on the gas ring. Her little cream bottle had frozen on the window ledge. She brought it in cupped hands and set it close to the flame.

Her notes were laid out by the typewriter, a neat pile in three red folders: Margery, Doyle, and Bartholomew Diggs. While the cream melted and the coffee dripped, she pushed a wine glass from the night before—purple dregs dried to the bottom— toward the corner of her desk. Her feet pressed on old newspaper, her ashtray was full. Molly sighed, rubbed her eyes, and scanned her chronology of events, so far as she knew them, from that first day at Vassar when Mary Twist had sat in Sabatier's class. She lit a cigarette, took out her pencil, and imagined Margery, lost that thought, and then imagined how Lyden might touch her, his hands on her waist, hers on his. She got up to tend to her coffee and her melting cream. She poured off liquid from around the icy core and it swirled into the black drink, little dissipating clouds. Molly sipped it while looking out the window, thinking of nothing, listening to the dog yap next door. She pulled a kimono over her nightgown and collected her things for the bath.

Dressed and dried, she drank a second coffee, peeled another orange, this time more neatly. In boots, a black coat with a fur collar, and a man's cap with the front brim bent, she tromped out into the snow for newspapers: *Times, World, Herald, Tribune, Sun, News, American.* The bakery window was fogged with steam, and Molly bought a poppy roll with butter. She bundled all her newsprint under one arm, pulling the roll from the bag to eat it before it cooled. Around the quiet corner and up the stairs; then, reaching the key toward the lock, she heard the telephone ringing downstairs. Conan Doyle's car would be arriving in ten minutes to take her up to the Sabatiers'.

The back seat bounced as they made their way up northern Broadway, traffic wretched near the drawbridge. Slowly uphill, and past Spuyten Duyvil, ice on the river, and ice-breaking boats headed south. The sky that morning was a perfect blue. Tree branches cast harsh shadows. She passed her notes to Doyle, and he reviewed them, glasses on the bridge of his nose.

"You've done the right thing," he said, patting her knee. "We can manage this better than the police can, and of course you'll have your story."

Professor Dingwall Bird slept, head against the window's curtain, spit collecting in his gray beard. Were it not for the rattle in his throat, Molly might have thought him dead. They drove the long way through vaguely remembered countryside, and then the car pulled up in front of the little cottage on the bumpy road.

"Of course," said Bird, reaching for a conversation lost on 72nd Street, "it's another argument for the immutability of the essence."

HOUDINI SEES them. He notes everything. A foot crunching snow, the cough of an exhaust pipe, the filing of a rope so it will break but appear whole.

The architecture of the place boggled Molly. She had written about it, imagined it, but not like this: the sunroom's metal and glass skeleton giving way to a tunnel and then a stairway, the risers angled but smooth, the wainscoting white, and the walls papered with delicate repetitive flowers. She could capture the details in print, but never her discombobulation.

Sabatier smiled as they entered. Doyle assisted him in the introductions. Molly knew Margery, but the recognition clearly was not mutual. The medium stretched out warm fingers, offering a smile, and Molly began to doubt herself: Was this face remembered faintly from college, Mary Twist, her old classmate, or was the discovered familiarity an illusion, a combined effect of obsession and fame? There was little small talk, they went straight to business, and Molly was asked to assist the nurse's examination of the medium. Wearing a beautiful silk dress, Margery led them upstairs.

Near Japanese prints hung framed photoprints of swirling, disembodied forms. At the second-floor landing a tiny window looked out at the road and farms and in the distance frozen water, all of it covered in snow. The rooms below the attic felt like a summerhouse in winter, neatly kept, unevenly heated. No one talked. They entered a study: a large rolltop desk near the edge of a window, and on the wall closest to the door a set of cabinets containing reference guides and medical texts. One window faced the woods; branches grew close to the glass. Margery drew the shade, a gesture so pure it seemed like playacting.

What had at first seemed to Molly a kind of couch or settee was in fact a medical examining table. Above it hung another handsome cabinet, this one stocked with small vials, tools for cutting and looking, scissors and pincers and scopes. The nurse worked the pearl buttons down Margery's back. Molly watched the curve of her neck, saw under her shoulder blades two lumpy scars, and the bandages Margery wore on her arms. She looked closer, seeking evidence, but the more she saw, the less she felt she understood. Margery spread herself on the examining table. The nurse greased her fingers.

"We don't have to," said Molly, gawking.

The nurse worked quickly, running practiced fingers up the calf, working the thighs and the sex, all her special knowledge on display, fingers in the vaginal cavity that produced the famous pseudopod. She palpated the belly, looked between the breasts, checked the mouth as if Margery were a horse, combed out the hair. She called out numbers—height, blood pressure, temperature—which Molly took down dutifully on a chart, but the figures felt to her encrypted, no way she could understand. And Margery offered up her body passively, as if it had been picked up in a store, or borrowed, or even—so it seemed to Molly—something the medium had once owned but recently abandoned. A crackling in the woods outside, as if a dog is rushing through the brambles.

Diggs is out there, knife and gun, seeking something he's seen: a black shape, a flash of silver. Light through the bare branches and dappled shadows, the ground beneath the snow covered in half-rotted leaves. Evergreens here and there, and rocks and branches, frozen puddles, not much of a path. Diggs follows. The footsteps are deep and emphatic, heels that break the surface ice and enter the mud below, and he feels taunted by them. He turns the edge of a fir, and there's the slope down to the even lawn, slippery with unbroken snow. The pagoda looks a sad reminder of summer. The infant statues wear caps of it, and their little hands are cupped in white. Diggs checks his watch. Only minutes until the séance. The footsteps run across the flat white ground to the pool. At the stony edge, they come to a miraculous stop. In the middle of nowhere, Houdini's trail vanishes.

SABATIER INVITED his guests to sit. It was her first séance. Molly followed directions. She was placed between Doyle and the medium, Bird across from her, and Sabatier's empty seat to Bird's left. The professor drew his thick velvet curtain. Molly glanced at the hands of Conan Doyle, then up to his face, the candle flame's reflection doubled in his spectacles. She hoped something magical might happen. She worried she would laugh.

"Welcome," said Sabatier.

He bound his wife at Bird's direction: short cords, carefully wrought. Molly had read about this, she knew the script, her interest lay more in interpretation than in action. Margery's white neck shone in the darkness, her dark hair faded into the gloom. Her eyes were shut, a blue vein throbbed on one lid, and her mouth was partly open, waiting to be gagged. Molly studied her, trying to memorize everything. She was composing sentences when all of a sudden the eyes opened and stared at her, magically. Molly could not look away: Margery was there—present in a way she had not been at the examination table—and her glance was intimating something, that she was trapped, that her bonds were more than metaphorical, that she knew everything.

Sabatier filled her mouth with plaster. The candle snuffed itself. The room went dark. Doyle gripped Molly's hand, and she reached out on her left for the mystic fingers of her neighbor.

"We ask for silence," said Sabatier to Bird's assistant, Dieter, who had set up his camera in a corner of the room.

Something is shining in the woods. A flock of pigeons rises suddenly to Diggs's left, cooing and clucking, wings battering, gray and purple against the snow. A rabbit crosses the long blank lawn. Church bells strike noon. Diggs sees someone across the grounds, behind the pagoda, just out of sight. A figure dressed in black and smiling, partly obscured by the pagoda's shade, the man is extending a powerful hand. Diggs draws his gun, leaps forward, fires, and the figure vanishes.

"Fucking," says Diggs, and his word echoes across the open ground.

The table rose, the spirits spoke. Ectoplasm oozed from Margery's ears, danced across the table, and took on the shapes of faces that screamed. It was an opera. She could not have imagined, without witnessing it, this brand of ecstasy. The bell box rang, tinny and dull in the muffled room. Objects flew through the air, but what was important were the silences between. The gripped hands in darkness, Conan Doyle's and Margery's, reassured her. This was intimate and private, yet collective. Molly felt it, the silliness, but also something nameless, present, and gone. She thought of her father, how he would scoff at this, and how her mother would withdraw, too, even if Molly could find words to explain it. The stunts and apparitions and superficial projections were beside the point. Nor did she believe she was hearing voices from beyond the grave. When you died you lost everything: the human body, the English language, everyone that you ever loved. A tickle in the heart, and then oblivion. But here and now was something else.

Diggs lights a cigarette.

Houdini stands across the lawn, bowing. Clean-shaven, hair slicked, he wears a tuxedo, cummerbund, and tails. Diggs aims his gun. He fires. The bullet sails. Houdini pinches it midair, drawing the metal from its flight as if it were a rabbit from a hat.

A tap on Diggs's shoulder, he glimpses the white glove. Diggs whirls but there's no Houdini. He jumps back. His left leg slips on the ice of the pond, which gives. Diggs loses his balance and tumbles, splashes, the ice breaking around his ears. He feels a ratcheting, a shock in his heart. He paddles and kicks and roars in pain. His pants get heavy, his shoes weigh a ton, and after the initial stabbing pains—burning, it could be fire—there's numbness and then warmth. His eyes blur. He reaches for the snowy marble edge.

He sees someone in front of him, Houdini, the white gloves, the black tuxedo, the terrible smile, and he is pulled from the water, convulsing and weightless. From the edge of the woods comes a detective, no longer with crutches but still with a limp. In the distance, sirens sound.

But in the séance room, there was only silence. Molly opened her eyes to perfect blackness and shut them to the same. All she wanted was a miracle, the kind she had experienced ever since she was a kid, communion with her dead brother, someone she had loved and lost, but this time it would be public, with a group, her most private feelings thereby ratified. Conan Doyle's grip was cold and dry, Margery's soft and glowing. Molly tried thinking of Carl and of Clarissa, tried asking them to come. That was the promise she had given Sir Arthur, that she would try to believe in Margery, and she did believe, but she could not say how, or in what. Grass grew and died, so did human beings. A rock spun through space and on top of that rock grew a thin layer of green, warmed by a ball of burning gas. How could any of us tiny temporary things grasp the grand scheme or say it was random? In Molly's left hand lay Margery's warm fingers. How could she pretend to know her? How could Doyle know anything?

A strange singing in the room, disembodied voices whose rhythm echoes Molly's heart's. Her questions come at her with their own recoil, and the line between "random" and "miracle" blurs.

The music gets louder. She can't tell for a moment if it's in the air, or coming from Margery, or if she herself is singing. Molly is possessed by a twin sense of ignorance and wonder. She may go on to write about Margery, but she will never understand the woman. And Conan Doyle? Who the hell is he? Houdini? All her massive ignorance is revealed to Molly. She understands nothing, she has no magic power. Lyden Silver? Her own dad?

Molly cannot see the future: how in the study Conan Doyle will pull from his pocket not a checkbook but a letter from Arizona, explaining Margery's marriages to Sabatier and to Diggs, how Sabatier, enraged, will draw his pistol, how Doyle will not wince, but instead will demonstrate conclusively and calmly the professor's guilt. Sabatier will plead that there was no attempt at murder, only an attempt to humiliate Houdini that got out of hand. Bird will ask, "How, Sir Arthur, can you know this?" And Doyle will say, "Elementary." Just then, uninvited, Houdini will step in. Molly doesn't see any of that—or Diggs in handcuffs, or Margery in a padded cell assaulted by visions of the coming century, stacks of matchstick bodies and black falling rain.

But in that séance room in the meditative quiet, she feels comfortable for a moment, a glimmering understanding not of herself but of her limits. It's a passing sense, and in the bustle of the next half hour— the revelations, the arrests, and the work to be done—it escapes her. The flash of comprehension makes its way to oblivion, lingering as only a memory of feeling, the sense itself never to return.